*W*hen lovely Miranda Heath, suddenly orphaned and penniless, turns for help to her father's old partner, Captain Bascomb, she finds herself plunged into a whirlpool of intrigue and danger. From the moment of her arrival at the gloomy old Bascomb mansion in the small New England port of Scots Harbor, Miranda becomes the target of a strange and violent conspiracy. She knows she must find the truth by herself. She can trust no one in the Captain's bizarre household . . . least of all the dark and dour young Brock McLean whom the Captain insists that she marry. . . . "More than a full measure of adventure, intrigue and mystery." —BOSTON SUNDAY HERALD

Fawcett Crest Books
by Phyllis A. Whitney:

- [ ] BLACK AMBER   23943 $2.25
- [ ] BLUE FIRE   24083 $2.50
- [ ] COLUMBELLA   22919 $2.50
- [ ] DOMINO   24350 $2.75
- [ ] THE GOLDEN UNICORN   23104 $2.50
- [ ] HUNTER'S GREEN   23523 $1.95
- [ ] LISTEN FOR THE WHISPERER   23156 $2.50
- [ ] THE MOONFLOWER   23626 $2.25
- [ ] THE QUICKSILVER POOL   23983 $2.25
- [ ] SEA JADE   23978 $2.50
- [ ] SKYE CAMERON   24100 $2.25
- [ ] SPINDRIFT   22746 $2.50
- [ ] THE STONE BULL   23638 $2.50
- [ ] THUNDER HEIGHTS   24143 $1.95
- [ ] THE TREMBLING HILLS   23539 $2.25
- [ ] THE TURQUOISE MASK   23470 $2.50
- [ ] WINDOW ON THE SQUARE   23627 $1.95
- [ ] THE WINTER PEOPLE   23681 $2.25

PHYLLIS A. WHITNEY

Sea Jade

FAWCETT CREST • NEW YORK

SEA JADE

THIS BOOK CONTAINS THE COMPLETE TEXT OF
THE ORIGINAL HARDCOVER EDITION.

All characters in this book are fictional and any resemblance
to persons living or dead is purely coincidental.

Published by Fawcett Crest Books, a unit of CBS Publications,
the Consumer Publishing Division of CBS Inc., by arrangement with Appleton-Century, an affiliate of Meredith Press

ISBN: 0-449-23978-0

Printed in the United States of America

31   30   29   28   27   26   25   24

Sea Jade

1. IT WAS FITTING THAT I HAD MY FIRST glimpse of the house at Bascomb's Point during the flash and fury of a violent thunderstorm.

The storm had not yet broken when my train from New York stopped at the Scots Harbor station. As the conductor helped me to the platform, a gusty October wind whipped at my skirts and mantle. I clasped my portmanteau in one hand and stood looking about me—eagerly and without fear.

My father's warnings had touched me not at all and my mind was filled with a romantic dream that I fully expected to become reality. Since my father's death some months before, the state of my fortunes had grown very nearly desperate. Unless I threw myself upon the charity of friends, I had nowhere to turn. Only Obadiah Bascomb could help me now. He had written to me in response to an appeal of my own, and I had come running, given wings by a sense of adventure, of expectancy, eager to meet the life counterpart of a legend with which I had grown up.

I know how I must have looked that day when I first set foot in the little New England town where my father, my mother, and I were born. Since I am no longer so tenderly, so disarmingly young, I can recall the look of that youthful Miranda Heath as if she were someone else. Slight and slender she was, with fair tendrils of hair, soft and fine, curling across her forehead beneath the peak of her bonnet. Her eyes were tawny brown, with quirked, flyaway brows above them. The wind undoubtedly added to the illusion of her flyaway look; the look of a fey, winged creature straight out of a make-believe world where love and pampering were taken for granted. A creature unaware that she was about to stray into dark regions for which nothing had prepared her. I could have scarcely have been more ill-equipped to face the household at Bascomb's Point.

So I can see myself, and my heart aches a little with pity, because I know now what was to come, and what fearful changes would be stamped upon that guileless innocence before it was banished forever.

For a few minutes that afternoon, as I waited on the station platform, it seemed that no one had come to meet me. I was about to look for help, when I saw a tall figure in a coachman's rain cape bearing down upon me.

"You're Miss Miranda Heath, for the Bascombs'?" he asked, and already sure of me, did not wait for an answer. "If you will go along to the carriage over there, miss, I'll fetch your trunk."

The need for haste under that lowering sky was evident, yet the whistling threat of the wind only exhilarated me. I cast a quick, identifying glance at my trunk standing alone on the platform, and then let myself go blowing down the wind like a small craft under full sail as I ran toward the carriage.

It did not trouble me particularly that only a coachman had come to meet me. Captain Bascomb's letter had been cordial in its invitation, and in my feckless way I anticipated no lack of welcome from the others of his household. My father had told me little before his death. I knew only that he had made the trip to Scots Harbor two months before his illness came to its inevitable end, and had called upon his old friend and partner, Captain Obadiah Bascomb. He feared to leave me alone and the plan had always been that I should write to Captain Obadiah for help if ever my need was great. Yet when my father returned to New York he was visibly shaken and his mind had been completely changed.

Under no circumstances was I to turn to the Bascombs for assistance, he told me. The captain was growing old, senile perhaps, and he had tried to drive some fantastic bargain. My father had refused unequivocally, wanting no such incarceration as might await me there. He used that very word, though it had no meaning for me then. In fact, so steeped was I in tales of Bascomb & Company and lore of the sea—my father's own doing—that I paid little attention to his words of warning when he insisted that the house at Bascomb's Point was one of ill-omen and that I was not under any circumstances to go near it. He did no more than identify the people who now lived there, and he would not discuss them with me. The captain's housekeeper, Sybil Mc-

Lean, was the widow of a former partner who had died at sea. Her widowed son and granddaughter lived in the house as well. The captain had married fairly late in life and had no children, but when I plied my father with questions about the captain's wife, he shook his head sadly. A strange woman, he said—out of her own place and often set upon by others in that household. He had seemed sorry for her, but he would say no more. It was as if by keeping everything shadowy and unrealized, he could shut the Bascombs out of my life from then on, forgetting that he himself had contributed to the legend that had fired my youthful imagination as no story book had ever done.

Perhaps I might have listened to him had life ever touched me with a heavy hand. Under the circumstances, my father's words only whetted my curiosity and did not penetrate meaningfully through the rainbow of my romantic dreams. All my life I'd heard of the Bascomb family, with its history of ships and sailing. I'd grown up spoon-fed on heroic tales of the tall ships—those winged ships that were the heart-catching clippers of the China run.

We were now in the late 1870's and the great days of the clippers had ended with the war between North and South. The queens of the sea had been reduced to ignoble duties on the oceans they had ruled for a brief ten years. Steam was replacing them in practicality, yet tales of their gallant reign would live forever.

My own father was Captain Nathaniel Heath, who had in his day been master of some of the swiftest craft to sail around the Cape of Good Hope and across the Indian Ocean toward the heights of Java Head. Once he had been a full partner in Bascomb & Company. I knew him as a man of fine intellect, with broad horizons, and a wide knowledge of the world.

Though my mother had died shortly after I was born, and my father had taken me from Scots Harbor as a baby and put me in the hands of his widowed sister in New York, I had grown up with only love and protection about me. I had undoubtedly been spoiled and coddled by my gentle aunt, protected in my self-centered illusions by the devotion my father had poured out upon an only child. No harsh sea gale had weathered me. Even my aunt's death a few years before had not destroyed my safe harbor because my father, long since retired from the sea, was always dominant in my life and I was content to make a home for him. In those days there was no impatience in me. I was still dreaming, still waiting for all the lovely things in life that were inevitably to be mine—simply because I'd been told that I was pretty and intelligent, and that everyone loved me. I had only to open my hands and wait, ready to give my own love and trust when the right time came and brought me—not a knight in shining armor, but more likely a brave sailor from the sea.

Then suddenly, at twenty-one, I was alone and almost penniless. Genteel positions open to women were few indeed. No one wanted to hire a governess who looked hardly more than a child herself. Yet when I tried to find work as a domestic, each interview ended quickly the moment the mistress of the house set eyes upon me. She was sure to consider me too slight and fragile for the work required. There was even one who told me bluntly that I was too pretty.

Unprepared to deal with reality, I did what my father had forbidden. I wrote to Captain Obadiah and told him of my plight. He responded at once. Nothing would give him greater happiness than to have the daughter of his old and dear friend come for a long visit. Surely a way would be found to solve my problems once we had talked together. My despondency fell away at once. Of course there would always be someone to love, advise and take care of me. How foolish that I had doubted it for a moment. My father, in his illness, had been unnecessarily alarmed. Captain Obadiah would rescue me and all would be well. To say nothing of the fact that in Scots Harbor I might even gain some knowledge of the mother I had never known.

Thus I was here, newly arrived, with my heart beating in eager anticipation. For was I not shortly to meet the personification of all the great sea tales my father had told me—Captain Obadiah Bascomb himself? Not that my father had ever portrayed the captain as thoroughly admirable. He had simply emerged as a hero in my own imagination in spite of the less than flattering picture my father sometimes painted of him. I could remember my father's very words: "Ruthless, iron-willed, stubborn, dynamic, lusty, unscrupulous . . ." Surely the strong stuff of which heroes were made.

Nevertheless, in spite of my own eagerness to meet Captain Obadiah, I knew I could not yet mean to him what he meant to me, so it did not trouble me that only a coachman had ventured into the storm to meet a stranger. The captain and his household would like me when they knew me, of course. They would help me, as it was my right to be helped. I never for a moment doubted this simple philosophy.

The barouche was before me and I opened the door and put my foot on the step, thrusting my portmanteau into the rain-curtained, leathery-scented interior. At once there was a burst of eerie laughter from within the carriage and a small figure squirmed away from me into the far corner of the seat.

"Ssh!" she warned, and put a finger to her lips. "Joseph doesn't know I'm here. I had to come secretly to meet you. You're Miss Miranda Heath, aren't you?"

This air of conspiracy appealed to me and added to my sense of adventure. I climbed in after my portmanteau and sat beside the little girl, glad to be out of the chill onslaught of the wind.

"I am indeed," I said. "And if you'll tell me your name I can thank you properly for coming to welcome me."

"My name is Laurel," she informed me. "But I didn't come to welcome you. I only came to see what you are like. After all the quarreling about you last night, I had to see you for myself."

Her words were startling and I saw now that her small face, sallow-complexioned in the gloomy interior of the carriage, bore me nothing but animosity. But while her words and manner puzzled me, I was not particularly distressed. I have always liked children and been at ease with them. This child, I judged, was about ten—an age toward which no adult should make quick, clumsy advances. Given time she would come around. Then I would understand such flights of fancy.

I settled back without answer for her taunting words and pretended to pay her no attention. My first glance had told me much about her appearance. She had huddled herself into an unbuttoned coat, but had troubled with no proper cover for straight black hair that hung in limp strands below her shoulders. Her eyes were nearly as black as her hair and they continued to stare at me unblinkingly.

When she saw that I would not pick up the conversational gambit she had flung at me, she cast a practiced eye at scudding clouds seen through an isinglass patch of window.

"We'll never make it home before the storm breaks," she told me. "Likely enough, we'll get blown right off the point into the sea, carriage and all."

"That will be rather uncomfortable for the horses, poor things," I said cheerfully.

The child thrust her black-browed countenance close to my own, staring at me through the gloom. "You aren't afraid," she said almost in wonder. "Why aren't you afraid?"

At that moment Joseph brought the trunk. There was a thud and the carriage swayed as he heaved it up to his seat, climbed aboard and flapped the reins. Wind blew through crannies in the curtains and the barouche shuddered under the impact of repeated gusts. The clopping of the horses' hooves had a purposeful, reassuring sound, however, as though our destination would be safely reached, whatever the elements might devise.

"Why aren't you afraid?" Laurel repeated, oddly urgent.

There was something almost touching about the child's antagonism, about the very limpness of unbrushed hair upon her shoulders, about a mouth that did not know how to smile and dark eyes too large for the pale oval of her face.

I smiled at her. "I'm not afraid of storms. I like them. Except for thunderstorms, perhaps, It's very silly, I suppose, but I've always been afraid of lightning."

She blinked once or twice and then returned to her steady, disconcerting stare. "I don't mean why aren't you afraid of the storm. I was only fooling about that. Joseph won't let us be blown into the sea. I meant—why aren't you afraid of *them* when they hate you so? They don't want you here, you know. You'll be sent away at once if they have anything to say about it. Or, if you stay, it will be the worse for you. I heard Grandmother say so."

How could I take her seriously? She was a child whose imagination had run away with her. This I could understand myself, being gifted with a fanciful imagination of my own. Though mine, fortunately, took a happier, more optimistic turn.

"Do *you* hate me?" I challenged her.

This time she turned her head away and looked out the window, not meeting my eyes. There was a moment or two of silence within the carriage before she answered me.

"I hate you most of all," she said. "I don't want you to stay! I've already put stones in your bed. If you don't go away, I'll put a witch's spell upon you. I'll put snake venom in your tea."

This outburst, so intense in its passion, so dismaying from

the lips of a ten-year-old child, chilled me in spite of myself. I folded my gloved hands, one above the other, and spoke quietly, evenly.

"Will you tell me, please, why you are so ready to hate me when you don't even know me?"

"My father hates you!" she cried. "Oh, I heard him last night when they all gathered in the library after the captain told them his plan. I listened in the hallway when they thought I was in bed asleep. My father hates you and so does my grandmother."

"But neither your father nor your grandmother knows me," I protested.

No words of mine were going to change her mind, however, and I sought another subject to coax her from this obsession with hating.

"You haven't told me your last name. What do you put with Laurel?"

"It's McLean," she informed me. To a degree I had succeeded, for now there was pride in her voice. "I'm Brock McLean's daughter. I'm Laurel McLean."

Again I smiled at her, on safer ground now. "Then you must be the granddaughter of the great Andrew McLean. I've always heard about him."

"I am!" said Laurel. "My father is a son of one of the Three Captains, just as you're the daughter of one of them."

For the first time her words struck a responsive chord in me. All my life tales of the Three Captains had been legion. My own father, like the other two, had sailed to Canton in the early days when that was the only port open to foreigners in China. "The Captains Three," the Scots Harbor cronies had been called: Captain Obadiah Bascomb, Captain Nathaniel Heath, Captain Andrew McLean. All were masters of their own ships early in life, and thus ready to captain the great American clippers they had sailed when China was opened to trade with the outer world. They were partners, too, in the Bascomb enterprises. Captain Obadiah was always mentioned first because the once-great dynasty of whalers and merchantmen had long been sailed by Bascombs, built in Bascomb shipyards, run by Bascomb merchants at home and abroad. A dynasty that had died as the family died, and clippers themselves vanished from the seas, though the name lived on.

"My grandfather, Andrew McLean," Laurel went on pridefully, "was more important than any of the Bascombs, really. Our family came from Aberdeen and settled Scots Harbor in the very beginning—before there were any Bascombs here."

"I know that," I acknowledged. "He designed a good many of the Bascomb clipper ships, didn't he?"

The child tossed her witchlike strands of black hair and something of a glow came into her eyes. "He designed the *Sea Jade*, and he built her too! She was the fastest of them all, and the most beautiful."

My attention quickened at the sound of that name, so long forbidden in my father's household, and I waited expectantly for her to go on. But Laurel flung me a sidelong glance and fell into sudden, unresponsive silence.

The wind had stiffened and rain clattered across the top of the barouche, drowning out all other sounds. The carriage rocked ominously, but we plodded steadily ahead. When thunder rumbled in the distance and there was a flicker of lightning, I could not help but wince. Gales I loved, strong winds that blew cleanly from the sea. But not the treachery of a thunderstorm.

Laurel reached out with a suddenness that startled me and touched a wisp of hair that had blown across my forehead. "It's like gold filigree," she said. "Like the filigree of a pin the captain's wife wears in her hair."

I laughed softly, for there was a wistful appeal in her tone and I thought she had softened toward me. Compliments warmed me and kept the cotton batting of love about me soft and intact. The child's seeming hostility had begun to distress me and I welcomed this apparent change.

"If it was a pin of gold filigree I would give it to you," I said.

At once her grasp tightened. She twisted the lock of hair about her forefinger and gave it a cruel tug. I cried out with the sudden pain and took hold of her wrist. I loosened the strand from her finger and tucked it beneath my bonnet.

"That hurt me," I told her, shocked and resentful.

Black eyes flashed triumph. "I know! And I'll hurt you worse if you do what Captain Obadiah wants."

"What does he want?" I demanded impatiently. The child had spoiled my sense of adventure, taken away from my eagerness to reach Bascomb's Point. I withdrew all effort to be friendly with her.

"I know what he wants," she said, the corners of her wide

mouth turning upward in a wickedly impish grin. "But I shan't tell you. Anyway my father won't let you do what Captain Obadiah wants. And it's my father who will have the last word. There are some who call him a black Scotsman and say he has all the stubbornness of a Scot. My mother was Scottish too, you know—Rose McLeod she was before she married. She could always coax my father to listen. But my mother has gone to her ancestors."

The strange phrase, following all the rest, seemed of a pattern and hardly raised a question in my mind till I remembered it later. I said nothing but sat in disconsolate silence in my own corner of the carriage.

All my high hopes and gay anticipation were being dashed by the efforts of this child, and much of the glow was gone from my day. Through the window on the leeward side of the carriage I could barely see out across the streaming landscape, but I tried to fix my attention upon it and ignore this unpleasant little girl. She would not remain ignored for long, however. Suddenly she leaned across me, gesturing.

"There! We're turning onto the point now. You can see the house if you look quickly."

I put my face close to clouded isinglass and peered out as the vehicle made its turn. I would have recognized the house anywhere from my father's long ago description of it. There were two houses joined together, really, two-storied, with the smaller part built around a central chimney. Wealthy Bascombs had later built the large adjoining house that made a wing of the earlier structure a whaling captain had built the century before. White clapboards had been set in simple lines, giving the house dignity and grace. The smaller structure rose straight from the ground, without adornment except for its neat green shutters, while a delicately columned veranda ran about two sides of the main house. This had evidently been a later addition for it did not encompass a front doorway clearly meant to stand alone in its elegance. Slim Corinthian columns framed the door's recess, with an elliptical fanlight above, and a few rounded steps leading up from the walk. All this was in my mind's eye, with reality added in no more than a glimpse through a rain-streaked curtain before the carriage turned along the road that led out upon the point.

"There's the lighthouse!" Laurel cried in my ear.

Again I had no more than a glimpse of a squat building of

15

gray granite with a tower rising above. I knew about the lighthouse, of course. In my father's youth it had stood upon this headland, warning and welcoming fishing and whaling vessels as they came to port. As a boy he had often climbed its tower. Now as he had told me, it stood long unused and a fine new lighthouse had been built across the harbor.

The carriage had come to a stop and by good fortune there was a respite in the downpour. Joseph jumped to the ground and opened the door, scattering raindrops. He exclaimed in disapproval at sight of Laurel, lifted her down without ceremony, and sent her flying toward the house. Myself he helped out more decorously, then turned back for my portmanteau and trunk.

I scurried through a white gate set in a white picket fence, and ran beneath dripping elms up a brick walk to the doorway. From somewhere behind the house a dog began to bark, full-throated and savage. It was a sound to make the hackles rise, had I been able to attend it fully at the time. But already Laurel had thrust the door open upon an unlighted hallway, and turned to gesture me in. I picked up my skirts and hurried up the wet steps and into the shelter of the vestibule.

It was then that the first of those strange, seemingly ordained moments of intense prescience occurred. Perhaps the child, with her hostility, had prepared me for this. My spirits had been dampened and there was an uneasiness in me where there had been none upon my arrival. I, who had expected only to be welcomed and made much of, stood suddenly hesitant upon this dark, unwelcoming threshold.

The dim hallway was not empty as I had first thought. Three people stood there in the gloom beyond Laurel's small figure. As I hesitated, waiting for someone to speak, to greet me, dismayed by the silence of the three as they stared at me, a sickening flash of lightning illumined the scene in utter clarity, etching the nearest details upon my sight, followed by a clap of thunder that shook the house.

A woman in a draped and bustled gown of some dark red material stood upon the stairs, the glass cylinder of an unlighted lamp in her hands. The look she bent upon me was almost malignant. In all my life no one had ever looked at me with such hatred before. I felt the ugly stab of it shockingly. Then darkness descended, all the more blinding after the flash of light, and I could hear movement in the hall. Wind blew through in a wild gust as a door opened at the rear, and again

I heard the mad barking outside. Thunder clapped, rattling panes, as lightning struck the earth not far away.

In the second flash I saw that the other two persons were men. One stood at the opposite end of the hall, where he had just opened the door. He was dressed in yellow oilskins and must have been in the act of going out when I appeared. He had paused, as if frozen in his tracks at the sight of me. I was instantly aware of a remarkable resemblance to Laurel—he could have been taken for no one but the child's father. In the flickering of light his dark, brooding eyes regarded me with almost as great an antipathy as did those of the woman on the stairs.

The second man stood nearer me in an open doorway with booklined shelves visible beyond his tall figure. The flashes of eerie, greenish light, now coming close together, showed me a face both handsome and mocking. For a moment his gaze held my own as if in challenge.

I closed my eyes against the livid flashes; the old terror full upon me. It was the only terror that had ever haunted my young life; a fear of sudden light, of light that changed and flickered. No matter what the source, such light always frightened me. I must have cried out, for the sound seemed to break the spell that held the three, releasing them from so threatening a focus upon me, releasing Laurel to speech.

"She's here!" the child cried. "Miss Miranda has come! I went to meet her. I've already told her we don't want her here."

I opened my eyes at once. The man in oilskins, Laurel's father, uttered an angry exclamation and vanished through the rear door into the storm. The second man gave me a faintly derisive bow and turned on his heel to disappear into the book-lined room. The woman came quickly down the stairs and set the lamp upon a table, concentrating upon lighting it. When she turned she offered me no hand in greeting, but stood looking at me in unblinking silence.

I recognized the look with a start. This was exactly the way the child had stared at me in the carriage and I knew where Laurel had found the manner she imitated. But where the child's gaze was bright and a little wild, this woman's eyes were very different. They were deep-set and seemed enormous above prominent cheekbones. Beneath the gray-streaked auburn hair that she wore in an old-fashioned style drawn severely over her ears from a central part, one almost

17

expected a dark intensity in her eyes. Instead, they were almost colorless, like shallow water, yet with an opacity unlike that of clear water. They were eyes that stared and yet looked curiously blind, as if this were a woman who already knew what she meant to see and would never have her mind changed by any fact that did not fit her beliefs. Held by this strange look—condemned by it—I could only stare in return and wait helplessly.

When she spoke at last, her voice was as colorless as her eyes, yet with a curiously penetrating quality. It was a voice that would be easily heard without needing to be raised.

"So you've come," she said flatly. "Under the circumstances, we cannot pretend to welcome you, though Laurel had no business telling you whatever it is she told you."

"I've told her nothing, Grandmother Sybil!" Laurel cried heatedly. "Only that we don't want her here."

"Go to your room," Sybil McLean said. "You had no business going out in the storm. You are in disgrace again."

The child threw me a wrathful look, as if her disgrace were my fault, and fled up the stairs.

"If you will come with me, Miss Heath," the woman said, "I will show you to your room. Captain Bascomb will see you as soon as he is able. He has been very ill, you know. His heart. I hope you will excite him as little as possible."

He had said nothing of illness in the letter I had received. I wanted to excite no one. I wanted only to solve my problem of how to live and regain some sense of a reasonable world about me. Nothing that was happening appeared in the least real. None of it could be happening.

In the hall upstairs a rail-thin woman in a black dress and white apron had just lighted a lamp against the storm. Darkness retreated as I followed Mrs. McLean's straight back and dark red skirts up the gracefully curving stairs. She led the way to a room at the rear of the house and gestured me into it. Again the woman had gone ahead and was turning away from the lighting of a lamp.

"This is Mrs. Crawford," Sybil McLean said.

The thin woman murmured words I could not hear, seeming no less hostile than the rest of the household. Then she glanced meaningfully at Mrs. McLean—almost as if she agreed with something that had not been said—and went out of the room. Only later would I realize the import of that look.

There was no fire on the room's cold hearth, and the storm outside made the air feel chill and clammy. Lightning flashes illumined wet panes of glass. I turned my back quickly upon glittering light, waiting while Joseph brought up my trunk and portmanteau. Sybil McLean said nothing until the man had gone. Then she turned that strange blank stare upon me again.

"I will let the captain know you have arrived," she said. "He will undoubtedly want to see you before supper, since he dines in his own part of the house and does not join us downstairs. That woman he has married gets his meals."

For all that my father had told me of Mrs. McLean's position in the captain's house, it seemed clear that she was no ordinary housekeeper. She had the autocratic air of one who knew her own secure place in an environment she considered superior to all others. There was a scorn and arrogance in the way she referred to the captain's wife that made me immediately sympathetic toward the woman she so dismissed. I recalled my father's words about Mrs. Bascomb being much set upon in this house. Perhaps we two would be friends.

I assured Mrs. McLean that I would be ready whenever I was summoned. After she had gone, I went to the double window near the bed and tried to see out through the glass. But while the thunderstorm was moving away, the sky had darkened early and black rain still came down, making the outdoors invisible. At least the dog had stopped its wild barking. Perhaps that dark-browed man in oilskins had taken the animal with him into the storm. I wanted no more of this impenetrable world of rain and I drew the curtains across to shut me securely in.

No warm water had been brought for my refreshment, but I poured cold from the yellow-sprigged china pitcher and bathed my face and hands in the big matching basin. I was glad to be free of my bonnet and I sought the mirror over a tall mahogany dresser in order to make myself presentable for the captain.

My own solemn expression in the glass startled me. It was as if I had glimpsed a stranger wearing my flesh and my garments. Deliberately I relaxed the unfamiliar frown lines and pressed my lips into a smile. When I had combed out the curls at the nape of my neck and brushed the pale fluff over my forehead, I stepped out of my wrinkled travel

19

costume and dressed myself in my favorite beribboned green faille.

My own natural optimism was returning. Surely some dreadful mistake had been made by those in this house. It was ridiculous to think that anyone could be seriously antagonistic to one so insignificant and harmless as myself. I had allowed the flashing of a storm, the words of a child to upset and frighten me, and that would not do at all.

Thinking of Laurel, I went to the bed to turn down the sheet and the bright patchwork quilts. Sure enough, a handful of sandy pebbles had been thrust into the center of the bed. The sight was so ridiculous that I could only laugh as I picked up the small stones and brushed sand out of the bed. As I dropped the pebbles on the dresser top, I wondered what had moved the child to so strong a prejudice against me. There seemed no sensible answer.

Ready now, I seated myself in a ladder-backed rocker to await my summons from the captain. How strange to realize that I had come at last to the very town where I'd had my beginnings. In spite of the bewildering lack of welcome I'd received in this house, there was an eagerness in me to seek out my own unknown roots, to know more of those from whom I was descended. Particularly more of Carrie Corcoran, who had lived here as a child and as a young girl, and who had grown up to become my mother.

My father had spoken of her often and readily, the sorrow of her loss always with him. He had told me of her Irish beauty and gaiety, of her affectionate spirit. Yet though his own words were spoken with loving warmth, it was always as though he held something back; as though in his thoughts he hesitated and did not speak fully, for all my urging.

There had been about my father a strangeness at times. He could withdraw into long silences that shut me out and left a core of loneliness at the heart of my otherwise happy existence. I knew my father had given up the sea while still in his prime, and sensed there were times when he brooded over this parting. The meager shore job he had held for a shipping company could never have satisfied him. The loss of my mother deepened his melancholy and when the mood was upon him I ceased to exist. It was as though he turned backward to live in a time when I had no being, could play no role in his life.

I had the feeling now that if I made my mother's acquaintance in this place I would not only be able to fill in the missing chapters of her life, but that I might also come to know more about my dearly loved father. The captain, surely, would be able to help me in this quest, and I began to look forward even more eagerly to my meeting with him.

When Mrs. McLean tapped upon my door, I was more than ready for my first introduction to Captain Obadiah Bascomb.

2. WHEN I OPENED MY DOOR TO SYBIL MC-Lean's knock, she stood for a long moment glancing over me with that look of antipathy in her pale eyes that I could not understand. She was noting, I'm sure, my effort to remove the stains of travel and make myself attractive, but there was no approval in her for anything about me.

"The captain insists upon seeing you now," she said. "It would be better to wait until tomorrow, but he will not. If he becomes at all excited, you are to leave at once. You must understand that he is ill and very frail. The doctor has warned us that his heart will not sustain any great shock or strain."

I nodded my understanding and followed her along the central hallway to where a passage connected the newer house with the old on this second level. A door opened upon a small stair landing that fronted a great central chimney. Mrs. McLean went to one of the other landing doors, tapped upon it, then ushered me into a large, cheery room in which a fire roared and polished furniture and shining brass gave off a fine gleam. A scent of faraway places seemed to rush toward me, exotic and strange.

As I stepped into the room I had a swift impression of shipshape captain's quarters. Then my attention focused on the area of lamplight and firelight close to the hearth. There a wizened little man sat in a huge chair that dwarfed him, his entire person lost in a nest of quilts, so that only his head emerged from their enveloping folds.

The shock of seeing him was great, for not by the farthest stretch of the imagination could such a man be the hero of my long-loved tales of the sea.

"Miss Heath is here," Mrs. McLean said, and stood aside to allow me to enter. She did not follow me into the room, but closed the door behind me and went away at once. I stood there hesitantly, aware again of a foreign scent upon the air. A scent that I could not immediately place, though I knew it was familiar.

From his nest this brown-faced raisin of a man waggled a beckoning hand at me. "Come here!" he commanded. "Come here where I can get a look at you."

His voice carried a ringing quality that startled me by its contrast to the rest of him. It was a voice that still gave evidence of having roared from a quarter-deck in its day. When I moved uncertainly toward his chair, his thin hand flashed out and grasped my own with surprising strength.

"Come down to my level, girl, so I can have a look at your face," he ordered me.

More than ever I wished myself elsewhere, wished that I had heeded my father's warnings. But there was nothing for it but to kneel on the hearth rug with the fire scorching hot along one side of me and allow lamplight and firelight to play upon my face. A pair of bright blue eyes stared at me from beneath shaggy white brows, and the strong, ungentle hand tilted my chin this way and that.

"You look like her!" the ringing voice said at length. "You're the spitting image of your mother. Even your eyes are like hers, with a touch of gold in the brown. I suppose you know we were all in love with Carrie Corcoran in the old days—Nathaniel and Andrew and I. But it was the one we least expected to win out who married her in the end. It's high time her daughter came home to Scots Harbor. You belong here, girl."

The Captain Obadiah of my imaginings was a tall, broadshouldered figure, at home in a storm with the deck tilting beneath his feet. He was a figure that bore no relation to this shrunken man with a voice ten times his size. The reality frightened me a little and I had no notion what to say to him. I murmured something about being sorry he was ill and not wanting to trouble him with my problems, but he brushed my words aside and shouted over his shoulder.

"Lien! Lien, come here! Confound it, woman, where are you when I want you?"

From the far shadows of the big room, where firelight did not reach and no lamp burned, the strangest of figurines came forward to astonish my eyes. She was a doll-like Chinese woman, dressed in a short coat and full trousers of pale green satin brocade. There was rice powder on her face and carmine paint upon her lips. Her glossy black hair was drawn simply back into a heavy knot, the coil thrust through with a butterfly pin of gold filigree.

My eyes dropped at once to her feet, for I knew much about China from my father, since it was a country he had loved second only to his own. This woman's feet, encased in embroidered slippers, had not been bound into tiny "lotus buds," so that she was able to move about as easily as I.

She came forward, bearing in small hands a tray of gold and black lacquer, with handleless cups set upon it. Gracefully, she bent to place the tray upon a low teakwood table at the captain's side. Again the spicy, foreign scent came to me and now I knew it was sandalwood.

The woman made a small, courteous obeisance to me. "If you please," she said in surprisingly good English, and offered me a cup. The captain dropped my hand and I rose from my knees to sit on a nearby hassock and take the fragile china from her hands, thanking her as I did so.

"This is my wife, Lien," the captain said.

I said, "How-do-you-do," looking at her with interest, for I had never before seen a woman of China. In spite of her strangely painted face, she was lovely to look at, with dark eyes that tilted exotically at the corners and full lips curved in a faint, courteous smile. Her age I could not surmise, except that she was no longer a young girl.

She returned my greeting softly and at once withdrew to the room's far shadows, not partaking of tea with us.

The captain drew my attention impatiently back to himself, as if he did not willingly share the center of interest with others for long. Though he had accepted a cup of tea from his wife, he did not sip it in a properly polite manner, but seemed able to drink it scalding hot. He drained his portion greedily and held his cup out to me to fill from the flowered pot on the tray before I had more than sipped my own. I found it a precious brew, pale green and fragrant.

"It was for the conveying of teas like this that we drove our ships to the limit back in the forties and fifties," he told me. "It took a ship with wings to deliver fine tea before the flavor faded. The company with the swiftest ships could command its own price."

I nodded agreement. "I know. My father has told me often of those voyages. And I've read about them in published accounts."

The captain's bright blue eyes studied me. "Did he tell you perhaps of the first voyage the *Sea Jade* ever made?"

The forbidden name had been spoken again and I tensed. "Not a great deal. Her first trip was my father's last and he never liked to talk about it."

"Hmph!" The exclamation emerged explosively. "He might well have felt that way! You and I need not talk of it either." The roar faded from his voice and he spoke to me more gently. "So you've come here at last, Miranda? Do you know how much this means to me—to have the old partnership drawn together once more under my own roof, close as it used to be? Ah, Nathaniel and I should never have quarreled!"

As I listened, a strange thing began to happen to me. It was as though the eyes and the voice of the man before me recreated the strong, stormy essence of all he had once been. Wrinkled brown skin and wizened body became irrelevant as I listened to him tell of the great days of Bascomb & Company. Of the days when the partnership of Bascomb, Heath and McLean had thrived and the company had rivaled the very trade of the British Indiamen on the seas. Those were the days when the three young captains had sailed the oceans of the world, continuing as partners the comradeship of experience they had known as boys in Scots Harbor. As I listened, the old spell came over me and the very room, with its ship's instruments of brass, its treasures of teakwood and jade from the Orient, the silent, exotic woman in the shadows and the fragrant tea steaming in my hands—all these wrought the old magic for me with a new, heady strength.

"Do you understand what I mean, Miranda?"

He bent toward me and held out his thin claw of a hand. But he did not snatch at me now. He waited until I put my own hand into his, giving him the trust I no longer wished to withhold, feeling myself—how foolishly!—safe at last.

24

"Do you see how it is?" he went on. "Old Obadiah Bascomb is still on deck. You are here and so is Andrew McLean's son Brock. There are some who say that Bascomb & Company is a name that has lost its power. The more fools they! With my help, the two of you who are its rightful heirs will bring it back. You'll do this for all our sakes, won't you, Miranda? For the sake of Nathaniel and Andrew and me?"

I had no idea what he was talking about, but I saw that he grew excited and I remembered Mrs. McLean's warning. Wanting only to soothe and quiet, I smiled at him warmly.

"I'll do whatever I can to help you, Captain Obadiah," I said.

The Chinese woman made a soft sound, as if of remonstrance, and came out of the shadows to stand near his chair. "This young person does not know what must be promised," she said in her high, light voice that carried an unfamiliar cadence, a faintly singsong quality, for all that the English words were correct.

Captain Obadiah looked at her with something of pride, speaking as if she were not there.

"That's prime English," he noted. "I wanted no pidgin from her, so I taught her the beginnings myself. With some polishing up of my own speech, of course. I wouldn't have her talking like an old sea dog. Ian Pryott did the rest."

"The young person must understand the promise she gives," the woman persisted.

"Go away, Lien!" The captain flashed in sudden anger. "You know better than to tell me what to do! Miranda will give me her promise. What else is there for her?" He turned to me impatiently. "How else can you live? What sort of life awaits you in New York? Working yourself into spinsterhood as a governess? Scrubbing floors for some female who'll not appreciate you or give you a home? Is that what you want?"

"It's not what I want," I said mildly, seeking only to quiet this rising excitement. "But I don't understand what it is that you ask of me."

The Chinese woman had not returned to her shadows. Instead, she went to a nearby cabinet and drew something from it. In her two hands she bore the thing back to the captain and knelt before him, offering it to him with her head bent as if in supplication. Firelight touched a golden gleam from the filigree pin in her hair, and sent red light down the broad steel blade in her hands.

The thing she held toward the captain was a sword, with a wide, curved blade on the order of a cutlass. The gesture, the vision of this kneeling doll-figure in green tunic and trousers seemed like something out of a play and once more I lost all sense of reality and personal involvement. What was happening seemed too much of the theater to be believed. Often, as I was to learn, Lien seemed to impart this sense of a performance. Or perhaps it was only the beholder's lack of firsthand acquaintance with far Cathay that resulted in this feeling of something unrelated to the everyday world. Perhaps this very fact played into her hands so that no one took her quite seriously and she could accomplish what she wished all the more easily for being considered a China doll.

Certainly the captain seemed undisturbed by the small figure kneeling so dramatically before him. He had calmed a little, for he was smiling now.

"You haven't done this in a long time, Lien," he mused and winked at me surprisingly.

I did not smile, for I could see Lien's face, hidden from the captain's view by her bent head. Her skin seemed faintly greenish beneath the rice powder and her eyes flashed a dark look, quickly hidden by the lowering of pale lids. I had a feeling of shock, and was no longer a mere spectator. Lien was far from acquiescent to all the captain's wishes.

The captain took the wicked blade from her by its hilt and held up the steel blade.

"This is a Malay cutlass, Miranda my dear. A pirate's sword. It came into my hands when my ship happened upon a mandarin's junk drifting aimlessly off the islands around the Canton estuary. The junk had been set afire and all aboard were dead except the mandarin's wife, who had hidden herself in a sea chest and thus escaped with her life. Never had I met a highborn Chinese lady before. It was a rare privilege to rescue her. Later she did me the honor to become my wife."

The woman raised her head and looked at him and at once his gentler mood vanished.

"I must do what I must do," he told her brusquely. "No one is going to stop me. Not you, Lien, or anyone else." He was in command of himself, and of us again. There was no tremor in his voice, though dangerous excitement stirred in his eyes.

"I will explain clearly what I want of you," he said to me. "Brock McLean is like my own son, as his father was like my brother. My family is gone, as your family is gone. I have no children by my marriage. Brock is the only one left who can take hold of the company after me and make it again what it should be. He cares about it as I have cared about it. He must be my heir."

This was all clear enough. I sipped the last of my tea and continued to listen. Lien reached courteously to take the empty cup from my hands. She did not go away but continued to kneel beside the captain's chair, her eyes downcast.

Captain Obadiah dropped the ugly blade with a clatter to the hearth beside him and went on. "Unfortunately, Brock is an embittered man. He has the curious notion that nothing will ever come right for him again. Whatever he touches seems to attract disaster. Or so he believes. He has determined never to marry again because he thinks he has nothing to offer any woman; nothing, in fact, to offer himself. If he will not marry, the future of the company will end with him. His child, Laurel, is a girl; and it is a grandson, at least by adoption, that I must have to carry on the line. So Brock must marry."

Still I did not see where he was heading. I sat on my hassock with my hands clasped about my knees, listening to a tale that was fascinating, but had little to do with me. Then the old man turned his clear blue look upon me and shattered my safe remoteness with his next words.

"I've brought you here to marry him, Miranda. This will be the solution to all our problems. Through you the dynasty of Bascomb & Company will continue. You will bear Brock a son to carry on our fortunes. I knew from the moment Nathaniel came here to see me that you held the solution in your own two pretty hands."

I must have gaped at him blankly. I know I gasped and could not speak at all for a moment. Then I protested in dismay.

"I don't even know Brock McLean! And he doesn't know me. What you suggest is impossible. Of course he will refuse and of course—"

"Don't waste my time with such nonsense," the captain broke in. Once more he reached out and grasped me by the wrist so that I felt the steel grip of his fingers, strangely frightening in a man so weak and ill. "You will do as I say —you and Brock. I have only a little while to live and I must see this settled before I go. Even if Brock should refuse, you are the one to bring him to his senses. You're pretty enough. And you aren't Carrie Corcoran's daughter for nothing. The three Captains will continue their rule of Bascomb Company and Scots Harbor through the two of you."

He had begun to shake with the fervor of his eagerness. The tremor of his lips as he tried to form further words alarmed me.

"Give me a little time," I beseeched him. "Until tomorrow, at least. Let me think about this. Let me meet this man you want me to marry. I'm not a pawn on a chess board to be moved without regard for my own feelings."

He gave up then, as he might not have done in the old days. He dropped my hand and fell back in his chair exhausted. At once Lien bent over him, wiping his brow with a handkerchief, motioning with her head for me to go.

I sprang up and ran for the door and neither of them spoke a word to stop me. I found my way to the newer part of the house and fled along the upper hall to the little room where I could shut the door and be alone. The contrast between the two sections of the house was extreme. Here in the newer part there was an aura of austere elegance and good taste. There was no wizened tyrant of a man, no scent of sandalwood, no exotic woman in Chinese garb, no savage blade to be offered in strange ceremony.

Yet the tenacity of the old man's will reached me even here. Within this small space I felt stifled and unsafe. I stepped to the window and looked down through the curtains. Though the late afternoon was still gray and lowering, the darkness of false night had lifted and it was no longer raining. The outdoors beckoned me. I flung my mantle about my shoulders and found my way quickly downstairs, slipping outside before anyone could question me. I wanted no encounter with Brock McLean, nor with his mother at this moment.

A stiff wind was still blowing, but it was a clear wind and I walked into it, past the lighthouse with its two chunky granite wings, and on to the very heights of the headland itself. Here scrubby juniper thinned its wild growth and gave way to a stubble of brown grass strewn with rock. Wild flowers would abound in this place in the spring, but now it was a dreary expanse of dead grass and barren outcroppings of rock.

Bascomb's Point was one of two opposite arms of land that nearly met at the opening to the harbor. To my left lay the calmer waters within, sheltered by land arms and by the long granite breakwater beyond. On my right lay the ocean. Its seas were running high in the wind, the white manes of the waves foaming as they raced toward the foot of the rocky barrier where I stood. I raised my face to the gale and let it tangle my hair and whip back my garments.

In what dusky light was left, I could make out a deeply indented, well-protected cove below the bluff on the harbor side. A fairly level ledge of land reached toward the water, its entire area strewn with piles of lumber that surrounded great wooden ribs standing up exposed, like the skeleton of a whale, to give evidence of a ship in process of being built. So this must be the place from which Bascomb & Company vessels had been sent down the ways for the last hundred years and more. On the far side of this ledge of beach several wooden docks ran out into quickly deepening water, beside one of which a small ship was tied up.

Still farther around the inner shore of the harbor I could see the clustered houses of Scots Harbor, with the white steeples of its churches rising among the lower rooftops. Alongside docks on the waterfront a forest of bare masts gave evidence of ships at permanent mooring. A scene that my father had told me was being repeated all up and down the coast now that the day of the tall ships was winding to its end.

The forests that had promised endless wood for wooden ships were thinning out. More and more iron ships were supplanting them, while steam supplanted sail. Across the continent steel rails were turning men's minds to quicker inland transport. Today, my father had said, Scots Harbor subsisted mainly on the efforts of its fishing vessels.

Below me the incoming tide sent white wavelets into the cove, while on the other side the stormy gray ocean churned and heaved. Directly opposite across the harbor entrance, the new white lighthouse pointed its slim tower to the sky. The lantern had already been lighted and was flashing its intermittent signal, while the unused lighthouse on this side stood dark. Once, through these two arms of rocky land, the *Sea Jade* must have sailed in all her maiden beauty. When I thought of how she must have looked, my very skin prickled at the imagined vision of billowing sails. How could iron ever replace the breathing, supple wood of a ship? How could clumsy funnels supplant white sails on the sea?

The sight of the water and my own imaginings had calmed me and quieted the alarm the captain's words had aroused in me. I could think more collectedly now. Many aspects of my lack of welcome at the Bascomb house were coming clear. Now I understood why Sybil McLean had looked at me with antipathy, wanting no forced marriage for her son, I knew why Laurel, picking up the angry contagion from her elders, had tried to frighten me away. The single glimpse I'd had of Brock McLean had told me how little he was willing to do as the old man wanted. But of course I could quickly set all doubts at rest. I knew now why my father had not wanted me to come to this place, and I would not stay. I would not allow Captain Obadiah Bascomb's highhanded notions to trap me into such imprisonment. I would leave as quickly as I could and never come back. By the first train I could catch I would return to New York.

And there I would face—what?

The challenge of that question made me catch my breath as though the very blast of the wind had snatched it away. But it was not the wind. It was my own dread of the struggle for existence that awaited me anywhere else but here.

I walked back along the cliff, trying to see the crescent curve of town more clearly in the gray light. There had been promise once that Scots Harbor would turn into a great shipping center like Salem or New Bedford. But the time of the tall ships had passed too quickly, and the whalers had moved farther north up the coast. The cluster of houses that made up the town had not spread out a great deal.

My mother, I knew, had been born in a small cottage down there. My grandmother had run her own little bakery shop, while my fisherman grandfather was away at sea. Carrie Corcoran had grown up among humble, hard-working people who had not always known what to make of her. "Like a nightingale in a sparrow's nest," my father had once said. Now my grandparents on both my mother's and father's side were dead, and there was no one to whom I might turn for help. There was no one who would lift a finger for me except Captain Obadiah Bascomb.

The treacherous thoughts came again, seeming to move of their own will. What of that dark-browed man who was Brock McLean? What right had he to dismiss me without knowing me? What right had he to judge and despise when he had never so much as spoken to me? Indignation brought with it a good leavening of courage. I, at least, would wait and see. I would withhold judgment until I had met and talked with this man. I would make no impulsively quick decision as he had made about me.

Thus, smugly virtuous, I opened a door in my thoughts—not to an acceptance of the captain's plan, but not to a total rejection of it either. I would simply wait and see. In spite of myself, a faint flicker of hope had stirred within me. It was not that the promise of wealth and family meant a great deal to me. It was the cotton batting of safety and love that I cared about. In that dream world to which I was accustomed, magic transformations were always possible. In the flicker of an eye the unknown figure of Brock McLean was taking on a certain romantic appeal.

The captain had said I was not my mother's daughter for nothing. But I was myself as well, and I had not been unpopular with what few young men I had known in New York. They were young men who had paid court to me decorously under my father's eye, with only playful encouragement from me. They had always seemed young and callow compared with the man I could imagine in my dreams. He, I suppose, was based on the pattern of my father, with a good lacing thrown in of Captain Obadiah's stronger brew. It was even possible that the unknown Brock McLean might fit into that dream. In my swift imagining it was not impossible that at the sight of me he would forget about never marrying again, that he would find himself willingly enough at my feet.

This weaving of fantasy was so pleasant that I smiled to myself, far more hopeful as I turned in the direction of the lighthouse. Perhaps the captain was wiser than I knew and had found a solution that was the right one for me after all. I began to feel cheerful and adventurous, and since I had no desire to return immediately to the house, I approached the lighthouse tower.

This unused structure was not nearly so tall as the newer

lighthouse across the harbor, though in its day the headland itself must have given it sufficient height. A flagged walk led across the brown grass of a lawn to a door set in the stone tower. Just behind the tower, and forming its base, was a small two-storied dwelling that jutted its wings to either side of the tower proper. Probably no one lived there now, though a flag hung from a pole over the front door. It was a flag I knew well from my father's tales—the yellow house flag of Bascomb & Company. Yellow to pay honor to China—unlike the more common blue and white flags of so many shipping concerns. The company's relations with the hong merchants of Canton had always been excellent. My father had exchanged gifts with old Houqua himself and had often spoken admiringly of the famous Chinese merchant who had headed the hongs in dealing with the west.

Lighthouses were a part of the story of ships and the sea, but I had never before set foot in one. I went quickly up the walk and mounted the low steps. The doorknob turned easily to my hand and I found that I could step inside. The moment I entered the entryway, with its iron rungs on my right, mounting circularly to the tower above, a fierce barking sounded close at hand. Alarmed, I half expected the dog to come leaping upon me, and I would have fled, had I not heard a man's voice chide the animal, so that it fell silent. I realized that the sounds came from beyond a closed door that led into one of the wings.

My heart began to thump a little at the realization that Brock McLean was only a door away. My daydreaming mood was still upon me and now I had no desire to escape. Undoubtedly he would control the dog, and it might be as well if there was an accidental meeting with this man, away from the house and the baleful influence of his mother.

I left the entryway that led to the tower and stepped into a spacious lower room, well lighted by two whale oil lamps that hung by pulleys from the ceiling. On one side its windows looked toward the captain's house, on the other toward the sea. This room appeared to open into two smaller rooms on either side, occupying the jutting wings, but these doors stood closed. The central portion into which I had stepped had been turned into something of a Bascomb & Company museum. On my right was a nearly life-sized boy, carved in wood and wearing the outfit of a sailor. He held the great brass housing of a ship's compass in his arms, and his blue eyes seemed to follow me as I went past. Suspended from crossbeams, or standing on pedestals were several figureheads, some cracked and weather-beaten, having sailed the seven seas, some as brightly and freshly painted as though they had never seen salt water. A likely possibility, I knew, since there were captains who had used their prize figureheads only when in port and stowed them safely in the hold out of harm's way when the ship was at sea.

Around the walls were hung framed paintings and photographs. Of these there was one that drew my interest at once. It was a delicately painted water color of a clipper ship, her sails puffed with wind as she sailed over neatly corrugated green waves, their crests etched in white. She was a black ship with a jade-green band painted all the way around her hull, and from the top of her mainmast flew the yellow Bascomb & Company flag. In the background were pictured blue-green hills that were stylistically Chinese. I bent to read the writing penciled on the mat and found the inscription: *Sea Jade,* Whampoa Harbor, and the name of a Chinese artist.

I stood entranced, studying every detail of the painting. This was the beautiful and dangerous ship that had broken all speed records in her day, and perhaps my father's heart as well. I knew that something had happened on that trip to make him leave his calling in spite of his never-ending devotion to the sea. I had been no more than two years old at the time and I knew nothing of what had happened. Later when I was older, a hush would fall when the name of the *Sea Jade* was mentioned, and sometimes my aunt would weep if I questioned her too closely, wanting to know more.

So rapt was I in study of the Chinese painting that I heard nothing until the nearby growling of a dog sent me whirling about in fright. The door across the room had opened. A man and a great black dog stood side by side, watching me. The dog was so huge that the man's hand lay upon its collar without his stooping.

Once I was sure the hostile animal was under his master's control, my attention was all for the man. He was out of oilskins now and I saw that he was tall and strongly built. Laurel had spoken of her father as a black Scotsman, and her description was apt. His hair was thick and dark and rather curly. Thick black brows arched above eyes that were nearly as dark, as he observed me coldly.

"Well? What do you think of her?" he asked.

It took me a moment to realize that he meant the handsome ship in the picture on the wall behind me. I felt flushed and confused and completely at a loss. This was not at all the manner in which I had imagined our meeting. It was I who should have come upon him unaware, with my smile in place and my courage high. Now I faltered as I tried to reply.

"I—I'm sure the *Sea Jade* must have been the most beautiful ship that ever sailed an ocean." My words were meant cravenly to placate, for Andrew McLean, this man's father, had designed and built the famous ship, as Laurel had reminded me.

"She was indeed," his son said curtly. "She was a clipper ship of great splendor and cruelty. She killed many a man in her day. My father among them."

I swallowed hard. Apparently my appeasing effort had gone astray. The dog growled low in its throat and I threw it a nervous glance which its master observed.

"You're right to be wary," he said. "Lucifer is not an amenable animal. But he is my friend and perhaps more to be trusted than most humans." With one large hand he gestured toward a glass case not far from me and I caught the glint of fine jade in a ring on his finger. "There's a model of *Sea Jade* that Captain Obadiah whittled out of white oak on one of her voyages. He did her justice, I think. Or very nearly."

I was glad to step to the case and pretend absorption in the graceful model the glass protected. I had the eye and the education, thanks to my father, to admire the clean lines, the grace of the prow, the unencumbered sweep of her decks, but it was the man who held my attention more than did the ship, though I could not meet his eyes.

"There were some who said my father built her too sharp so that she wasn't safe on the seas, but she proved her critics wrong," he went on. "She stayed afloat and lost herself in no storm."

"What became of her?" I asked.

His expression darkened. "The captain sold her years ago when she no longer made money for him. Perhaps she wound up as a slaver, running Chinamen to Peru to work at collecting guano."

To be involved in so tragic a trade seemed dreadful for all that gallant beauty.

34

Brock McLean spoke again, his tone suddenly low so that there was almost a growl in it like the dog's.

"You've seen the captain by now, I suppose?"

I nodded. "Yes, I've seen him."

"Then you know of this wild plan of his?"

The scorn in Brock McLean's voice cut through any last wisps of my daydreaming. I managed to draw my gaze from the ship and look at him from beneath lowered lashes.

"Yes," I said. "He has told me what he wants of me."

"And you've given him the only possible answer, of course?"

It was clear what answer he expected me to give. I could only shake my head feebly, feeling the wind-tangled curls tremble against my neck.

"I said I would answer him tomorrow. He was growing excited and he seemed very ill. I didn't want to disturb him further just then." To my own ears I seemed to be making feeble excuses.

"So you postponed your decision?"

The man spoke to the dog and commanded him to sit. Then he took his hand from the animal's collar and came toward me across the room. I did not know which I feared most at that moment—the man or his dog.

"I can understand," he said more quietly, "how tempting this offer of Captain Obadiah's must seem to you. It's quite evident that you would have everything to gain and little to lose."

The words were bracing in their import. They touched a chord of indignation in me and I summoned a few shreds of my vanished courage.

"Of course!" I told him. "I would have everything to gain —except love."

In my mind this argument had seemed the ruling one. But the sound of my words must have appeared unutterably naive, for Brock McLean smiled grimly.

"You're right about that. I hope the fact will weigh sufficiently with you so that your answer—upon proper consideration—will be a firm 'no.'"

"It will be 'no,'" I assured him, hating his arrogance, his cynical doubt of me, detesting him more than I'd ever had cause to detest anyone in my entire young life. "I hope," I added, "that the disappointment won't upset the captain too much."

"He's a tough old rascal," Brock McLean said. "And he's weathered worse than this. If you mean what you say, then the matter is settled."

"Isn't it already settled if you've rejected the plan yourself?" I asked him more boldly.

For an instant his dark look wavered from my face toward the view of lighted Bascomb windows. To my surprise I sensed a hesitation in him, something that suggested uncertainty. This alarmed me even more than his scorn. If a man like Brock McLean could be swayed by the captain or perhaps bought by him, my own resolution might not hold strong enough to save me.

I found myself echoing his own words in an effort to taunt. "It's possible that you would stand to gain even more than I by doing as the captain wishes. I can understand how tempting the offer might seem to you."

My derision went home and I saw anger flash in his eyes. He gave me no answer, but turned on his heel and went back into the room from which he had come, calling the dog to follow. I did not watch him go, and thus missed a certain physical fact about Brock McLean that I did not become acquainted with until later. A fact that had, above all else, influenced his life.

I waited until I heard the door close behind those two kindred spirits and then I picked up my skirts and fled from that place. I ran down the flagged walk with the wind behind me and scurried like a child toward the one haven I knew— the tight little room that would shield me from the assaults Bascomb's Point was making upon my temper and my emotions. I had never been so deeply angered before, or so shaken. Nor could I remember having wanted so much to hurt anyone as I had wanted to hurt Brock McLean. Tears were stinging my eyelids by the time I hurried upstairs and opened the door of my room.

The child, Laurel, sat cross-legged on the bed waiting for me, and she missed nothing of my distraught state of mind.

3.   ONCE MORE I WAS FORCED TO BRACE MY-
self. I could not face this child with tears in my eyes. Now
the anger roused by her father was ready to vent itself upon
her.

"What are you doing here?" I demanded. "I don't believe I
invited you into my room."

She sensed the turmoil in me and used it at once to
strengthen her own position. "My room is next door." She
waved a casual hand at an open door between our rooms. "I
came to see what you did with my stones. I wouldn't want
you to throw them away. Why are you angry? Why are you
nearly crying?"

I stood before the dresser mirror and busied my hands,
combing out tangles the wind had set in my hair.

"The stones were easy to remove," I told her. "The sand
was not. Why should you want to do such an unkind thing?"

"To drive you away, of course. You've seen my father,
haven't you? That's why you're upset. That's why you're almost crying."

In the glass I could see her, peering at me through lank
wisps of hair with eyes that were like her father's.

"I've seen him," I said.

At once she became agitated. She slid long thin legs from
beneath her petticoats and I saw that her striped stockings
were twisted and wrinkled, and one of them was torn. Who
cared for this child? I wondered.

"You're not going to stay here, are you?" she demanded,
coming close to stare upward into my face with her grandmother's unblinking look. "You're going to tell Captain
Obadiah you won't do as he wishes, aren't you?"

"I am indeed!" I said and was once more startled by the
unfamiliar sharpness in my voice. "There's nothing in the
world that would make me stay in a place like this and I
would certainly never marry your father."

Laurel tossed back the black strands of hair with a gesture

that was suddenly triumphant. "That's fine. The sooner you leave, the happier we'll all be. We don't want the daughter of a murderer here."

I was too shaken to behave sensibly. I pounced upon the child and shook her hard, demanding what she meant. She turned her head with the swiftness of a small animal and sank her teeth into my hand. I snatched it from her shoulder with a cry and held the red indentations to my lips.

At that moment Sybil McLean appeared in the door I had left open to the hall. She stared at us for a moment and this time I stared back with equal hostility. She was a tall, full-bosomed woman in her dark red gown. At her throat the white ruching was immaculate. Tiny jade earrings made a surprisingly exotic touch at her ears. I was aware again of a subdued intensity, of a barely restrained malevolence toward myself.

"So she's bitten you, has she?" Mrs. McLean said. "I thought we had cured her of the habit. You've no business here, Laurel. Go to your room at once. Your father will hear of this and there will be no supper for you tonight."

The child threw us both a hateful glance, snatched up her pebbles and walked through the door into her own room without hurrying. Her grandmother changed the key from Laurel's side of the door to mine. When she had locked it, she took out the key and placed it upon my dresser.

"You'd better keep the door between you locked. There's no telling what the child will do next."

With my new contrariness, I came perversely to Laurel's defense. "It was my own fault," I said. "I shouldn't have lost my temper."

Mrs. McLean regarded me in her autocratic manner, as though no remark of mine could carry weight or import. Her very bearing had the effect of making me feel young and awkward and ignorant.

"The captain has asked me to say that he wishes you to have supper with him tonight," she informed me.

I responded with what little dignity I could summon. "I'll be happy to do so. I'm glad to know he's feeling better."

"I'm not sure he is, but he will listen to no advice. I can only hope that you will try not to disturb him. The *Chinese* woman will come for you when it is time." Her underlining of the word "Chinese" gave evidence of her low regard for Lien.

She swept about with a swish of her bustled skirt and left me alone. This time I closed the hall door and bolted it. I felt more relieved by the captain's invitation than anything else. He was the one person in this house who appeared to have any liking for me. It would be far more comfortable to dine with him than to find myself at the table downstairs with Sybil McLean and her son.

From Laurel's room there came no sound, though I stood for a moment at her door, listening. In spite of my bitten hand, I felt sorry for the child. She gave evidence of knowing nothing of love or of any gentle treatment and I thought this quite likely, having met her father and grandmother. I wished I could dismiss her words about my being the daughter of a murderer as easily as I had dismissed other things she had said, but however foolish, they remained to haunt me. In a way I knew how she must feel—small and helpless, living in an atmosphere of disapproval and without affection. What else could one expect but a striking back at those one fancied as enemies? Even I, who was older and should have known better, had reacted in the same way this afternoon. I had bitten no one, but I had slapped out with an ugly taunt that was unlike me. Worst of all, I could not regret it.

I sat in the rocker once more and tried to soothe my ruffled feelings by moving gently back and forth. The dog was barking again from the rear of the house where his kennel must be. So he and his master must have returned home.

What fitting companions they made—that dark-brown man and the black dog, Lucifer! Both oversized and bad-tempered. Both burning of eye and ready to attack. Both wholly male in a sense that I could only shudder from. My father, for all that he had been master of a ship at an early age and had subsequently lived a hard life at sea, had been a gentle man in his own home. With me he had been endlessly patient and loving and forgiving—even when I sometimes behaved as a spoiled child must, wanting my own way. Even Captain Obadiah, for all that he was a shadow of what he must have been, and could take cruel hold of my hand, attempting to bend me to his will—even he had a sweeter, more affectionate side. But there would never be anything of love in Brock McLean or that black dog of his. Unless it was for each other. It was fantastic of the captain to think he might force such a marriage upon me.

In no more than fifteen minutes Lien came tapping on my

door. If she was surprised that I had to unbolt it, she gave no sign.

"You will come, please," she said.

I followed her exotic little figure toward the captain's quarters and she said nothing at all on the way. I could not tell whether her silence indicated disapproval, or the shyness of a foreign woman.

This time it was a pleasure to step into that warm, bright room with its scent of sandalwood. I saw that the captain had left his nest of quilts and stood beside an open window, looking out into the darkness while a cold, salty breeze blew in from outdoors. This was the first time I had seen him on his feet and I was surprised by the evidence of sturdiness he gave. His face and hands were wizened, but the strong bone structure of his body still lent him considerable height and breadth.

Lien ran to him at once and sought to draw him back to his chair. But though he leaned weakly upon the window sill, the captain stood his ground.

"The dog's been barking his fool head off," he said. "There's someone prowling around down there in the back garden."

Lien bent to peer through the opening and said that she saw no one.

The captain snorted. "If you'd forget that vanity of yours and get yourself glasses, you might be able to see beyond your nose. Take a look out there, Miranda, my girl. Tell me what you see."

I drew a fold of drapery behind me to shut out the lights of the room and looked down into the dark garden. From the lower windows of the new house a faint illumination had been flung across leafless bushes and flower beds. As I stared, I saw movement upon a path. A man stepped into the light and looked up at the captain's windows. For an instant I glimpsed a heavily bearded face, the shine of a head that was nearly bald. The dog was barking madly now, and the figure faded into shadow even as I looked down.

"There is someone there," I said over my shoulder.

At once the captain pushed past me to roar out the window in his surprisingly lusty voice, demanding to know who was down there and what he wanted. There was no answer and the captain seemed satisfied that he had frightened the fellow off.

"No matter," he said as I closed the window. "We keep the downstairs door locked at all times. Don't we, Lien?"

His wife bowed her glossy black head in agreement. "The door is locked. Come to your chair, please."

"Tomorrow I'll find out what's going on," the captain said, leaning on Lien's arm as he moved back to his chair. "I like all hands on deck and accounted for. With no stowaways."

Lien brought the small teakwood table and placed it before the captain. Then she drew up a chair for me and began to serve the meal. To my delight, the food was Chinese and I was able to eat as skillfully as the captain with my chopsticks. My father had been fond of Chinese dishes and we had enjoyed them often at home. Lien had cooked shrimp and bits of lobster and other sea food in a savory sauce, accompanied by vegetables done so slightly that they were still crisp, and the rice was fluffy and dry.

It troubled me that the Chinese woman would not eat with us, but the captain shrugged the matter aside.

"In her own country she would eat with the women, never with the men. Here she prefers to eat alone."

The relationship between these two puzzled me—perhaps because it matched no pattern with which I was familiar. The captain seemed to depend upon his wife in many ways, yet he treated her with the casual manner he might have bestowed upon a servant. What the woman herself thought or felt I had as yet no way of knowing.

The captain watched with approval as I began to eat. "You're hungry as a sailor, girl. It's a fine thing to savor good food. I like a hearty eater."

Lien did not at once sit down apart from us to her own meal, but hovered nearby, ready to replenish our bowls at the slightest look from the captain. More than once when she came near, I glanced at her feet, wondering at what must be considered their abnormal size for a well-born Chinese woman. The captain caught my look.

"Well may you stare," he said, again speaking as if she were not in the room. "Lien is a most fortunate exception to a miserable custom. Her father was a scholar of some note in his country—a forward-looking man who wanted to see the barbarous custom of binding girl children's feet come to an end. As it must one of these days throughout China. The Manchus, who are the country's rulers, have never adopted the custom themselves. It is thanks to her father's foresight that Lien is able to walk normally."

I glanced at the captain's wife, wondering how a scholar's daughter must feel living unaccepted in this strange household, and put to almost menial service by her husband. As I finished my second bowl of rice, thankful not to be dining with the others in the new house, I wished again that a friendship of sorts might be possible between us.

"Thought I'd get you away from all those long, lugubrious noses," Captain Obadiah said, grinning at me wickedly over his chopsticks. "The only fellow in the house with a sense of humor left is Ian Pryott. Have you met him yet?"

I recalled the man who had stood in the library door upon my arrival and said I had not. The oddly mocking bow he had given me hardly served as an introduction. But so quickly had the occupants of this house made me edgy and uneasy that I welcomed the thought of someone who might be unrelated to the McLeans, and thus more friendly.

"As Brock has been my right hand for the last few years, Ian has been my left," the captain explained. "His father sailed before the mast on a few voyages of mine. Lost at sea, he was. The mother died a long while back and the boy was left an orphan. I took an interest in him and since his taste for the sea lies only in books, and not in sailing, I gave him a bit of education and put him to work in the company as a clerk. But he's proved himself worthy of something better and lately I've given him the task of recording a history of Bascomb & Company, and I've moved him into the library so he can be close by when he wants to consult me, or when I think of a story for him. Nights he stays over in a second floor room nearby in the old lighthouse. He's ambitious and talented. I like to see a young man who's out for making something of himself and who won't give up, even when circumstances are against him. Brock could do with more of that quality himself. Ian manages to be cheerful too —which is more than I can say for the rest of this pretty household. He's helped Lien with her English and taught Laurel her lessons as well."

"Laurel doesn't seem at all a happy child," I said.

"She's not," said the captain and I saw too late the opening the subject gave him. "She needs a mother badly. You'll do wonders for her, I know. Sybil doesn't care for children, and Brock has forgotten he's a father. But you'll change all that."

I had no intention of changing anything. I shrank from the way he so readily leaped to the conclusion that I would stay and that everything was already settled. As I gave my attention to the handling of chopsticks, my lack of response must have reached him, and he sensed my opposition.

"Sybil has probably been snubbing you," he remarked. "You must pay no attention, my girl. Her nose is out of joint on more scores than I can keep track of. Once you're mistress of the house, you can give the orders."

I could imagine nothing I wanted less. "How could I possibly live in a house where everyone dislikes me, where no one wants me?" I protested.

He surprised me by reaching out to touch my hand across the table. "I want you," he said gruffly.

The gesture touched me as nothing else could have. I felt a flash of affection for this old man who had been a hero to me through all my growing-up years and who was now only a shadow of himself. He sensed a softening in me and took crafty advantage of it at once.

"When you look like that you're a dead ringer for your mother. You bear her a startling resemblance, you know. Ian will be interested in this. It's a part of Scots Harbor history —the role your mother played."

"What role did she play?" I asked, moving toward safer ground.

But he was too wily for me. "The role of the everlasting Eve, of course. Just as she wound Brock's father around her little finger, so you'll wind Brock around yours. It doesn't matter that he's afraid of you now. That's all it is, you know—the instinctive male fear of the trap. How could he resist you when you look the way you do, and when your mother's blood runs in your veins? You'll know how to deal with him, how to bring him to his knees."

The thought of Brock McLean on his knees, beseeching me for my hand in marriage was a startling picture. And a tantalizing one. Improbable, of course, however much I might like to see him there after his treatment of me—if only for the enjoyment I would have in refusing him.

"He's been without a wife for too long a time," Captain Obadiah ran on. "It's five years since Rose died. He's ripe for loving, but the town women aren't good enough for him, to

43

my way of thinking. You're the one to change his mind about marriage. You can do it if you try."

There was in me a faint prickling of temptation to try. A feeling based mainly on my desire to punish that arrogant man. My lips must have curved in a smile for the captain nodded at me.

"You've caught the look, girl. Use it on him! He likes gentle girls like the wife he married. A tepid little body, I always thought. I've never cared for meek women, but you can fool him until he's willing to bend. Then when you're married, you can do what you like with him. You know that, don't you?"

His words brought me back to reality. To play-act in my mind at the subjection of so frightening and scornful a man, was one thing. To marry him was another. I turned my smile directly upon the old man, coaxing him away from the subject.

"I saw your model of the *Sea Jade* over in the lighthouse. Was she really as beautiful a ship as that?"

He seized the bait I offered, perhaps more because of the ship's magic name than because of my coaxing.

"She was a beauty indeed. Everyone claimed that Andrew built her too sharp for safety. But I proved them wrong. Andrew had a notion that he was the only man alive who could sail her through a typhoon, but I proved him wrong too. Between us—the *Sea Jade* and Cap'n Obadiah—we made a record that has never been broken, before or since. No other ship ever touched it. Seventy-four days back from Canton!"

"Mr. McLean said the ship killed his father. What did he mean by that?"

"As a manner of speaking, I suppose you could say that she did." The captain's laugh had a sour sound. "Though indirectly." The thought must have been an unpleasant one because all mirth went out of him. He leaned toward me again and grasped my wrist, not affectionately this time, but so tightly that I winced. "I'll not wait till tomorrow for your answer, girl. These days I can't be sure of tomorrow. So I'll have your promise now. I've seen you for myself. I can tell your worth. You'll raise fine sons for Brock. Promise me now that you'll marry him."

I was suddenly afraid of this willful old man who still had such strength in his fingers. I cried out that I could give no such promise. That I could not, would not marry Brock McLean.

He flung my hand away from me so sharply that it struck against a teacup and sent it flying, spilling pale green liquid across the table. The cup crashed upon the hearth and at once Lien came to kneel before the fire and sweep up the shattered fragments. Her regret over the destruction was visible in her every movement. When I looked back at the captain I saw that an ugly expression had come into his eyes. "He's ruthless," my father had told me and I knew that this would be true.

"Did Nathaniel ever give you an account of what happened aboard the *Sea Jade?*" the captain demanded of me.

I shook my head, not wanting to hear the story, whatever it was, if it must come to me from prejudiced lips.

"Do you want to have Nathaniel's good name destroyed —and he not here to speak for himself? Do you?"

"I don't know what you mean," I said. "My father's good name speaks for itself."

The old man went on relentlessly. "I have only to tell the truth about that first voyage of the *Sea Jade*—as I didn't tell it at the time. Nathaniel was my good friend. I was willing to lie to save him. But if you refuse me now, if you do not do as I wish, I can publish the truth. It's not a pretty truth, my girl. It will destroy Nathaniel's name in the record, and it will undoubtedly hurt you as well."

I was shocked and frightened, yet within me some small wellspring of strength that I had never before tapped surged up to give me a stubborn courage as I answered him.

"If you did not tell whatever you had to tell when the thing happened, then I don't believe you will tell it now. And I will not marry Brock McLean for such a reason."

The ugly look that had frightened me vanished abruptly and he startled me by laughing. To my astonishment, the sound had a hearty, approving ring, as though I had somehow managed to do the right thing.

"You've called my bluff!" he roared. "A little trick of a thing like you! You're right, girl. Whether I like it or not, you're right. The old story is dead. What's done is done and I'll not undo it now. I'm pleased you've got the backbone to stand up to me. Never could endure a namby-pamby-afraid-of-her-shadow female like Rose. I don't mean you've won, my girl. You'll do as I want and you'll do it soon. But I like the fact that you're a scrapper."

A scrapper? I had never thought of myself in such a light, and his words brought me no ease. Captain Obadiah was one accustomed to having his way at all costs. I did not want to remain in this house to find out what he would try next to force my will to his. The sooner I escaped him the better. I must find out about trains for home. I must get away from this place.

He had just signaled to Lien to remove my empty bowl and his own half-eaten food, when I saw his look change. He was staring fixedly at the door behind me, while a flood of crimson rushed into his face. He made a choking sound and put a hand to his throat.

I turned and saw in the doorway the same bearded fellow I had glimpsed in the garden. He wore a seaman's jacket and trousers, and there were boots on his feet. His bald head was bare and he touched a mocking forefinger to his temple.

"Tom Henderson at your service, Captain Bascomb," he said.

The captain pulled himself to his feet, fighting for the power of speech. "Why . . . are . . . you here?" he managed hoarsely.

The man's grin was cocky. "You know well enough why I'm here, Cap'n. You knew I'd come back someday and then the jig would be up. You knew that, didn't you?"

The captain stared at him for a long moment of violent, inward struggle. Then he fell back, slumping in his chair. Lien rushed to him, bent over him. She spoke to me without glancing around.

"Bring them from the other house. Quickly, please!"

I sprang up and found as I turned toward the door that the bearded sailor had disappeared. I ran through the passage to the other house and breathlessly down the stairs. In the hallway below, Mrs. Crawford, bearing a tray of dishes, had just emerged from the dining room. When she saw me she blocked the doorway, her thin face registering disapproval.

"You can't go in there now," she said flatly. "Mrs. McLean doesn't like to be disturbed at mealtime."

From beyond I could hear the sound of voices, the small clashings of silverware and china.

"Let me by!" I cried. "The captain is ill!"

I think she might have disputed my entrance to the room even then, had not Brock McLean heard my voice and told her to let me in. I brushed past the woman, impelled by Lien's urgency. They were all there at the table except the banished child: Mrs. McLean, Brock, Ian Pryott.

"The captain is very ill!" I told them as they turned startled looks in my direction. "His wife wants you to come at once."

Without pausing to ask questions, Brock left the room with a limping stride. For the first time I noted that some physical handicap interfered with the motion of one leg. I could see that it gave him difficulty, though it did not slow him now. His mother rose with less haste and moved toward the door. When I would have accompanied her, she spoke to me curtly.

"Please do not come with me. You have done nothing but disturb him ever since you arrived."

She swept past me with the haughtiest of airs, and at her going I heard a sound behind me. I whirled to find Ian Pryott looking down at me from his tall height.

"Why does she treat me like that?" I asked, choked with indignation and hurt. "I have done nothing to harm the captain."

"I can tell you easily enough," he said. "Your grandmother was a shopkeeper, your grandfather a fisherman. If it's any comfort to you, my mother ran a grog shop and Mrs. McLean treats me in the same way. It is an offense to her sense of what is proper for the McLeans to have us in the house."

He spoke quietly, without bitterness, though his look was wry. When I would have left him to return to my room, he touched my arm lightly, arresting me.

"Don't go, please. I'm glad of an opportunity to talk to you, Miss Heath."

Was it possible that someone in this house could treat me kindly? I measured Ian Pryott with more caution than I would have been capable of only a few hours before. He was younger than Brock by a few years, I judged. Perhaps thirty to Brock's thirty-five. He must have been as tall as Brock, for I had to look up at him, but he was far less stocky of build. There seemed a wiry strength in the man that I sensed through the very touch of his hand, as though some life force pulsed strongly to his very finger tips. His hair, brushed back from the forehead, was only a little darker than my own pale locks, and his eyes were the gray of the ocean off Bascomb's Point. As I was soon to know, they were eyes never to be easily read. Even in such a household as this, Ian was able to remain his own man.

He smiled at me with his quick, wry way of seeing past the façade a person might present to the world, cutting home to the truth, however unflattering. Whether he was handsome, as I had first thought, or whether his face was ill-proportioned and uncomely, I could never fully decide, for the sculpture of its planes received the light irregularly. And in any event, it never seemed to matter.

I must have studied him as unblinkingly as Sybil McLean had studied me, for his smile broadened. "If I pass muster, Miss Heath, let's leave the captain to the good ministrations of others for the moment. You don't want to go back there immediately, do you?"

"The captain is very ill . . . perhaps I should . . ." I broke off, knowing he was right. Concerned though I was for Captain Obadiah, I knew Mrs. McLean would not allow me to help. While I hesitated, Ian Pryott gestured toward the library across the hall.

"You need to catch your breath," he said. "You'll be more comfortable in here."

We left the elegance of polished mahogany, of fine linen and silver, and went into the smaller room I had noted the first time I had seen Ian Pryott. Here books crowded the shelves and a fire burned cheerily in a narrow grate. Near a window stood a desk heaped with papers, books, and writing materials—undoubtedly to do with his work of recording Bascomb & Company history.

He brought a chair upholstered in yellow damask and seated me before the fire. It was a lady's chair, small with a gracefully rounded rosewood frame, and it seemed out of place in this room of mahogany and leather and masculine simplicity. As if it might have been borrowed from a drawing room for the comfort of feminine visitors. As I was later to learn, it was Laurel's favorite chair.

My impromptu host remained standing, an elbow resting upon the white marble mantelpiece near the inevitable model of a sailing ship under glass. Here the fire seemed to burn with less exuberance than did the huge, old-fashioned fire in Captain Obadiah's room. The very contrast was

48

somehow relaxing and I realized for the first time the strain I had been under ever since my arrival at Bascomb's Point. My hands, as I held them toward the fire, were shaking a little and once more I felt close to tears. Ian Pryott's gray eyes missed little. He went to a table, poured me a glass of wine, and held it by the slender stem until I took it and sipped a little.

"There," he said, "that's better. The color's coming back into your cheeks. The old man has given you a bad time, I'm sure."

This was the first person in the Bascomb household who had been truly kind to me, who wanted nothing of me. I sipped more of the wine and set the glass on the small table beside me. Then I burst ridiculously into tears.

4.

IAN PRYOTT LEANED AGAINST THE MANTEL and watched me weep into a scrap of handkerchief. I was accustomed to being consoled when I wept over the most inconsequential matters. But this man made no further effort to comfort me. At length I grew ashamed of my tears and stole a look at him, to surprise a curious expression upon his face. It was a look that seemed inquiring, wryly questioning. It was not at all a look that said he liked and admired me, or even that he was sorry for me. Apparently I had been mistaken in thinking him kindly inclined toward my plight.

I dried my eyes and straightened in my chair, ready to face my problems again. After all, I wanted pity from no one.

"I'm sorry," I said. "I feel better now."

"Would you like to tell me what caused the captain's upset?" he asked, ignoring my apology.

I had no hesitation about telling him and he listened with that faintly sardonic smile touching his mouth. What I related about the appearance of the bearded man did not surprise him.

"Old sea dogs are always turning up out of the past to

49

call on the captain," he said. "Some of them just want to yarn awhile about the old days. But in his time the captain was one of the most hated ship's masters on the China run, and there are still those who bear him a grudge. When they come back to pay him off, they have to be sent about their business. Brock and Lucifer will take care of him if he's not wanted about."

I shivered. "That dreadful, ugly dog!"

"Lucifer is all of that," Ian Pryott agreed. "Since you would scarcely meet the animal while he was alone, I presume you've also met his master?"

I did not want to talk about my meeting with Brock McLean and I left the words a statement, rather than a question. "The captain told me you are writing a history of Bascomb & Company," I said. "That must mean the history of Captain Obadiah as well. Will you put in what you've just mentioned about his being hated by some of his crews?"

"Of course. He'd not want it different. No weakling ever made a good clipper ship captain. To get the speed he needed, a captain had to ask everything of both his ship and his men. He had to know to the last square inch how much sail a ship could carry in the teeth of a storm, and he never hesitated to send his men aloft at the last minute, no matter what the weather. Those clipper sailors were a tough and rugged crew. They needed a master strong enough to handle them."

"My father was a clipper ship captain," I offered proudly.

"Yes, I know."

"Yet I've never seen a gentler man."

Ian Pryott smiled and left the subject. "What are you going to do now, Miss Miranda Heath? I've heard about the captain's plans for you."

I gave my answer quickly. "I've already told the captain I won't marry as he wants me to."

Ian Pryott seemed surprised. "Do you think he'll accept such an answer as final?"

"What else can he do? I mean to leave as quickly as I can. I want to catch the next possible train away from Scots Harbor." I leaned toward the man at the mantel, suddenly eager. "Will you help me? Can you tell me about the trains and help me to get away?"

He shrugged slightly. "Perhaps I might. But you'd only

have to come back. The captain will never let you get away now. The sooner you face that, the sooner you can take steps to save yourself. Though not, I think, by running away."

"Save myself?"

His fair eyebrows lifted slightly and I knew well enough what he meant: save myself from Brock McLean. This I intended to do, of course.

"Mr. McLean likes me no better than I like him," I said heatedly. "There can be no question of marrying him—ever."

Again Ian Pryott surprised me. He bent toward me and put a forefinger beneath my chin, tilting my face to the light.

"It's a good thing Brock is too much shut up in his own prison to look out and see what is being offered him. It might be the worse for you if he looked your way. Perhaps the worse for him too."

I did not wince from his finger or his studying gaze, though I did not understand what he meant. After a moment he dropped his hand and took a turn about the room away from me. I felt suddenly uneasy, as though this man might know something that I did not, as though he withheld something from me. His next words surprised me further.

"Very well," he said, "I'll help you get away. There's a train tomorrow morning at eleven o'clock. I'll get you aboard it if that's what you want. I don't know that it will do you much good, but perhaps you had better try."

"Why does the captain want this marriage?" I asked. "The fact that there was once a partnership between the three families has no meaning now. That is a sentimental reason and he doesn't seem a sentimental man."

Ian Pryott returned to the hearth and stood looking into the fire as he considered his answer. "Perhaps Captain Obadiah is more sentimental than you'd suppose. For another thing, he likes his own way and he can never brook opposition. Nor does he ever forget a defeat. Nathaniel Heath is the only man who ever bested him. Captain Obadiah wanted Carrie Corcoran for himself. But in the end she made another choice. Now you are going to pay for what your mother did. You're not only your father's daughter, you're Carrie's daughter as well—the daughter of Obadiah's one true love, because of whom he never married in his younger days. Now he's answering Nathaniel, and Carrie too, by bringing you here. He means to tie you into the Bascomb fortunes through your marriage to Brock."

"But he can't do that!" I cried. "I won't let him. I understand now why my father didn't want me to come to Scots Harbor. Were you here when my father visited the captain? Did you meet him?"

"Briefly," Ian Pryott said. "He was closeted with Obadiah most of the time. They had a few strong words that made the walls reverberate."

"Did Brock McLean meet him?" I asked.

Ian shook his head, unsmiling. "Captain Obadiah saw to it that Brock was sent away when he knew your father was coming." Again there was that faintly evasive look, as if something were being withheld from me.

I pressed him further. "What will happen if the captain dies? Won't the money and control of the business go to Brock anyway, whether he marries me or not?"

"I should think it would go to the captain's wife."

"Lien? That would put everyone's nose out of joint," I said, taking some pleasure in the thought.

"It would indeed."

"What is she really like—this Chinese woman? The captain said you taught her English."

"Perhaps I helped. She's quick and intelligent. She went almost faster than I could lead the way."

"My father hadn't told me that she was Chinese, but he hinted that she had a hard time in this house. Mrs. McLean seems to resent her presence."

"That's putting it mildly. Mrs. McLean has never discovered that her own particular culture is not necessarily the center of the world. For the Bascombs and the McLeans Scots Harbor, the company, and Bascomb's Point are at the heart of the universe. All roads must return to this hub."

"My father wasn't like that," I said. "He always wanted me to read and learn about other people and places. He wanted me to respect the right of others to look at things in a different way. Since I could not travel abroad in reality, he saw to it that I traveled in books."

For the first time Ian Pryott smiled at me with no wry twist. "Good for Cap'n Nat. But this would make you a hard pill for the others to swallow. If you stayed."

"If I were going to say I'd like to be friends with Lien," I told him. "I've never known a Chinese person."

"She's not easy to know, though I've tried to stand on her side. At least I've taken the trouble to learn more about her than Mrs. McLean has."

"Lien frightened me this afternoon," I said. "She brought out a dreadful looking knife and went through some sort of ceremony by offering it to the captain."

"The Malay cutlass? She must be furious with him."

"I felt she disliked me," I said. "She wanted him to tell me the truth, but I could sense her intense dislike for me all the time I was in the room. Why should she feel that way?"

Ian had turned to his desk and he stood fingering papers upon it idly. "Why shouldn't she? If the captain marries you to Brock and changes his will, she'll be left with only her dower rights."

I pondered the logic of this. "Perhaps that would be the best way, after all. How could she run the business, or manage the captain's wealth?"

Ian was suddenly impatient and I glimpsed again the mocking facet of his character that left me uneasy. After apparent kindness, he could step back abruptly, as if he washed his hands of me and my problems, and laughed at me for expecting more.

"Ask the captain if you want to know," he said. "There's a small legacy for me in any case, and a job to be finished, no matter what the outcome is. After that I'll look for work elsewhere. I'll not seek employment with the company if Brock McLean is in charge. I like him no better than he likes me. I never intended to stay here indefinitely in any case. When I've served the captain I'll go."

At least his vehemence against Brock was somewhat reassuring. "Since we share the same feeling about Mr. McLean and his mother, perhaps I can count you my friend as well as Lien's for the little while I must stay in this house?"

The hint of mockery that disturbed me in him had vanished. He regarded me almost warmly. "I will be your friend for however long you stay, Miranda Heath," he assured me.

I rose and held out my hand. "I want to leave tomorrow, if that is possible. I shall be grateful for your help."

He took my hand in one of his and covered it with the

other. There was an unexpected sweetness in his smile, as if he liked me already and even wanted me to like him. I felt comforted, though perhaps with little reason, since Ian Pryott could have so little influence on my fortunes in this house.

I told him I would count on him to aid in my escape on the morrow. But now I would return to the captain's rooms to see how he was progressing, no matter whether Mrs. McLean wanted me there or not. Ian went with me as far as the door and as I climbed the stairs he stood looking up at me gravely until I was out of sight.

I found my way to the landing in the old house and rapped upon the captain's door. In a moment Mrs. McLean came to open it. When she saw me she shook her head and put a finger to her lips.

"There's nothing you can do. He's had a dreadful shock. It will be a miracle if he recovers. Please go to your room and don't return unless you are sent for."

I wondered if she was sending me away against the captain's wishes, but I dared not oppose this woman who so openly disliked me. Without answering, I turned away and retraced my steps to my room. There the air seemed chill and damp and the fire remained unlighted. I did not want to set match to it now and decided to go to bed at once. My day had been long and wearing, not only because of my trip, but because of the extremes of emotion that had beset me. I bolted the door to the hallway once more, though I was not quite sure why I wanted it locked. When I looked for the key to Laurel's room on the dresser, I found it missing. There was no sound from beyond her door and I tried for the knob. The door was locked—probably from the other side. I did not mind. It was not that strange, unhappy little girl whom I feared in this household.

I undressed quickly and pulled my warm flannel nightgown over my head. The livid scar that had marred my left shoulder since babyhood seemed to ache and burn as it sometimes did when I was worried, and I rubbed it with absent fingers. Our family doctor had told me that such aching was purely of my imagination and that the injury I had received as so young a child could not trouble me now. Nevertheless, the nervous reaction remained.

Before I got into bed I stood for a moment at the window, looking down into the same garden area that was overlooked by the captain's windows. Though blocks of light from the older house patterned the garden in geometric squares, no bearded face stared up at me. The dog was silent now and nothing stirred among the shadows.

From this rear window I could not see the point of land that extended into the ocean, nor was the old lighthouse in view. But across the harbor the newer light flashed, alternating a period of darkness with a period of light. I knew I would not sleep with that flickering against my window and I drew the curtains tightly. Then I ran across the bare floor to where a bright oval of rag rug before the bed lent warmth and softness to my feet. A moment later I was shivering between cold sheets, pulling the quilts up snug around me.

I did not sleep. Where the night had seemed quiet before, now the sounds of a strange place seemed to murmur all about me. The sea wind howled more fiercely, it seemed to me, than the city winds to which I was accustomed. This point of land thrust itself unsheltered into the open, to be jostled by ocean gales and dashed with spray. I could hear the sea breaking with a roar upon the jagged rocks of the ocean side, then sucking back in the undertow, only to crash again, endlessly. My romantic dreams of ships and the sea had somehow never provided me with a sound so monotonously ominous.

Even the little room with its locked doors no longer seemed a harboring place. Lying there in bed, I had the curious feeling that some whispering of secrets went on in its shadow —as if the very walls talked to one another in sibilant sounds that mingled with the distant hissing of the sea.

I lay sleepless for a long while and the old loneliness which had haunted me at times deepened a hundredfold before my weary body brought me surcease and I dropped into uneasy slumber.

Perhaps I slept for two hours, or three. Once when I jerked awake, I heard a grandfather's clock downstairs striking midnight. I listened, counting until all was silent and I fell again into unhappy dreaming. Now my dreams took on a tinge of evil. I dreamed of some danger that came upon me with a pulsing of light, that beat against my eyelids and threatened my very life. I started up with a cry, to find the light was real.

Someone stood beside my bed holding a candle that

smoked and flickered in a draft of air, blinding me. In fright I struggled away to the far side of the bed. The woman holding the candle was the captain's wife, Lien.

"Do not fear," she said. "I am sorry to wake you. But you must come now. Come at once."

I flung a fearful glance at the hall door and saw that it was still bolted. She noted my look. "It is locked. I have entered through the child's room. The captain has not recovered from the shock he has suffered. Perhaps he is dying. You will come to him at once."

Still dazed, I stepped into the stinging cold and thrust my feet into slippers, pulled my warm wrapper about me, let the long braid of my hair hang down my back. Lien went to the hall door and slid back the bolt. But before we left the room she spoke to me softly.

"It is perhaps the end for him. You may as well promise what he asks. Give him peace. It does not matter now. It will not change your life."

The cold draughtiness of the hallway shocked me awake and I hurried after Lien as she returned to the captain's rooms.

There the fire still burned in the grate, though less energetically than before. The old man sat beside the hearth, enveloped in bright quilts. Brock McLean stood behind his chair, watchful and dark-browed as always, as if he habitually scowled. His mother sat somewhat apart across the room, though as watchful as her son. Neither looked at me or greeted me as I entered.

At least the room's warmth was a relief after the shuddering cold of a New England autumn night. The captain saw me at once and a thin hand darted from his quilts to beckon me close.

"Expected to find me in bed, didn't you, girl? But I'd rather die on my own quarter-deck instead of in bed like any landlubber. Come here, girl."

His voice was fainter than before and it cracked more than once, as though he were fading fast. I could feel only pity for him—pity for all who were strong and bold, to whom age and weakness eventually comes. I dropped to the hassock where I had sat at his knee earlier and took his frail hand into my own.

"I've only a little time left," he told me. "I must make my last plans at once. My will must be changed. Except for a few legacies and my wife's dower portion, all must go to Brock, who has been like a good and loyal son to me. You and he must have sons of your own to assure the future of Bascomb ships upon the seas."

Behind him Brock McLean leaned forward and put a hand upon the old man's shoulder. I saw a compassion in his face I had not glimpsed before, and it came to me that this hard, cold man loved the rascally, still heroic captain.

"But first," the old man went on, gathering a last strength into his voice, "I must have your promise, Miranda. As Carrie's daughter you are already dear to me. This way you will be cared for always. Give me your word that you will marry Brock so that I can change the will."

I looked helplessly from one to another of those in the room. From her far corner Sybil McLean watched me with antipathy. Still her son did not meet my eyes. Only Lien was trying to tell me something from the place where she knelt at the captain's right hand. Her slanted, foreign eyes held my own with insistence and now I remembered what she had said to me in my room. If I gave my promise it would ease the captain's dying—yet it would not matter. There was no time for will changing now. There was only time to give him some peace of mind in his last moments.

Yet still I could not speak. Afterwards no one would hold me to such a promise, I knew. Least of all Brock. It was already too late for the will to be changed in his favor. Yet somehow I could not give lightly a promise I did not mean to keep. I did not want to betray this dying old man with a lie.

He was quick as before to sense my resistance and turned his head feebly. "Help me with the girl," he said to Brock.

For the first time Brock looked at me, a challenge in his eyes. I could only shake my head, holding out against them both. Brock McLean leaned past the captain and grasped my hand in his strong, fierce clasp. There was a cold fire in the look he bent upon me—a fire that seared, yet had no warmth. At the grip of his fingers about my own, a shock seemed to run through my body.

"Give the captain your promise," he commanded.

All strength drained from me. I could hold out against them no longer. I could not, after all, deny this old man what little comfort my words might give him. Numbly I bowed my head.

57

"I will marry him if you wish it, Captain Obadiah," I said.

At once there was sound and movement in the room. Brock withdrew his hand from mine with a quick, sharp gesture, almost as if, having imposed his will, he flung me from him. Mrs. McLean made a sound of outrage, quickly suppressed, and moved to the center of the room. Lien stirred slightly in her kneeling place on the floor, her breath escaping in a long sigh. Even the fire contributed sound as a red log fell with a thud that sent sparks aloft in the grate.

I saw that the captain's eyes were brighter now and a flush bloomed in his cheeks. He was looking at me with an expression of gleeful triumph that made me wonder if I had been tricked, and if he was far from dying after all. If that was the case, I would not keep my promise. I would fight them all every inch of the way.

"Get Joseph," the captain told Lien, his voice stronger now. "Send him at once to summon both Dr. Price and Mr. Osgood. He is to bring them here as quickly as he can. I'll do no dying until my wishes are executed."

"Joseph is waiting," Lien said. "The carriage is ready, as you ordered. I will tell him."

She ran from the room, moving swiftly, yet quietly in her soft-soled slippers. I could feel the trap closing about me and I started to speak, to protest, but Brock uttered two words, silencing me.

"Be quiet," he said.

Again his look set his will above my own and I was still. I thought helplessly of Ian Pryott, too far away to help me —the only person to whom I could have turned for aid.

The captain's hand seemed feverishly hot and dry about my own. Its pressure had weakened, but he did not let me go. Without hope of escape, I sat upon my hassock, waiting for whatever was to come.

5.

THE WEDDING CEREMONY WAS BRIEF. DR. Price, the minister, arrived first. In a daze I stood beside Brock, aware that the room was too hot and that hatred toward me burned beneath the surface. Even while Brock and his mother conceded to the captain's wishes, I knew how greatly they despised me. I was the price of inheritance for Brock. A price he could not escape paying. I wished he could know that my distaste for him was equally strong.

As the minister looked at him inquiringly, Brock drew a ring from his little finger—a gold ring set with a jade stone that I had noted before on his hand—and put it upon my own fourth finger. It slipped on loosely, and in that dazed moment the fact that the ring was too big for me seemed a more vexatious detail than anything else.

There were other inconsequential distractions—as if I must give my attention to anything except what was happening to me. Once I heard the black dog howl in the distance and the sound seem prophetically menacing. Wind rattled dry leaves on a nearby tree and a bough scraped against the window. The night was a black entity outside, pressing against the house, and the voice of the sea spoke again and again, sounding its own mournful counterpoint to the events in that room.

Sybil had come forward to stand at her son's elbow. Firelight gleamed in the fading auburn of her hair, and her bosom moved with the deep anger of her breathing. Lien remained beside the captain, her eyes downcast as if she would hide her thoughts from all in that room.

Captain Obadiah waited impatiently until the last words of the ceremony were spoken. Then he asked testily for Mr. Osgood, the lawyer. Where had the man got to? Why wasn't he here? Joseph came in to say that he had gone first to Mr. Osgood's house and the lawyer had promised to come as quickly as he was able. He would ride his own horse, so Joseph had not waited for him.

If there had been trickery on the captain's part, it had not lasted long. He was truly fading now. The will to wait, to hold onto the parting threads of his life was weakening before our eyes.

"Ian!" he gasped to Lien. "Bring him here at once. Tell him—paper, pen—!"

Lien fled. The captain's hand tightened briefly about my own. "Lean closer, girl. For . . . your ears . . . only." He flashed his old look of command at Brock. "Stand back, the rest of you. I'll speak to her alone."

Dr. Price stood apart uneasily with Brock and Mrs. Mc-Lean. I bent toward the captain and his hot dry breath brushed my cheek as he spoke softly in my ear.

"Watch for storm signals, girl. Reefs ahead. You can weather . . . a good little craft. The whale stamp . . . follow the whale stamp. On the China run."

He was trying to tell me something and I did not understand.

"What do you mean?" I whispered, leaning to catch his least whisper.

His words came spaced between the gasps of his breathing. "Only half . . . the story . . . find . . . the whole. I always meant to . . . meant to . . ."

Even as I tried desperately to catch his words, his meaning, the clutching fingers loosened about mine and he lay back and closed his eyes as if he had gone to sleep. Ian came into the room with Lien upon his heels, but they were already too late. Dr. Price bent over the old man, then straightened to look at Brock.

"The captain has made his last landfall," he said.

I glanced at Ian and saw his eyes upon Brock's jade ring on my wedding finger, saw the sardonic smile touch his lips. I knew what he was thinking—that I had been bought by the captain after all. Everyone would now think that was why I had agreed to this mad plan.

For the moment, however, no one paid any attention to me. Lien was wailing aloud, a strange foreign keening that had no place in this New England room, and seemed more a rite than an expression of grief. Brock gathered the old man up in his arms, a frail burden, and carried him into the adjoining bedroom.

Again I saw the difficulty with which Brock moved his right leg, as though the trouble might reach all the way to his hip. Yet there was no lack of physical strength in the man and he carried the captain in his arms with ease.

Joseph was sent off again, this time to fetch the doctor. No one needed me. I had served my single purpose—futile now, since Brock would not receive his inheritance after all. In me there mingled pity for the captain, stunned recognition of my own position as well as fear of what was to come— all stirred into a turmoil of confusion. I could not bear to remain in the captain's rooms, and I slipped away to the newer house. If any noted my leaving, I was not called back or pursued.

Once more I shot home the bolt of my door with a ringing of metal. I lighted a candle and faced the cold, strange room. It seemed new to me now, like a place I had never seen before. But it was I who was changed, I who had become even more a stranger to the room. The ring burned my finger, loose as it was. I took it off and laid it on the dresser where Laurel's pebbles had rested so innocently earlier in the day. There was no innocence about the jade ring. It was an indication of barter, of purchase, of contract made and sealed.

Lien had left Laurel's door open when she came to bring me to the captain and it remained ajar. I went to draw the key from the other side where the child must have placed it, and stood for a moment looking about a room that was smaller than my own. Candlelight from my own doorway reached through and faintly illumined the child lying asleep on her pillow. There were streakings of tears that had dried upon her cheeks and when I bent closer I saw that her pillow was damp. She turned restlessly under the light, but did not waken, and I stood looking at her, thinking in disbelief that I was now the stepmother of this pitiful and unfriendly little girl. But though the word repeated itself in my mind, I could not accept or believe in my new identity. I moved as if in a dream from which I must surely waken.

When I returned to my room, I closed the door between, though I did not, after all, lock it. My head had begun to throb and my body ached with renewed weariness as I got into bed again. Yet I could not at once fall asleep. I lay tensely awake, listening to the house. At times the sound of distant voices came to me. There were occasional hurrying steps on the stairs, or in the hallway outside my door. Yet no one came to summon me on this incredible wedding night.

Now and again in past daydreaming I had thought of what such a night would be like, warming myself with un-defined visions of tenderness and love. Never had I expected to lie cold and alone on my wedding night, as forgotten—once I had done the captain's bidding—as though I did not exist.

Not that I wanted anything else after that hasty, unreal ceremony. All I asked under such circumstances was to be forgotten. Yet the captain's passing left a lonely void. In spite of what he had asked, he had championed me. Now I was wholly alone and without a defender.

The events of the night began to run ceaselessly through my mind and I could not stop the wheel from turning, or blank out the pictures. In every detail I lived again what had happened. I recalled the very feeling of Brock's hand upon my own when he had forced me to his will. How much he must have coveted the captain's legacy that he would accept a bargain he so plainly abhorred. As details multiplied I even found myself wondering for the first time about the wife who had died five years ago. "Rose," the captain had called her, and he had dismissed her as too gentle and "namby-pamby." Yet Brock must have loved her deeply. Did his bleak, harsh qualities stem from despair suffered after her death? If so, how bitterly he must resent this unwished-for marriage that had been forced upon him by Captain Obadiah.

Not even the thought that I might have had a friend in Ian Pryott could comfort me now. He, at least, might have helped me to escape, but now it was too late. I did not want to remember the way he had looked at me in the cap-tain's room when he saw that the marriage words had been spoken and that I had accepted this bondage.

Tossing in my bed, trying to find some respite for my throbbing temples, I gave myself to thinking of the captain. At least I had tendered something there. I had eased his dying. The Captain Obadiah of my meeting tonight was not at all the hero I had pictured, yet I had begun to realize that the essence of the man he had once been still burned within his frail being. He was still capable of command, of ruthless action, yet of affection and tenderness too. Once he had loved my mother deeply. Perhaps she had fled from his approach as I had fled from Brock McLean's. *Fled?* I ques-tioned my own thoughts, startling myself. I had not fled at all, really. "I *am* Mrs. Brock McLean," I repeated to myself, but the words meant nothing.

If the captain had lived, I might have learned to be fond of him, as he seemed so quickly ready to be fond of me. In the end he had tried to tell me something, to warn me of some danger ahead. But his voice had wavered and the words had faltered too soon. What had he meant by that hurried reference to a whale stamp? To *follow* a whale stamp? What had he meant about half a story? The words were meaningless gibberish, a part of the nightmare.

It was a long while before I fell asleep. Then, although my dreams were disturbed and sometimes frightening, I could not remember them in the morning when I wakened. I opened my eyes only to a sense of apprehension. Beyond my curtains the sun was high and I knew the hour must be late. For a moment I lay dazed and drugged with heavy sleep. It was the thought of my marriage to Brock McLean that wakened me fully. I rolled out of bed and ran barefoot to the dresser. The cool green of jade in a gold ring told me that this particular thing had not been a dream.

All the frightening implications of my situation swept back to envelop me. Last night I had been too stunned and weary to believe, or even to fear. Now I began to face my desperate situation, to turn and twist in its confines, seeking some answer, some escape. The fact of my marriage to Brock McLean could not be set lightly aside, yet somewhere there must be an avenue of escape. I knew he could not want me for his wife any more than I wanted him for husband. Ian Pryott, I thought—I must find Ian. When I explained, he would understand how my hand had been forced, how helpless I had been with all of them against me in that room last night. Somehow, somehow, he would know a way out.

I had sensed in Ian a quiet purpose that I had found in no one else in this house. Perhaps because he had long had to struggle with adversity, he was the stronger for it and would not easily be brought to despair. At the moment, I was overwhelmed by the events that had overtaken me. Yet at the same time there was an unyielding core of stubbornness in me that would not give up, a budding of strength that was new to my experience, since it had never been needed before.

I dressed hurriedly and went into the upper hall. All the doors were closed to shut what warmth there was into the rooms. No one was in sight. As I moved toward the stairs an oriental scent drifted up to me from the floor below.

Somewhere down there incense was burning, and at once I knew why.

There was a sudden rush of sound behind me and a woman gowned in bustled black went past me down the stairs with a great rustling of skirts. It was Sybil McLean and she gave me not so much as a glance, let alone a greeting, but simply passed me by as though I did not exist. I followed the scent of incense and arrived just behind Mrs. McLean at the open door of the front parlor.

Within I glimpsed a coffin and Lien kneeling beside it. She was already dressed in what I knew was the white coat of a widow, as though she must have had such apparel long prepared. At each end of the coffin had been set a brass container of sand in which sticks of incense were burning.

I was close enough to see what happened. Mrs. McLean stalked into the room and snatched up three incense sticks, to break them off and bury the smoking heads in sand.

"I will not have such heathenish practices indulged beneath this roof!" she cried. "You have no business in this part of the house at all!"

For an instant something flared in Lien's eyes as though she might give vent to indignation toward the other woman. But if she was so moved, she controlled the impulse and rose calmly, gracefully from her knees to face the American woman, who was so much larger and taller than herself.

"I am the captain's wife," she said with dignity. "What is proper will be done."

I heard Mrs. McLean gasp and I could sense the very pulsing of her rage. For a moment I thought she might strike out at the slight figure in white coat and trousers. Instead, she managed to regain her self-control and wheeled to stalk past me from the room—again as though I were invisible.

Lien saw me and bowed courteously. "Good morning, Mrs. McLean. I hope you have had good dreams."

I barely returned her greeting, for there was a reproach with which I must confront her. "You told me my promise to the captain would not matter. But it did matter. So what am I to do now?"

She observed me with mild interest. "I wished to see him at peace before he died. You are of marriageable age and more. It is better for a woman to have a husband. You will be well cared for now, as the captain wished. He had great concern for—" she hesitated, perhaps in faint mockery, "—the daughter of his old friend, Captain Heath."

I saw that it would be useless to offer further reproach. Her concern now appeared to be for the earthly remains of Captain Obadiah. I stepped closer to the coffin and looked down upon his face. The lines of struggle had been wiped away and he looked younger than when I had seen him last night. This morning I gazed upon him without feeling of any kind. I bore him no love, yet I could not hate him either, this man who had so trapped me and changed my life.

Lien murmured sadly in her careful, though strangely accented speech. "All is wrong within this house. When the hungry spirits of the flesh depart from the body there is danger to the living. It is necessary for a priest to perform the proper rites so that such spirits do no harm to those who remain. This has not been done. Now the evil spirits of the body have invaded all this house. Because of uncivilized and unenlightened ways, misfortune lies ahead."

"We believe differently," I protested, but she appeared not to hear me. She lighted the broken sticks of incense from those already burning and replaced them upright in the sand.

I did not stay to argue with her but wandered toward the rear of the house and the kitchen, finding myself hungry. As I passed the door, I looked into the library, but the room stood empty, with no fire in the grate. So Ian Pryott was elsewhere this morning.

In the kitchen Mrs. Crawford's tall, lean figure moved stiffly from stove to table to sink as she went about her work. When I said, "Good morning," she wiped her hands deliberately on her apron and turned to regard me with open disapproval.

"So you got what you came for, *Mrs. Brock*," she said.

Her insolence implied more strongly than anything else had done that I was of no consequence in this house. It told me that she knew very well what had happened and that for her there was only one Mrs. McLean in this household.

"I wonder if I may have some breakfast?" I asked, pointedly ignoring her remark.

"Fix what you like," she told me and went back to her sinkful of dishes. "If you come to meals with the family, you'll be served with them. If you come late, you'll have to make out as you can."

Her rude assumption that my position in the house was hardly better than that of a scullery maid was clear, but I could think of no way to assert myself. In fact, I had no idea what my position in the family was to be, or what authority, if any, would be allotted to me. I made myself some tea and found bread and butter and a dish of preserves. Then I sat down at the kitchen table to eat.

While Mrs. Crawford might hold me in low regard, she was nevertheless willing to use me as a receptacle for a running stream of talk. In Mrs. McLean's presence she had been silent, but as I was to learn, she liked the sound of her own voice.

The funeral, I quickly gathered, was to be this afternoon, and there would be many there from the town to mourn a fine, important man like the captain. Afterwards they'd be coming to the house for an early supper, and she'd have her hands full with the baking. How this sudden marriage of Mrs. McLean's son was to be explained to the townsfolk, Mrs. Crawford could not imagine.

I took a swallow of tea and set my cup down firmly. "I am Captain Nathaniel Heath's daughter," I said with some dignity. "Perhaps you've heard of him in Scots Harbor?"

She twisted her thin neck to throw me a scathing look. "Half good blood doesn't make all good blood. I remember your mother—and your grandmother and grandfather before her. Irish trades-people and fisher folk! Not fit to marry with the likes of the McLeans. It's a disgrace to bring you here and set you down in the company of a lady like Mrs. McLean!"

I choked on a crumb of bread and when I had recovered, I rose from my place at the table. "No matter how long you may have worked here, Mrs. Crawford, you've no right to speak to me in such a manner," I told her heatedly.

Her bony shoulders moved in a shrug that dismissed my words. "I'll not be here long, I can promise you that. If the captain's will leaves everything to the Chinese woman—as they say—then I'll be walking out the minute I can leave."

I would not listen to her longer, but spread a second piece of bread with butter and took it with me as I went out of the room. Behind me I heard a mutter of "good riddance."

I knew I must escape the house and get outdoors in order to recover from the heavy atmosphere of hostility. When I had put on my outdoor things I let myself out the front door with no word to anyone, and found myself greeted by a warm, Indian summer morning. It was a beautiful day to explore my surroundings and I felt lightened and more cheerful out of doors.

Avoiding the point itself and the lighthouse, I walked back along the road I had driven down with Laurel when we had arrived in the storm yesterday—so long ago! Now the sky was clear and blue with only a few distant puffs of white cloud. The waters of the protected little cove glistened quiet and serene below the cliff and from where I stood I saw that a path zigzagged downward through scrubby brush toward the lumber-strewn expanse below. There seemed no activity down there at the moment. Undoubtedly the captain's death had caused all work to stop for a time of mourning.

A stand of pine woods lay between me and the bluff path, with a way winding through the trees. I walked toward it and entered the woods. Here beneath the pines it was shadowy and cool, the air pungently scented and amurmur with the whispering of branches overhead. In a few moments I was in the open again, with the sun on my head. A rocky path dropped away down the bluff.

I could see that the village lay along the curve of land that continued inward beyond the cove occupied by the shipyard. It was the ship-building area that interested me now, however. I started down the path, pulling my skirts free when they caught in the brush, drawing strength and reassurance from the very warmth of the sun. It seemed as though I had been cold ever since I'd arrived at Bascomb's Point, and bright sunshine was welcome. The northeaster had blown itself out, and even the breezes from the sea blew more gently and warmly today.

The path dipped steeply toward a wide ledge of ground well above the reach of high tide. On the right were various buildings, probably sail-loft, rope walk, and tool shops that serviced the building of ships. On the beach rose a hull in construction, its bare ribs curving upward from the keel, the ways that would eventually launch it running long rails down into the tide. All was quiet here today, the cove empty of activity.

I picked my way across ground strewn with wood chips that carpeted pebbles and sand, finding my way among barrels and lumber piles as I moved toward the dock area that served the cove. The wharves were empty of supply craft today and only one ship rode at her mooring, masts and yards glistening white in the sun above a black hull. While she carried no furled sails in her rigging, she looked ship-shape and well-cared-for.

As I came closer the blunt prow told me she was probably an old whaler. Lettered along the hull was the name *Pride of New England*—a name I would have recognized as belonging to a Bascomb ship, even before I noted the yellow house flag flying from her mainmast. All seemed deserted at the moment, but a gangplank connected the ship with the dock and I walked toward it, suddenly eager to go aboard.

I was still so very young that day, so ready to be distracted from my troubles, not yet fully aware of the implications my situation might hold for me. I still thought stubbornly in terms of escape, in terms of some miraculous solution to my problems.

Wooden steps led to the dock and I climbed them and walked across unevenly spaced boards that let me look through to gurgling water beneath. The wet brown pilings were barnacle-encrusted and the wood in places had the furry look of age. Clearly this dock was little used these days, for all that the ship at its side seemed clean and well kept.

In New York my father had taken me aboard various craft and I was no stranger to ships. I had always counted it a treat as a child to be taken to South Street where the great bowsprits reached out above the street to the second- and third-story windows of the warehouses they faced. The thought that here was a ship that I might have all to myself brought a further quickening of eagerness to my step.

As I walked along the dock I looked up toward Bascomb's Point where the captain's house stood out boldly, high above me, its double structure gleaming white in the morning sunlight. No one seemed to move up there, and if anyone watched from those far windows, I did not care. There was no one nearby to stop me from exploring.

It was not until I reached the cleated gangplank that a breeze brought me a snatch of song and I paused in surprise to listen. The voice was thin and light, but the words and the tune were familiar. Someone aboard the *Pride* was singing an old sea chantey.

The voice was a child's and as I reached the rail I saw Laurel McLean in the stern of the ship. She stood behind the great wheel, with oversized spokes in her two small hands. I knew she was far from reality at that moment, steering a ship at sea and singing as lustily as her piping voice was able. As I stood at the rail a man's voice chimed into the song, drowning out Laurel's thin tones. Had I heard a masculine voice sooner, I might have turned back. Now there was no time, for I was already in full view. I jumped down to the deck and looked hastily around. The male voice had been silenced by my appearance and though I gazed forward the length of the ship, the owner of it was not in sight.

Laurel behaved as her grandmother had behaved toward me earlier. She went on with her make-believe steering and kept on singing as if in the pretense that I did not exist. Wondering if she had been told of her father's marriage and would thus be all the more antagonistic toward me, I walked back to the wheel.

"Good morning," I called. "I like your song. Can you tell me where this ship is bound for?"

My acceptance of her game surprised her into an answer. "We're bound for Californiay!" she shouted. "Around old Cape Stiff and up the Pacific coast."

I knew her imagination had transformed the clumsy whaler into a graceful clipper, and I understood very well the spell that lay upon her. Looking up at bare rigging I could almost see full canvas billowing as we breasted the seas with a fair wind. I could hear the very creaking of timbers and the hum of the rigging as the ship headed on at full speed. All these things my father had given me and sometimes I almost felt that I too had sailed the oceans in a clipper ship.

"Can you use an extra hand before the mast, cap'n?" I asked Laurel.

She almost smiled at me, then pursed her lips and scowled instead. "I want no landlubbers aboard," she said. "And especially not you." Then gave up her make-believe. "I thought you were going home today."

So no one had told her. That was a mistake, I thought, but I was the last person who should have to instruct her in the unhappy news of her father's marriage.

"Who was singing with you just now?" I asked, postponing the matter of my leaving.

Laurel turned her head to look at me directly. The wind

had blown several limp strands of hair into a snarl that whipped across her face. Her dress was as careless and untidy as before and there was a rent in the skirt which seemed to indicate that she dressed as she pleased, with little adult supervision. Hostility was clearly evident in her expression and I thought she would not answer. Then a notion seemed to seize her and a sly smile touched her lips.

"This ship is haunted," she told me. "There's an old whaling captain's ghost who is my good friend. When I come aboard he talks to me and sings with me. He has a fierce black beard and he will frighten you if you meet him. He won't like your being aboard, you know. If you want to get safely away, you'd better run for it at once."

I looked at her more soberly, for I well remembered a man with a fierce black beard.

"Is your ghost also bald-headed?"

Again she was taken by surprise and forgot to scowl. "Yes, he is. How did you know?"

I turned and made my way quickly along the slightly slanting deck toward the place where the try works were. Here there was a great brick stove with an iron cauldron set into it, under which a fire could be lighted. It was here that oil was tried out of the huge chunks of whale blubber. My father had shipped on a whaler once as a boy, but while there had been excitement in the chasing of the whales, he had hated the business of getting the whale cut up and aboard. He had been sickened by the smells and the blood and the slippery decks. Sailing a ship at sea meant more to him than such butchery.

Around the structure of the stove I came upon what I expected. The man with the black beard whom I had last seen in the doorway of Captain's Obadiah's room, sat cross-legged on the deck, where he must had dropped out of sight when I appeared at the rail. He made no effort to escape me now, but got up with the ease of a born sailor at home on a deck.

I noted the fellow's skin had a tanned, weather-beaten look—the mark of a man recently aboard a ship. He squinted his eyes as he stared at me and I saw a sudden flicker of surprise cross his face—as if he recognized me, though he could have had no more than a glimpse of me last night. He recovered speedily and regarded me with a jaunty, confident air that had, nevertheless, something furtive about it.

"I don't seem too able, playing ghost for the little lady," he said. "You've shown me up for certain, miss."

"Captain Obadiah looked as though he thought you a ghost when he saw you last night," I reminded him sternly.

"I'm no ghost," he said, unperturbed by my words. "Who wants me can find me easy enough. Just ask for Tom Henderson."

I liked neither the man nor his manner. Beneath his easy insolence there lurked an evident threat.

"Do you know that the captain is dead?" I asked. "That is what your sudden appearance accomplished last night. You gave him a shock he did not recover from."

A blank look seemed to slip like a mask over the fellow's face and I could not tell whether my news was a surprise or not. He shrugged slightly and did not answer me. It was clear that he would not grieve at the passing of Captain Obadiah Bascomb. Clear too that he'd had enough of my company. He touched a finger to his temple in a salute more mocking than respectful and went around me on the deck.

"I'll shove off now," he said. He waved to Laurel, sprang down the gangplank and jogged along the dock. I stood watching and in a few moments saw him take the road that led into town.

When he was out of sight, I turned to Laurel. "What was he doing about this ship?"

For once the child had no objection to giving me an answer. "He said he'd shipped aboard the *Pride* as a boy. He said he wanted to renew her acquaintance. But he made a face when he said it. Maybe he just wanted a good place to hide. A place where he could watch the captain's house. That's what he was doing with a spyglass when I came aboard."

"Then we'd better report him to your father," I said.

"Why should we? I don't tell my father anything," Laurel said darkly. "This is the captain's ship—"

She paused as though suddenly realizing that she could no longer speak of the captain in the present tense.

"Captain Obadiah's grandfather built her," she went on. "She's not working now, but Captain Obadiah had her kept shipshape and he wouldn't sell her. He liked a deck under his feet, he always said, and he liked a captain's cabin so he could get away from landlubbers. He used to keep secrets in his desk down here. He told me so. Some day he was going to show me how to open the secret drawers."

Laurel took her hands from the wheel and turned to look out across the quiet cove toward the waters of the harbor. I knew with a pang that she had turned to hide a grief I had not suspected.

"I'm sorry about the captain," I said. "I'm terribly sorry."

"We were good friends." She spoke fiercely over her shoulder. "My grandmother says it was *your* coming here that killed him. You made him suffer so much that it broke his heart and he died of it. Why don't you just go away and let us all alone?"

I stared in dismay at her quickly averted head. How was I to combat so wicked a falsehood? If the captain had been disturbed by my coming, it was no fault of mine. Under the circumstances it seemed doubly unfair and unwise for Sybil McLean to further prejudice this child against me.

"Sometime I'd like to talk to you about all this," I said. "I'd like to tell you about my being here."

She hunched her shoulders, rejecting me, and I knew this was no time for persuasion. I left her alone and retraced my steps along the deck, moving forward into the blunted curve of the prow that was so unlike the sharp cut of a clipper ship. There I stood leaning upon the rail, reaching out along the bowsprit with one arm, trying to forget the land before me and feel myself at sea. I must have been lost in my own effort at make-believe, as Laurel had been lost in hers, for I did not notice the man who stood amid the scattered timbers of the shipyard looking up at me, until he hailed me across the ribbon of water.

"Ahoy up there, Mrs. McLean."

I looked down with a start and saw Ian Pryott on the shore below. The sun shone on his bare head, glinting it with gold as he looked up at me with a strange excitement.

"Stay right where you are for a moment!" he cried. "You've just given me a tremendous idea. How would you like to pose for a figurehead?"

I had no idea what he meant, but the notion delighted me. "I'd love to," I said readily, with never a thought for the difficulties such a promise might involve. "Come aboard and tell me about it."

He shook his head. "Not now. You've set the house in a stir by disappearing. Mrs. McLean wants to be sure you're

72

fitted with proper mourning clothes for the funeral, and she could find you nowhere. Brock has been sent to search for you, so I thought I'd come and warn you."

My small adventure had given me a brief respite, but now all my troubles surged back redoubled, and the fact must have betrayed itself in my expression.

"There—I've done it!" Ian said in regret. "You've lost the exhilaration I saw in you just now. Don't let them do that to you, Miranda. Fight them for the right to be happy!"

I was surprised at his vehemence, but there was little fighting spirit in me at the moment. "How did you know where to find me?" I asked despondently.

"I happened to see you go down the bluff and I watched until you disappeared aboard the *Pride*. Then I followed to warn you."

Apparently he had not seen Tom Henderson talking to me. I would have told him about the incident, but Ian glanced over his shoulder toward the bluff above the shipyard.

"Here comes your husband now. He's probably spotted you from above, just as I did. I'll see you later, Mrs. McLean." The way he spoke the name I now bore carried a sting of mockery, for all that he had seemed friendly a moment before.

Already Brock was plunging down the path, the severity of his limp hardly evident on steeply pitched ground. Ian gave me a quick salute before he strode off in the direction of town. I did not want to be found here in the prow watching Brock's approach and I turned away, wishing there were some place where I could hide and never be found at all.

In my turning I nearly stumbled over Laurel, who had come up close behind me. The angry hurt in her eyes alarmed me.

"Why did Ian call you 'Mrs. McLean'?" she demanded. "Why did he dare to call my father your husband?"

I moved toward her, my hand outstretched in a pleading gesture. "I'd like to tell you about it."

"Then you *are* married to him!" Laurel cried. "You lied to me. You said you would never marry him. You said you would go away."

There was rising hysteria in her voice and I tried to quiet her, tried to explain as gently as I could.

"It was the captain's dying wish that I marry your father. It wasn't possible to refuse him. His state was so grave that we believed there was nothing else to do but give in. We didn't mean—"

The child did not wait to hear me out. Stricken, she darted toward a door in the deck where stairs led below. Before I could call out or stop her, she had disappeared down the open hatch into darkness. I ran to the opening and looked down the steps, but I could see nothing. The scuttling sound of her feet reached me from below. Though I called to her, she paid me no heed and after a moment there was complete silence, as if she had been swallowed into those darksome hollows that existed below decks.

Behind me I heard the sound of heavy, uneven steps upon the wooden dock and I knew Brock had reached the ship. In a moment he would come up the gangplank and there could be no escaping him. I stood where I was to await the man who was Laurel's father—and, whether I wanted it or not, husband of the girl who had been Miranda Heath.

6.

IN THE MOMENTS THAT I WAITED, I strove to calm my sense of turmoil. I dreaded this face-to-face meeting with Brock McLean—the first since that hurried ceremony last night.

At least my concern for the child gave me the courage to stand up to him. He set the gangplank swaying as he came up it and a moment later he had vaulted through the opening in the rail to land lightly on the deck. When he saw me waiting for him, close at hand, he displayed his exasperation at once.

"So this is where you've got to? I guessed as much since you're a captain's daughter! But after this you might do us the courtesy of letting us know where you're off to."

"I had no idea anyone remembered my existence," I told him. "When I saw your mother this morning she did not speak to me. And I'm sure you've given me scant thought since last night when I served your purpose in an effort to secure your inheritance."

What a dark-browed, glowering man he was, I thought, half afraid that he would give way to his temper and reach out to give me a good shaking. If he did, I would fight back, I told myself—and was astonished at such a thought. I had never felt like this before.

"We'll not discuss the matter now," he said roughly. "My mother wants you. Come along to the house at once."

I shook my head. "Not until Laurel is safely on deck again."

"What are you talking about?"

I pointed to the black oblong of the open hatch. "She's down there in that dark, frightening place, and I don't mean to budge until you've brought her up. Apparently no one troubled to tell her what happened last night. She's just learned the truth and I'm sure it has been a dreadful shock."

He had the grace to look startled and perhaps faintly apologetic. "Then I've waited too long. I was trying to find a way to break this to her gently, since she has a great antipathy toward you."

"Thanks to your mother, and to you!"

The hint of apology was gone. "We will discuss this another time. For the moment let the child stay where she is until she is ready to come up. She knows this ship like the inside of her own pocket. There are lanterns down there if she wants a light. She'll come out when she's hungry enough."

He turned toward the gangplank, clearly expecting me to follow.

"I'll go after her myself," I said.

In spite of his angry astonishment, I started down the ladder. As I descended I found it was not wholly dark below, for the square of sunlight thrown through the stair opening above showed me an area of cabins fore and aft, an open door to the ship's galley and other quarters stretching dimly away. For the first time I sensed the curious metamorphosis that was always to occur when I descended into the depths of the *Pride*. Above decks all was sunny air and gleaming spars and a salt sea wind. Below there was a smell of old rot, of rancid oil and spaces too long airless. Above decks she was a well-kept ship; below she seemed a neglected derelict. I had never before known what claustrophobia meant, but I understood it now. The very timbers seemed to curve in upon me and I had thoughts of sinking ships, of

75

sailors trapped and helpless while water poured in upon them from above.

I called to Laurel and my voice echoed hollowly along the passageway. Now I could make out still another opening to the lower hold. As I moved reluctantly toward it, light flickered below. Laurel must have lighted a lantern and gone down still another level. I did not wait to see if the man above intended to follow me, but started down a second, steeper ladder.

By the time my feet touched the boards of the lower passage in the very belly of the ship, the light had been extinguished and here the darkness was complete. I had no knowledge of which way to turn. The blackness of a pit hemmed me in and there was that queer-smelling airlessness in which the odors of wood and dust and a lingering aura of whale oil intermingled. I called to Laurel again, but she did not answer.

Then, to my relief, a light moved above me and I saw that Brock was swinging down the ladder with a storm lantern in his hand. The shadows leaped away to gather in far corners and for the first time I could see what lay immediately about me. Huge, curving timbers reinforced the bulging sides of the ship, like the bare ribs of a whale rising about me. A wooden catwalk formed a foot passage on either side of the center structure. Everywhere else the bottom of the ship was filled with broken rock for ballast, in absence of any cargo. Forward stood a row of casks, empty now, but perhaps once the redolent containers of oil. Even with the coming of light the sense of menacing oppression lay heavily upon me.

Brock came down the last steps and stood behind me, holding his lantern high. On a pile of umber-colored rocks nearby lay whitened bones—the skull bones of a small whale. I longed for the clean sea air above. But first Laurel must be found.

Her father shouted for her, setting the echoes crashing eerily about us. Forward in the prow of the ship a scrabbling sound reached us as the child tried to crawl farther away over the ballast stones. At once her father swung the lantern in the direction of the sound and we could see her curled up against the very timbers of the ship's side, her knees drawn into a huddle, her face hidden against them. I knew her father meant to shout at her again, and I ran forward along the walk and called to her more softly.

"Laurel, come with us now. We need to talk to you in a more comfortable place. It's too dank and dusty and dreadful smelling down here. Come along, dear—let's go back to the deck."

She raised her head and blinked in the glare of the lantern. "I don't want to go back! I won't have you for my mother! I'm going to stay here until—until I turn into bones like that whale!"

Her father snorted impatiently. "That will take a long while and I'm not going to stay down here and turn to bones with you. Get along above now and no more nonsense. Why aren't you at your lessons?"

I whirled about on the narrow walk to face the man behind me. "Will you stop shouting! You're only frightening the child. Be quiet a moment, please, and let me talk to her."

He looked as if one of the timbers had rebuked him, and was surprised enough to fall silent.

"Please come," I said to Laurel, holding out my hand.

"If I come he'll beat me," the child said.

"I've never beaten her in my life!" Brock shouted, angrily. "Get out of there now or I'll come after you."

I blocked his way with determination. "He shan't beat you and he shan't punish you," I assured the little girl, angry enough to be bold about my promises. "If I am to be a part of your family—which is something I never asked to be —then I'm going to have a voice in what happens from now on. If I'm to be your stepmother, then I'll have some say about you. Do come out, Laurel dear. Come home with me."

I think she did not really want to remain in this oppressive, stale-smelling place. She waited a moment longer to see if her father would contradict my words. When he merely breathed heavily behind me, sputtering under his breath, she crawled toward me over the rough stones and pulled herself upright on the walk. Then she ignored my outstretched hand and ran past us, edging around her father, and scrambling up the ladder as fast as she could go. By the time we had climbed after her and stood on deck again, she was far away, racing toward the bluff with torn petticoats flying. I filled my lungs with air, glad to be above decks again.

Brock watched the child go, scowling. "A fine influence you're going to have," he said to me. "Encouraging her in disobedience! Don't take too much upon yourself—Mrs. Mc-Lean."

All the fight went out of me abruptly. How little I could aid the child, when I could do nothing to aid myself. I bent to brush tawny dust from my mantle and then walked toward the gangplank. He reached the rail ahead of me and held out his hand. I did not look at him as he helped me to the dock. Nevertheless, I was acutely aware of him and I withdrew my hand as quickly as possible from his touch. I would have hurried ahead, had I not become aware of the labored effort he must make because of his leg. It was only considerate to slow my steps, whether I wished his company or not. However, as I was to learn later, Brock McLean was more than sensitive toward any effort by others to accommodate to his slower gait. He could hurry when he chose, but he did not often choose.

"Go ahead," he said roughly. "My mother is waiting for you in her room. I've something to do down here."

I left him in relief and returned to the house by way of the path up the bluff. When I neared the top I paused for breath in my headlong flight and looked below me. Brock stood near the water's edge, his back to the cliff, looking out toward the harbor's entrance and the ocean. There seemed to be something of defiance in his pose—as though he were a man beaten down, yet not wholly bested by fate. There was nothing I could do about his problems and I had enough of my own. Having recovered my breath, I hurried on to the Bascomb house.

There I went first to my room to fling off my things. Next I knocked on Laurel's door and when there was no answer, I looked inside. The child was not there and I could take no time to search for her. I only hoped she would not hide herself away in some other strange place before I had been able to talk with her sensibly. I had begun to fancy myself in the light of Laurel's champion—the defender of a mistreated child; someone to stand between her and a cruel parent.

But now I must present myself to Mrs. McLean and I went reluctantly along the hall to her room at the front of the house. The moment she called to me to come in and I stepped into her presence, I could sense her bitter resentment toward me. She stood beside a bed on which several black dresses had been laid. She herself was already gowned in full mourning and the unrelieved black made her skin seem sallow, and her pale eyes more washed of color than ever. Behind her a small fire burned in the grate, lending a secret whispering to the otherwise silent room.

I was aware of wallpaper printed with some prickly purple bloom that seemed a fitting background for the woman herself. Then the portrait that hung above the mantel caught my eye and I saw nothing else. This, I knew, must be Andrew McLean.

The artist had not painted his subject in the role of sea captain, for he wore the garments a gentleman might wear at home. His black jacket had wide lapels of velvet, and his collar stood high above a wide black tie. There were pearl studs down his shirt front and double strands of gold chain looped across his vest. But it was the man's face that arrested my attention.

He was an older Brock, with thick, rather curly black hair combed carelessly back from a broad forehead. The eyes look piercingly into mine and the mouth was set in a stern line above a square, cleft chin. On a table before the seated figure drawings for parts of a ship had been spread, and he held a pencil in his hand. It was as if he had just looked up from his work to question the observer's purpose with him. He looked like a man who would be strong-willed and easily angered—again like his son. I found myself wondering what Sybil McLean had been like when she had married this man so many years ago.

Now, as I stared at the portrait of her husband, fascinated by its lifelike quality, she waited in watchful silence.

"My father admired him tremendously," I said. "He spoke often of Andrew McLean's genius in the designing of ships."

The woman who had been Andrew's wife looked at me with her strange pale eyes in which no fire burned—though sensed that fire was there, banked and hidden, burning somewhere deep within her. There was a volcanic hint of it in her voice when she spoke, contradicting my words.

"Nathaniel Heath hated my husband. He was wickedly jealous of his talents. If Nathaniel ever said anything good of Andrew in his later years, it must have been to subdue the accusations of his own conscience."

There was nothing I could say in the face of such bitterness. I wondered if the woman were a little mad. Every word she spoke to me, every gesture she made in my direction seemed to hint at fury restrained behind her cold, pale stare.

I did not look at the picture again, but moved toward the dresses on the bed. "Your son said you wished to see me."

She clasped her hands before her, the fingers intertwining. "You must be suitably dressed for the funeral this afternoon. I notice that you are not wearing black for your father."

"My father hated to see me in black," I told her.

She gestured toward the bed. "I have found a few things that you may be able to wear. The style is not the latest, but I think that hardly matters. It is important to show proper respect for Captain Obadiah in public. There will be enough talk about this sudden wedding as it is."

I picked up one of the frocks. "I'll take the dresses to my room and try them on."

"Try them on here," Mrs. McLean ordered. "I want to see how they look on you."

I did not want to disrobe before her critical stare, but I began unhooking my waist from the back of the collar down. She did not help me. When the hooks were freed, I slipped my arms from the sleeves, dropped the dress to the floor and stepped out of it in my ribboned corset cover and white petticoats. I disliked revealing the scar on my bare shoulder and I put up my hand to cover its ugliness from her gaze. To my distress, she came toward me at once and snatched my hand away.

"What is that? What have you done to yourself?"

"It's only a birthmark," I said. That wasn't true, but I did not want her to think that my aunt had been negligent in her care of me. The accident had occurred when I was very young.

Mrs. McLean challenged my words at once. "It is not a birthmark. It is obviously the scar from a burn," she said, and shocked me by reaching out a forefinger to trace the area of the mark with a light touch that sent a shiver through me. It was as if she took some perverse pleasure in her discovery.

"How ugly it makes you," she went on. "My son will be repelled. He cannot bear physical marring. The contrast with *her* will be all the greater."

I had jerked away from the touch of her hand with a repugnance of my own. The thought of having Brock McLean see the scar on my naked shoulder left me shaken. I snatched at a word she had spoken to distract her from my distress.

"Her?" I repeated.

Again she gestured toward the bed. "Rose. My son's first wife. These are her gowns, of course. She was rather small, as you are, but plump and well made. She had a perfect little body with the creamiest of skin—not a blotch on her anywhere. I know. I washed her myself after she died."

I caught up one of the dresses and pulled it over my head, and in the instant while my face was hidden I struggled to regain my self-control. This woman wanted to upset me, and I must not let her succeed.

"She was a good deal larger than I am," I murmured, wriggling into the sleeves, dropping the fuller skirt of another day over my petticoats.

Once more Mrs. McLean descended on me. She reached beneath my arms and pulled handfuls of the goods tight on either side, smiling faintly, as if she enjoyed what she was doing.

"I shall take in the seams for you," she said. "You're not as full in the bosom as Rose was. I'm sure it must be distressing to wear her clothes, but I don't know what else we can manage when there is so little time."

"Why should I mind?" I asked. "I never knew her. She means nothing to me."

"Do you think Brock won't remember all he has lost when he sees you in a dress of Rose's? She had these things made when her father died. Only a year or so before her own death, poor young thing. Of lung fever. It was a great tragedy. They were so perfectly suited to each other, she and Brock. He has been a broken man ever since."

I pulled myself from her grasping hands. The woman must indeed be mad to say such things. Why did she hate me so? Whatever the cause, I must make my own feelings clear at once and free myself from any false position. But her behavior had upset me and my voice was not altogether steady when I spoke.

"Please understand that what has happened in the past does not concern me at all. I am not in love with your son. I had no desire to marry him. His devotion to his first wife is something I can only applaud. I'm sorry if wearing her dresses will remind him of his unhappiness. If you think too much harm will be done, perhaps it would be better for me to wear my own clothes and forget about dressing in black."

She did not advance upon me again, but went to a chair beside the fire and seated herself well away from me. She seemed not at all taken aback by my rejection of her words. The sly smile still curved her lips as though the hoped-for prospect of my suffering entertained her mightily.

"You may not love him yet," she murmured, half to herself, "but the time will come when you will beseech him for a glance, a word, and your heart will break when he will not look at you. Women find him fascinating, irresistible—but he will never forget Rose. She had everything a woman might have for him—everything!" Her voice rose on a note of triumph, as though I were already beseeching her son for a glance. "Rose came of good blood, of a fine New England family," she added. "She was one of us. While you—with your dreadful background!—you are that creature's daughter!"

Managing to hold my temper, since I knew she would listen to no words of mine in defense of those good, humble people who had been my mother's parents, and of whom my father had always spoken with affection, I flung another look at the portrait of Andrew McLean in its place over the mantel. Here was a further possible reason for his wife's dislike for me. Since I had come to Bascomb's Point I had heard that all three partners—Obadiah, Nathaniel, and Andrew—had been in love with Carrie Corcoran. If Sybil McLean was aware of this, if her husband had loved Carrie, then indeed she might entertain hatred for Carrie's daughter.

She was staring into the fire and had not seen my quick glance at the portrait. I fancy she had expected some indignant outburst from me that would have given her opportunity to hurl further vituperation upon me. But when I said nothing, she chose a new course and went on in quieter tones.

"Of course you can save yourself—if you choose. You can run away."

I had turned my back on her to face a tall cheval glass in order to see how the dress might be altered to fit me. Now I stared at her averted head in the mirror, caught by her last words.

"What do you mean—run away?"

"Back to New York." She caught my eyes upon her in the mirror and her look intensified. "Something might be arranged. I could let you have a little money, perhaps. After all, the marriage was wholly a matter of expedience—and a mistake."

"You mean it was a mistake because the captain could not after all fulfill his own part of the bargain and change his will? Thus I am of no use to you or to your son?"

"Of what use could you possibly be?" she demanded. "If you go away everything will be forgotten in a little while. My son has no desire to marry again. What has happened will not matter."

"What if I should want to marry?"

She threw me a scornful look, implying that no one would want me.

What she suggested was a possible solution. Perhaps I might choose this course of escaping from a dreadful situation. But I would not run away behind Brock's back at the mere instigation of his mother. I would first tell him what I meant to do. It was even possible that he might help me to leave if I faced him with my request. All these things I thought quite honestly. There was in me still a naïve, well-intentioned belief that sincere effort would bring about an honorable answer to my problem.

"I will consider your suggestion," I told Mrs. McLean and took off the black dress.

She seemed agitated as she accepted it from my hands, as though the fact that I did not immediately seize upon her advice disturbed her. Perhaps she really thought I might have some design upon her son. If that was so, I felt inclined to let her worry.

"Was Laurel the only child of the marriage?" I asked as I put on my own dress.

Mrs. McLean had risen to open a handsome box, inlaid with a Chinese scene in mother-of-pearl and ivory. From it she took thread and thimble and small gold, birds'-wing scissors, delaying her answer.

"I would have liked a fine grandson," she said at last. "A boy to resemble his grandfather. Their first child was a boy, but he died when he was two years old. The second was a girl—stillborn. And then Laurel, who is a changeling if ever I saw one. She is like no one else in the family."

I remained silent, thinking that Laurel resembled her father, and perhaps her grandfather, far more than her grandmother was willing to admit. There was something in her as well of her grandmother's deep-rooted resentment against life.

I had still another question I wanted to ask as I struggled with the last hooks on my bodice.

"Did Brock never want to follow in his father's steps? Did he never long to go to sea?"

"The sea!" Mrs. McLean echoed the words as though she rejected all that had to do with ships and the sea. "The sea took my husband. He was buried beneath its waves. And it would have taken my son too, had it not been for the war. Young as he was, he had his master's papers and he had made a voyage as captain of a ship. Sometimes I thank God for the shot that shattered his hip in a sea battle and set him forever upon the land. If I were you, girl, I would not mention the sea to my son."

I was growing tired of being addressed brusquely as "girl" by the members of this household.

"My name is Miranda, Mrs. McLean," I told her quietly.

Pale cold eyes dismissed me. "Perhaps you had better go now and prepare to move your things into your husband's room at the front of the house across from mine. I will get to work on Rose's dress and have it ready for you this afternoon."

If she had meant to surprise me, to take me aback, she had succeeded. Such a move was the last thing I wanted. Indeed, since little notice had been taken of me last night, I had begun to think that not even the outward conventions of marriage would be expected of me.

"I'd prefer to stay in the room I now occupy," I said. "After all, this is not a real marriage." Yet even as I heard them, my own words sounded like the pleading they were.

"You have no choice in the matter," she told me with curt satisfaction. "I offered you an avenue of escape which you have refused. Now you will find out that the marriage is real enough. My son has given the order that you are to be moved into the front room."

I very nearly ran from her presence, feeling shocked and not a little frightened. Nevertheless, all my new, inward stubbornness was aroused. I had no intention of being forced by Brock McLean into the true role of a young bride. If he so much as lifted a hand to touch me, I would fight him with all my strength. I would cause a scandal in this house if there was any attempt by him to consummate this ridiculous marriage. Thus, talking heatedly to myself, I bolstered my courage and my determination.

Later, however, when Joseph came upstairs to move my trunk and few possessions, I could not countermand his orders. It was not with the servants that my battle must be joined. I must regain my freedom from Brock himself, and I would not flee ignobly and in fear.

He did not reappear that morning. I supposed he was away taking care of the details of the funeral. There was considerable coming and going of visitors to the house by now—of friends arriving to condole and to pay their last respects. Lien remained in quiet charge of the front parlor where her husband's body rested, while Sybil McLean, unable to dislodge her from her dutiful role, moved in and about ignoring her.

The noon meal was hurried. Brock was still absent and Ian Pryott I saw not at all, though I looked into the library more than once, hoping to find him there. On an occasion when I encountered Laurel in the hallway, she glowered at me with bleak dislike, as though I had betrayed her. As perhaps I had. I could guess that some punishment had been dealt her that I had no way of blocking, and I realized too late that I had made her a reckless promise, impossible for me to keep.

Not until afternoon did the household assemble in its entirety. By that time I was wearing Rose McLean's hastily fitted dress. How I looked could not have mattered less to me. There were problems more real to be met.

For the first time I must take my place in public on Brock's arm—to all appearances his wife. The ordeal was one I could not face with equanimity. During the drive to the cemetery, in the carriage with Brock, Laurel, and Mrs. McLean, I held myself stiffly erect. I was as silent as the man at my side, determined to betray nothing of my inner trepidation.

7.

GRAY CLOUD BANKS WERE MASSED ABOVE the country cemetery where Bascombs had been buried for more than a hundred years, spoiling our beautiful day. That the afternoon should put on mourning for Captain Obadiah seemed fitting.

Of the once large clan of Bascombs no family member remained to grieve his passing. But the captain's friends were many, and in lieu of blood kin, the McLeans stood nearest the grave. I leaned correctly on my husband's arm and wore his ring upon my finger, but I could not believe that such things made me Mrs. Brock McLean. Again I had the sense of watching a play at which I was merely a spectator.

Not far from our small grouping stood the captain's wife. There had been no one else to attend Lien and Ian Pryott had stepped in to accompany her to the cemetery. He stood beside her now, supporting her fragile weight upon his arm. Lien had chosen to cover her exotic white garments with a long black cloak which hid her entire person from view, its hood engulfing her head and shadowing her face. Once, above her bent head, Ian's eyes met mine and he gave me that quizzical look I was coming to dread—as though he laughed secretly at us all, and especially at me.

As I stood there, listening to the minister's sonorous words, which seemed to have little to do with the real Captain Obadiah, I was again more intensely aware of small impressions than of those with larger import. My mind could grasp and believe in the twittering of sparrows in a nearby tree, and the look of them, gray as the branches on which they perched. From the direction of the road where our carriages waited, I could hear the creak of wheels and harness, the stamp of hooves, an occasional neighing, and low voices as coachmen talked among themselves.

I felt no more moved by the scene before me than were the horses or the sparrows. The coffin had been lowered into raw earth and whatever lay there had no meaning for me, no relationship to me. I could no longer identify the wizened old man who had so changed my life, with the hero of those childhood legends I had loved.

When Dr. Price, the same minister who had married me to Brock, spoke his last words and cast a handful of earth upon the coffin, a sudden outburst of sobbing startled us all. Laurel, standing on the other side of her father, had burst into stormy tears. The sound returned me abruptly to a sense of reality and I was oddly grateful to the child, however indecorous her sobbing seemed in this silent place where all emotion had been hidden and suppressed. One of us at least, was able to mourn Captain Obadiah in a manner that came from the heart.

When earth had fallen upon the coffin, the group about the grave began to break up. Mrs. McLean drew the weeping child away, and Lien turned toward the carriages, with Ian still accompanying her. Only the man at my side did not move except to release my hand from his arm, as though he wanted to stand alone and unhampered. I stepped back a little and waited, watching him. As I did so a new and fresh awareness came upon me without warning.

It was as if I saw Brock McLean in a new light, removed from any effect he might have upon my own life. Here was a man who had been cruelly defeated at every turn. Injury to his leg had kept him from the sea. Only a few years before he must have stood in this very place grieving over the loss of his wife. Even the work to which he had given himself since his injury might be taken from him because the captain had not acted quickly and wisely. Yet there was sorrow in his manner as he turned from the grave.

On impulse I spoke to him softly. "I'm sorry. I'm very sorry."

If he felt grief, the sound of my voice banished all evidence of it. He looked at me with distaste, as though I had said something foolish—as perhaps I had. That I was sorry for all that had befallen him in the past I could hardly explain. Nor was such feeling on my part anything he would welcome. I felt ill-at-ease again, and to cover my lack of composure I spoke a thought that had occurred to me earlier.

"While we're here," I said humbly, "will you show me where my mother is buried?"

I would not have been surprised if he had refused, but to my relief he did not. He allowed the others to return to the carriages and without a word led me along grassy aisles to a sloping hillside where a weeping beech tree stood near the far side of the cemetery. Here, where the beech cast its shadow, stood an unpretentious headstone of New England granite. Though granite seemed somehow inappropriate for one who had lived so gaily and fully as the girl of whom my father had so often told me. No sentiment had been inscribed upon the stone, but merely a name. I bent to read the letters: CARRIE CORCORAN HEATH.

In my imaginings I had felt that when I stood in this place she would become real for me. But the woman who was buried here was a stranger—someone I had never known, someone who had nothing to do with me. I hardly knew I spoke aloud.

"I wish I could find her," I said.

There was no sympathy in the man who stood beside me. "What good would it do you to find her? Why should you want to?"

I knew I would receive from Brock McLean no understanding of a loneliness and a need which seemed to have redoubled now that I found myself in this place and devoid of all feeling. Yet I sought to make him understand.

"I want to know all about her, all there is to be discovered, I want her to stop being a stranger to me—someone I've only heard about from others. I want to know my mother."

"And when you find that she was a coquette who liked to collect men's hearts—what have you then?"

It angered me that he should say such a thing when she could not answer for herself. At least I, her daughter, was here to answer for her.

"How do you know she was like that?" I demanded. "Just because she was pretty, because she was someone who attracted love—"

He did not let me finish. "I know because she destroyed my father. I was old enough at the time to see it happen. She hardened him and made him a bitter, unforgiving husband to my mother. All because he'd loved Carrie Corcoran as a young man and tried to forget her by marrying another woman. But Carrie never let go of anyone she could subjugate. You've seen what my mother is like now—a shell of what she once was. I have only sympathy for her—and pity. My father made her suffer because she could not be to him what Carrie had been. Do you think you are not a painful thorn in her side, looking as much as you do like your mother?"

"But that's not my fault," I began.

He cut in upon my words at once. "What does fault matter when every glimpse of you wounds her? How do you think she must feel having you thrust into our midst where you must become a part of our lives whether we wish it or not?"

He was speaking with a deadly control that was more searing than anger, and I felt chilled and not a little frightened. Still I tried to answer him.

"So now, whether it's reasonable or not, you must try to punish Carrie Corcoran through me?"

His laugh had an unpleasant ring and he cut it off abruptly, perhaps remembering where he was. "You are a foolish and romantic child. What you, personally, may feel or be, is nothing to my mother. Or to me, for that matter. It's the opening of old wounds that is hard to live with."

"Then let me go," I pleaded. "All you need to do is let me go."

He turned sharply from me and started toward the carriages, walking quickly so that I had to run a little to keep up with him. He seemed to manage his wounded leg more evenly when he hurried than when he moved slowly and deliberately. There was no question now of setting my pace to his.

Mrs. McLean stood beside the carriage, receiving the condolences of friends. I could tell at once, however, that she watched for Brock. I glanced about for Ian and saw him helping Lien into a carriage, tucking her voluminous cloak about her. He caught my eyes in mockery, as if he congratulated me on playing so well the dutiful role of a McLean wife. His look dismissed me from any communication with him as if I had gone over to the clan of McLean.

Increasingly it seemed that there was no one to whom I could turn as night itself awaited me at the end of the day. Always the room at Bascomb's Point waited for me. That room which I must now share with Brock McLean. Fearfully I glanced at the sky. But though the sun had vanished behind scudding banks of gray cloud, there was still light in the heavens. A little of the afternoon was left.

Brock handed his mother and me into the barouche, but when we looked around for Laurel we saw that she had run off to Lien's carriage, to ride with Ian and the captain's wife. I wished I might have done the same, even though there was no welcome for me there either.

Again we were silent on the drive back to the house, except for a single comment Mrs. McLean made about the mourners who were coming to the house for supper.

Brock did not speak, and I sensed in him a smoldering, as if he could barely contain himself politely. When we reached Bascomb's Point, he did not go inside to play the role of host, but whistled the great black dog out of its kennel. Then man and dog went off together in the direction of the point.

I ran upstairs and stepped to the front window. Somewhat to the right of the lighthouse I could see the black dog and the black-browed Scotsman standing at the edge of rocky cliffs on the ocean side. They faced a sea that was as bleak and gray as the sky it reflected. I had the feeling that I had tested a dangerous fire that afternoon in the things I had said about my mother. What did he expect of me, this man who was so unwilling—and so undesired!—a husband? Last night I had been forgotten, but would I be again?

Still garbed for out-of-doors, I stole downstairs. The last traces of incense had been aired from the front parlor. Lien no longer stood guard beside a casket but had retired to her own part of the house. The furniture had been set to rights and friends of the family were gathered in the room, their voices less subdued, now that the funeral was over. Had I been accepted in this house, I would have offered to assist in the kitchen, or tried to make myself useful in some other way. But I knew that Mrs. Crawford would not welcome my help, nor would Mrs. McLean. It would be enough if, of necessity, I put in an appearance at suppertime as Brock's wife.

I slipped past the parlor door unnoticed, and once outside I wandered again toward the old, unused lighthouse. When I entered the building and looked about, I found the place empty, with no sounds coming from beyond closed doors off the main room. I went to one of the doors and opened it. What I found was an unexpected place of wonder.

Within the room the odor of raw wood, of shavings, of paint, were strong and fresh. It seemed that a wood carver of considerable skill plied his art here. Figures of animals and objects and small human forms crowded the shelves. I gave these scarcely a glance, however, because of the figure that occupied a raised platform in the center of the room. I might have taken it for a conventional wood carving of a woman —somewhat larger than lifesize—had it not been for the slant at which the figure was lashed to a standard, extending into the room as if intended to breast whatever gales might bluster across an ocean. It was, of course, a ship's figure-head.

The carving was in a strange state of partial completion. Its body was garbed in lovely jade-green robes that swept backward, as if in a strong wind—robes that were complete in every detail, as though the carver had worked lovingly over each fold of simulated cloth. The woman's hands were held before her, hidden in the wide cuffs of her sleeves. Her breast, gently molded, lifted to meet the elements she faced. Yet in surprising contrast to this detailed perfection, the head, above slender shoulders, remained a block of raw wood. No effort had been made to complete its shape, or to form the headdress. Nor had the features been so much as indicated.

What a strange way to work, I thought—to finish all else, even to the applying of color, while the most important element of the entire figure still remained untouched.

I recalled Ian Pryott's moment of eagerness when he had seen me leaning forward in the prow of the whaler. He had asked me then if I would pose for a figurehead. Was it he who worked in this room? He who had created this faceless lady? Had he thought to use me as a model to complete the carving?

But this could hardly be what he intended, for the figure-head represented a woman of China, and mine was an oc-cidental face. Something stirred vaguely in my memory. Had there not been a story of just such a strange combination that I had heard of long ago? Some tale of a figurehead in oriental dress but with an occidental face that had once caused a decided stir upon the seaways?

As I stood pondering, a man's voice spoke to me from the doorway. Startled, I looked about to see the bearded seaman, Tom Henderson, standing there. I did not like this man. There was something nefarious about him, something vicious in the way he had deliberately frightened the captain. And why should he now remain in the vicinity of Bascomb's Point? His sudden appearance gave me a queerly trapped feeling—as if I had been approached by the presence of elemental evil. He stood between me and the door and I sensed that if I tried to push past him he would keep me from leaving. I stood where I was, striving to conceal my trepidation.

"I thought I recognized you down there on the ship

this morning," he went on. "But it didn't come to me till later that you're Carrie Corcoran's daughter. The spitting image of her too, as many must have told you in Scots Harbor."

"Carrie Heath," I said curtly.

He showed me the grimace of a smile in his nest of black beard. "I was coming to Cap'n Nat in my own good time. That's why I've took an interest in you, as you might say. I sailed under your pa in my day, and never did I see a better ship's master. I was his second mate long before I had the bad luck to be first mate for Cap'n Obadiah Bascomb."

I did not care to hear my father's name, or Captain Obadiah's, on this fellow's tongue—whether in praise or otherwise. "If you don't mind—" I said, and moved toward the doorway.

He did not budge from my path, but nodded his bald head in the direction of the carved figure. "I wonder why they'd be making another *Sea Jade* figurehead?"

I flung a startled look at the lady in her jade green robes, and suddenly, out of distant time, words drifted back to me—words uttered by my aunt and broken off as though she had not meant to speak them:

"It was your mother, child, who posed for that famous figurehead on the *Sea Jade*. There were some who said she would bring only ill-luck to the ship . . ."

Then my aunt had checked her tongue and would never thereafter speak of the *Sea Jade*'s figurehead.

"How do you know this is a replica?" I asked Tom Henderson.

He grinned wickedly at the carving. "Not likely I wouldn't know! As I was saying, I sailed as first mate aboard *Sea Jade* under Cap'n Obadiah."

He left the doorway and came into the room, to stand closer to me than I liked. I could smell the grog on his breath and the unpleasant odor of an unwashed body.

"Only a few weeks ago I saw the real figurehead," he informed me. "The very one your ma posed for, setting all those tongues awagging at the time."

Despite my distaste, he had caught my interest. "The real one? What do you mean?"

"O' course you'd hardly recognize her for the weathering," he said. "But she's still in place aboard the ship."

"Do you mean the *Sea Jade?* But where is she? Where did you see her?"

He grinned again. "Old Tom knows a lot o' things that maybe you'd like to know. This one I'll give you free. The ship's standing in dock at Salem this very minute. No good to anybody now. Could be they'll turn her into a coal hulk. But that's not what I want to talk to you about, miss."

He wheeled away to a window where he stood looking out, speaking to me over his shoulder, as though he knew very well that I would not run away.

"You've done all right for yourself, haven't you, miss? Marrying a McLean and all that. There'll be money in your pocket—where Cap'n Nat had none. So maybe you'd be ready to spend a mite of it for benefit of hearing a story I could tell."

I looked at him with increasing aversion. "I have no money. And if I had, I wouldn't pay you to make up lies." I moved toward the door, but he went on talking, knowing full well that I'd stay to hear him out, whether I wanted to or not.

"Could be you'll change your mind, miss. I'll be hanging around the *Pride* a few days more to see what may turn up. Any time you want to talk to old Tom, you come on down there with a little silver jingling in your pocket. I'll tell you a tale to make your hair stand on end. A tale to make your blood run—" He broke off and turned from the window. "There's somebody coming!"

With his sailor's gait he crossed the room, flung up the window sash on the ocean side and straddled the sill, pausing there to look back at me. "Don't forget now. You'd best look me up and hear me out." Then he dropped to the ground and disappeared from sight.

A moment later Ian Pryott came into the museum and found me standing before the figurehead, the window still open on the far side of the room.

"The seaman who frightened the captain is still around," I told Ian hastily. "He was here trying to sell me some sort of information. He wanted me to come down to the *Pride* to talk to him." I pointed toward the window.

Ian leaned through the opening to look out before he closed the window sash. "Give him short shrift when he comes around, Miranda. If I run into him I'll warn him

off. There's no one here will pay him blackmail money—
if that's what he's after. Not now that the captain is gone."

"Then you think that is all he wants?"

"What else can he want?" Ian returned to where I stood
beside the carving, his manner toward me still cool, remote.
"What do you think of her?" he asked almost carelessly.

"Even without a face she's very beautiful. Is she yours?
Why did you carve her?"

"The *Sea Jade* story has always fascinated me, and I do
a bit of whittling now and then, as you can see." He gestured toward the shelves around the room. "This time I decided to try something more ambitious."

"Whittling!" I echoed. "This is as good as anything I have
seen in the art collections in New York. But what will you
do for her face?"

"I'm not sure. I found some old pictures that gave me the
pose and general details of the figurehead. But I've needed
something in the round to use for the face. Lien wants to
pose for it. She feels that this time the figure should have
a face to match the robes."

So he did not mean to mention the moment this morning
when he had thought of me as a possible model. He turned
to a shelf where tools lay and began picking up one instrument
after another, replacing them absently, as if he waited for
me to go away so he could get to work.

"It would be wonderful to see her in place aboard the
Sea Jade," I mused.

Ian laughed shortly. "I think that is hardly possible."

"Why isn't it possible? Tom Henderson says the *Sea Jade*
is in dock in Salem right now. He thinks she may be turned
into a coal hulk. That seems a shame with so beautiful a
ship. Could she not be purchased and brought home again?"

Ian heard me in astonishment. The idea excited me the
more I thought about it, and something of my own feeling
seemed to catch fire in him.

"What an idea! But only the captain could have done it.
There's no one left to care."

"You think Brock would not be interested?"

"He'd never touch her." Ian was emphatic. "Not that ship.
Not when his father died aboard her. You can forget the
notion—unless you have exceptional influence with your husband."

His last words stung. I stayed for a moment longer, trying

to find some way to reinstate myself with this man who had earlier offered me friendship and now judged me so unfairly. But there seemed nothing more to say to him. His back was toward me and I went out the door without speaking to him again. Outside I found a vast bank of darkness climbing the eastern sky. Reluctantly I started toward the house.

There was no sign of Brock McLean and his black dog on the sea cliffs, nor did he appear within the house, or for supper that night, even though he owed the guests the courtesy of his presence.

The meal seemed endless to me, thanks to the role I must play as a new bride in this household. Many were the curious glances cast in my direction, and several ladies tried to draw me into conversation. But Sybil hovered close and watchful, ready to break in when anyone grew too curious. Plainly Mrs. McLean was looked upon with respect and not a little awe, so no one pried too far with me in her formidable presence. As soon as it was possible to do so, she excused me from the gathering on the pretext that I had endured two long and trying days.

Thus dismissed, there was nothing for me to do but go upstairs to the large bedroom that had waited for me all day long. There I found a fire burning in the grate to take away the nighttime chill. I was no longer a forlorn, unwelcome visitor for whom no fire would be lighted. Tonight I was a forlorn and unwilling bride.

8.

THE HOUR WAS NEARING MIDNIGHT. I stood at a front window of the room that I had discovered was once Rose McLean's. The lamps were out and there was no light except for a single candle I kept burning on a bureau. By this time I knew every detail of the room and I had gained some encouragement from the fact that there were no evidences in it of Brock's possessions, though there were small indications that his wife had once occupied it.

I had quickly discovered that a door at the rear connected

with a smaller room. Opening it, I found this to be the room now occupied by Brock McLean. It was as orderly as a captain's cabin, from the narrow bed to the sturdy, compact desk that might have served its time at sea.

Rose's room was more elegant. Its articles of furniture could have been made in Salem. The pieces were simple and clean of line, perhaps with a Sheraton touch. There was a large wardrobe, which I found locked when I tried to hang my clothes there. On a small walnut desk with an open dropleaf, I noted a scrimshaw inkwell, and a daguerrotype miniature in a scrimshaw frame. Skillfully carved ivory roses circled a pretty young face that looked out from the picture. I picked up the small portrait and studied what was undoubtedly a portrait of Rose.

When this girl had been younger than I she had married Brock McLean. Perhaps he had been different in those days from the black-browed man he had become in his mid-thirties, with his life fallen about him in ruin, his wife dead, himself lamed, and any ambition he might have had to sail the seven seas defeated. I could hardly blame him for detesting me under such circumstances. This I scarcely minded. What I dreaded was the possibility that he might try to punish me for the role I had unwittingly played in these recent events.

The one article of furniture in the room from which my eyes slid repeatedly away was the four-poster bed that dominated the central space with its fluted mahogany columns and oblong wooden canopy. A bright patchwork quilt that covered the bed—perhaps made by Rose's own hands—had been turned down at one corner to invite me. But I could not bear to get into that huge expanse, even though the fire had died by now and I shivered here by the window in my nightgown and wrapper. Cold though I was, I would wait until I heard Brock come up and go to bed in the next room. Only then would I feel safely forgotten and able to lie down and sleep.

The view from this window was unlike the one I'd had in my smaller room. Here the harbor and the flashing beam of the new lighthouse could not be seen, but I could view most of Bascomb's Point, with the older lighthouse bulking between me and the ocean. The tower where the lantern had once shone was dark, but a light burned downstairs in the dwelling part of the building. I knew by now that Brock had an office over there, as well as his main office at Bascomb & Company in town. And of course Ian's workroom was there, where he had carved the figurehead.

The night was gusty, with a haze blowing across the face of a three-quarters moon. So thin and gauzy were the clouds that the night seemed brightly lighted outdoors. As I stood there, a lamp upstairs on the second floor of the lighthouse came on behind shutters, and I knew it must burn in the room Ian occupied. As I watched another light was extinguished in the lower right wing. A man came out the door and down the moonlit path, accompanied by a great black dog that moved close to his master like a sinister shadow.

Brock was coming home.

My heart began to thud unevenly as man and dog approached the Bascomb house. I stepped to one side of the window, lest the man look up and see me there. The emotion that filled me was a strange mingling of fright and uneasy excitement. The question of whether I might learn to love such a man came unbidden to my mind. I dismissed the thought at once, with distaste for my own treacherous weakness.

The two did not enter by way of the front door below my window, but went out of sight around the house, presumably to settle Lucifer in his kennel for the night. At length a door opened at the back of the house and I heard Brock's uneven progress up the stairs.

When he knocked upon my door, I could not manage an answer because of the trembling that ran through me and seemed to close my throat. He had to knock a second time before I could speak my "Come in" clearly. I faced the doorway in trepidation, not knowing what I might expect from this man who was now my husband.

"Good evening," he said with stiff formality, and closed the door behind him. "I've brought you a proper wedding ring. I'd like to take back the jade ring I used for a makeshift last night, since it belonged to my father."

I had not worn the jade ring since the funeral. It lay upon the bureau where I had placed it when I moved to this room, and I gestured toward it without speaking. He picked it up and put it on his little finger. Then he took a jeweler's box from his waistcoat pocket and held it out to me.

"Will you try this, please, and see if the fit is right."

I did not want to wear his ring and I took the box reluctantly. He stood watching me and once more I was aware of the height and breadth of him, of his dark look fixed so intently upon me. With fingers that were all too uncertain I opened the clasp, took out the plain gold band and slipped it upon the proper finger. It fit well enough, but I took it off at once and replaced it in the box.

"The ring is for you to wear," he said curtly.

I shook my head stubbornly. "I'll not wear it."

"Put it on your finger," he ordered. "You will wear it as my wife."

When I made no move to obey he came toward me with barely suppressed impatience, took the ring from the box and slipped it onto my finger.

I snatched my hand away the moment I was able. "I shall take it off as soon as your back is turned," I said, but I felt as Laurel must, futilely opposing a force far stronger than I—a force in full authority. Perhaps I was all the more defiant because I did not like my own reaction when this man touched me. I had not liked the tingling shock that had gone through me last night when he had grasped my hand, or the repetition of that feeling now.

He paid no attention to such feeble opposition. "Get into bed where you'll be warm," he said. "You're shivering your head off."

I moved toward the bed, afraid and icy cold, yet compelled by his voice, his words. I kicked off my slippers and got clumsily beneath the covers. Then I sat up against the huge pillows with the quilt pulled to my chin and stared at him. He came to the foot of the bed and I sensed in him the cold fire I had been aware of before. But now there was something new as well—a sort of angry elation that was frightening in itself. It was as though he might have something of his mother's tendency to take pleasure in inflicting hurt.

"What a great disappointment it must have been to you that Captain Obadiah died before he could change his will," he said. "Now his fortune will go to the captain's Chinese wife. Even the control of Bascomb & Company will be in her hands. Instead of the wealthy husband you expected, you must now find yourself married to a poor clerk."

I regarded him furiously. "Perhaps you've won your just

deserts. You married only to gain power and wealth."

He went on in the same cold voice, being very explicit. "You're right. I would have given anything and everything to have the ship-building in my hands. The money doesn't matter so much. But this was my father's work as well as the captain's, and it has become mine. I owe it to my father's memory to bring the company back into a position of importance in the world of merchant ships. This I would have done. Now, instead, I find myself married to a woman who has brought me nothing but defeat. What you say is perfectly true."

I hugged the quilt beneath my chin and watched him over drawn-up knees. The sheets seemed as cold as the air to me and my shivering had not ceased. I was ready now to plead. There was nothing to gain by fighting this man.

"Let me go then," I begged him. "Let me return to New York. I mean nothing to you, and if you'll let me go, I'll trouble you for nothing."

"So you're timid as well as foolish! Now that you've lost your gamble, you're ready to run away. What do you think you would make of your life married to a husband who was never present? Nor will I accept the reverse—living apart from a woman who has become my wife. If I must have a wife, then I will have her here. Besides, you're wrong about one thing. Perhaps you mean more to me than you guess."

There was something in his words that made me shrink against my pillow. He went on as if he had begun to enjoy himself and I sensed again the dark elation in him.

"Tell me, have you ever heard your father speak of that first voyage of the *Sea Jade?* Has he ever told you about the death of Andrew McLean aboard that ship?"

All my life I had known that something lay hidden in the shadows waiting to pounce on me. I had sensed it when I was very small. I had felt it in my father's grieving for his lost career, in the brooding silences into which he sometimes withdrew. Always I had turned away from this thing with a fear of the unknown. But now it was in the open. There could be no holding back knowledge that I did not want.

Brock McLean did not wait for my assent or denial. "My father was murdered on that first voyage. He was shot down while doing his duty. Murdered by your father, Nathaniel Heath."

I could only stare at him in shock and horror. He came around the end of the bed, caught up my left hand roughly, staring at the gold band that circled my finger. Then he flung my hand from him.

"No," he said, "I will not let you escape so easily. You will remain here as my wife—for however long you live. But not to be cherished and loved. Nathaniel Heath's daughter can hardly expect that of me. The captain has played his macabre joke, but the outcome will not be as he expected."

I continued to watch him, unable to think, to feel. The man was as withdrawn from all kindly human emotions as was his mother. He crossed abruptly to the connecting door between our rooms, and then paused to speak again, his voice empty of feeling as if his rage against whatever drove him had drained suddenly away.

"When my wife was ill," he said, "I moved into this adjoining room so as not to disturb her. It is the room I occupied as a boy in this house, and I have remained there since. You may have the larger room for yourself. The outward conventions of marriage will be observed, since there is a connecting door, but from now on neither of us will use it. In public you will appear to take your place as my wife. You will do as you are told in this house. And you will not again interfere with my disciplining of Laurel. The child is not your affair."

On a warm flood of rousing anger my own ability to speak swept back. "What you've said is a lie! My father was a gentle person. He would never have harmed anyone. I don't believe a word you've said about him."

"You knew him on the quarter-deck, did you?" Brock taunted. "No man was gentle there or he would not last as master of a clipper ship."

I was no longer cold and shivering. Life flowed through me in hot tide. I would not submit to such injustice, or listen to such lies. When he would have gone into his room, I stopped him with a word: "Wait!"

At my tone he paused impatiently.

"I cannot help the position I am in," I said. "That I'm your wife is as much your fault as mine. But since this has happened to me, you need not expect me to play a passive role in this household. If you insist on keeping me here, you'll not find me submissive and meek. I'll not accept your accusations against my father. I'll do my best to learn the truth and publish it. Nor will I keep my hands off when it comes to your neglected daughter. I meant what I told her earlier today. She doesn't want me as a mother, but perhaps I can be a friend to her in this friendless place."

The man in the doorway flushed to the dark roots of his hair. He took a step toward the bed, and I rushed on, buoyed up by my own anger.

"What's more, I'll do my best to make a reasonably happy life for myself in this house. I won't wear black after these few days. And I won't live in a pattern of gloom. Not if I have to fight you all!"

My last words came out in a despairing flood because I could not keep on in the face of that look of muted violence in his eyes.

When he spoke, he managed to do so with ominous restraint. "You're a ridiculous child who has been flung into a situation too big for you. I'll try to remember that. But don't push me too far. I've endured more than most men would endure with equanimity. If you persist in setting a course upsetting to the rest of us, it will be the worse for you."

I thought I could see his mother in him and though he spoke with deadly calm, I was more afraid of him than before. Yet I had to make one more attempt at freedom.

"Then let me go back to New York! I won't trouble you there."

"You'll stay at Bascomb's Point," he repeated. "Eventually there may be some use we can put you to." With that he went through the door and closed it after him in a contained manner that seemed worse than if he had slammed it in a rage.

I got up to blow out my candle, and in the moment of rising I heard a whisper of feminine skirts outside the door to the hall, and the faint creaking of a board beneath a foot. I held my breath, listening. Somewhere a door was closed ever so softly, and I knew with revulsion that Sybil McLean had been in the hallway listening to everything we said. It must have given her great satisfaction to know there was to be no love-making between Brock and me. If she too believed the story of Andrew McLean's death, I could better understand her detestation of me. To have me the daughter of the woman her husband had loved, and the man who was supposed to have murdered him, must indeed be painful to accept. But no matter what fury drove her, such action sickened me.

I went back to bed and huddled beneath the quilts. Realization of my own words and action had begun to frighten me. What had I gained by infuriating this man? How could I carry out such rash avowals as I had made? Yet I must —I would! Not for a moment did I believe the dreadful claim he had made against my father. I would find a way to disprove his accusations and then I would somehow leave this house. It was outrageous that Brock McLean should think he could imprison me here in this mockery of a marriage. Not for nothing was I Captain Nathaniel Heath's daughter, and the daughter of Carrie Corcoran Heath as well!

The thought of my mother and all she had been in her young life returned to me and I began to speculate. How would this mother I had never known have dealt with such a situation? Apparently she had won the heart of more than one man and I wondered what her spell had been, her secret ability to charm. Surely Carrie would have known how to bring the cold angry man in the next room around to doing as she wished. My father had always said that I looked like Carrie, perhaps that I was even prettier than she had been. Brock McLean had regarded me without interest or liking from the first, yet if Carrie had lain here in this bed, he would surely not have remained in cold rejection of her beyond that unlocked door.

Yet I hardly wanted him otherwise—this man who had so mercilessly accused my father. What I wanted was to hurt him, punish him, pay him off for the injury that had been done me.

To comfort myself, I began to dream again. I could imagine Miranda Heath—no, Miranda McLean!—turning into as fascinating a woman as Carrie herself had been. What a delight it would be to refuse the importunities of Brock McLean, to show him my indifference in the face of ardor. How cruel I would be, once he . . . My revery was broken into by the sound of creaking bed springs from the next room. My foolish dreaming was dissolved in an instant. This was the sort of self-indulgence I must put aside forever. I was married to a man who despised me and was unlikely to change. Instead of dreaming of the impossible I must find the strength and wisdom within myself to carry out at least the beginning of those promises I had made.

Perhaps one thing I could do would be to make Brock McLean so much trouble that he would be glad to send me away. Perhaps I might make him feel that he could not endure my presence for another day. Then I would be free. I could well imagine myself infuriating, tantalizing, maddening him until he was ready to pack me off and forget me forever. This was no mere dreaming, but a plan for practical action. Yet I had never wanted such warfare in my life. I had wanted only to be loved, to love, to be gay and quietly happy. Since none of these things were to be possible for me in this house, warfare would have to be the pattern, whether I was suited for it or not.

A reflection of light that lay in a pattern on my wall vanished suddenly. A lamp had gone out in Ian Pryott's room and I thought of him again as the one person who still might help me. If not to get away, then perhaps in other ways. He had no liking for Brock—that had been evident. And he was the historian. Surely he could help me to disprove the lying story Brock had told about my father and what might have happened on that first voyage of the *Sea Jade*. At least Ian was not wholly part of this Bascomb's Point household. He was an outsider like myself, and if I could reassure him about my own motives concerning this marriage, perhaps he would again be willing to befriend me.

Holding this thought in my mind, I was able at last to sleep.

With the coming of sunlight and a new day, I rose the next morning rested and refreshed. I was free, at least, of one dread that lay beyond that closed door to Brock's room, yet I no longer felt so inadequate as I had in the dark hours. Spiteful thoughts of revenge were not for me. I remembered Ian saying, "Don't let them do that to you, Miranda. Fight them for the right to be happy." In some ways I must change because growth itself was change. But there were ways in which I must remain true to myself and to my raising. I had conceived something of a plan for action. Now I must carry it out.

Again I put on the black dress that had been Rose McLean's, wondering about Brock's wife as I did so. Had her way in this household been an easy one? I supposed it must have been, since she had been cherished by her husband

and approved by his mother. But I must not think of that. It was from this place in which I stood that I must make my start.

I found the unrelieved black not unbecoming in contrast to fair skin, and my newly burgeoning sense of purpose lent a brightness to my eyes that I noted and approved as I brushed my hair. I could do with a look that denoted spirit and courage. Instead of the current style of curls that fell at the nape of the neck, I tried a smooth blond coil at the back of my head to give me a more mature air. There must be no more dismissing of me as a feckless child by Brock and his mother.

As I dressed, I listened now and then for sounds in the adjoining room, and only then did I feel uneasy. Either Brock was still asleep, or he was up before me, for I heard nothing beyond the closed door.

That he had risen earlier, I discovered as soon as I went downstairs. The family had just gathered for breakfast. Brock was seating his mother, while Laurel, dressed in black like her grandmother, stood waiting for her elders to take their places. Someone had troubled to see that she was properly dressed for the funeral yesterday, but this morning her hair was awry again, and the lace collar of her dress was torn.

Ian was not at the breakfast table. As I was to learn, while he sometimes dined with the family, he more often ate in town, or fixed himself a simple meal in his lighthouse quarters. Usually he did not appear at breakfast time, but rose when he pleased and went to his work at whatever time he desired. The captain had demanded no regular hours of him, but only that he give his best to the task of recording company history.

Sybil McLean murmured a distant, "Good morning," while Brock said nothing at all to greet me. He did not, in fact, so much as glance at me. This morning he looked glowering and ill-tempered, and at the sight of him a pulse of wicked excitement began to beat in me. Here was my chance to prove that I was no empty dreamer. I would show this man who had forced marriage upon me and then humiliated me, that he had a woman to deal with—not the ridiculous child he had called me. I went to him as he turned from his mother's chair, put a hand on his arm, and rose on tiptoe to kiss him lightly on the cheek.

"Good morning, dear," I said.

I expected anger. I expected some heated outburst. Instead, my teasing effort could not have fallen with a greater thud. Brock merely looked at me with contempt. His mother noted his reaction and smiled mockingly, knowing well enough that I was playing a role. Laurel eyed me resentfully and imitated her father by not speaking to me. My intent to carry the situation off gaily collapsed about my ears and I sat down in the place that had been set for me, flushed and ashamed, and thoroughly embarrassed.

Mrs. McLean continued to regard me with her mocking look. "The dress is too full for your figure, but it will have to do for the moment. It is a frock that belonged to Rose, Brock my dear. I disliked having to use it, but there was no other choice. I will have Hettie Bright come in soon and work on suitable mourning for your wife."

If Brock minded that I was wearing Rose's dress, he showed nothing of his feeling. In fact, he showed nothing of any feeling at all after his first contemptuous dismissal of me. He ate in silence the food that was placed before him and ignored me completely.

Once more I attempted to assert myself, at least with Brock's mother. "You need not trouble. I've decided not to wear mourning. I don't care for black and it seems pointless to wear it, since I hardly knew the captain."

Still Brock said nothing. It was as if he had removed himself to some far place in his thoughts where I did not exist and could not trouble him.

"We shall see," Mrs. McLean promised darkly, and ignored me thereafter as she spoke to Brock. "Do you suppose you could persuade the Chinese woman to wear something besides those outlandish clothes, now that the captain is gone?"

"Let her alone," Brock said. "The town is accustomed to her dress by now. Have you learned anything further about the fellow who showed up so suddenly and frightened the captain? Has he been around since?"

Laurel spoke up, pleased to give information. "I know who he is. His name is Tom Henderson and he's an old friend of the captain. He told me so. I talked to him on board the *Pride* yesterday."

"You are to stay away from that ship," her father told her curtly. Then again to his mother, "I must find out what the fellow wanted. Why he came here."

Mrs. McLean, I noted, was staring at her plate and she spoke without looking up. "There's no need to concern ourselves. Mr. Henderson came to the house a few days ago and I talked with him. He is just another seaman whom Captain Obadiah treated badly in the past. He had reason enough for his grudge and he felt the captain might be persuaded to do something for him, since he was in need."

"Is that how he got into the house night before last?" Brock asked. "Did you let him in?"

His mother's pale eyes met his own and I sensed again the inner force of the woman, concealed so much of the time by her restrained and pallid manner.

"I have no idea how he got in. I told him I would intercede for him with the captain and try to get him work."

Whether she was lying or not, I could not tell. I was certain that if letting Tom Henderson into the house to frighten the captain had served that purpose, Sybil McLean would have done exactly that.

Brock studied his mother somewhat grimly. "It was the violent shock experienced at sight of this fellow that caused the captain's death. There is no doubt about the fact."

"The man is still around," I offered. "He even tried to sell me some story he had to tell if I would listen."

"How does it happen that you were talking to him?" Mrs. McLean demanded, her voice sharp, as though some guilt on my part were involved.

Before I could answer, Brock dismissed our words. "Just see to it that neither of you talks to him again. I don't want his kind around."

Thus silenced, we said nothing more for the rest of the meal. The exchange had left me thoughtful. Yesterday, when I had dismissed without interest anything Tom Henderson might tell me, I had not known about the accusation against my father. Now I found myself wondering if, after all, this seaman might have something of importance to tell me. Nevertheless, the thought of seeking him out alone aboard the *Pride* was not to my taste. Undoubtedly I would meet him again as I moved about the locality and my questions could wait for that time.

After breakfast Laurel slipped away from the table as soon as she was excused. Her lessons under Ian's supervision were to be dispensed with for a period of mourning. When the other two had no further word for me, I went looking for her. This time I found both Laurel and Ian Pryott in the library. Absorbed in a book, Laurel sat curled in the small chair I had sat in on my first visit to the library. Ian was at his desk, busy with his writing.

The moment the child heard me enter, she started guiltily and slammed her book shut. Noting her reaction, Ian looked up and smiled at me.

"We thought it was Grandmother come to chide us for having our nose in a story book again. Since it's you, come in and join us."

But Laurel was on her feet, staring at me in her usual hostile manner.

"You said you'd keep me from being punished yesterday. But I was sent to bed with only bread and milk for supper. So I will never believe you again."

"I'm truly sorry," I told her. I could not admit to her that my promise had been recklessly given, before I realized how very little influence it was possible to exert in this household.

She continued to stare at me with her wild, bright gaze. "I don't like you to wear my mother's clothes. My father should make you take off that dress."

"I'm not going to wear it after today," I said. "There was nothing else for me to put on, since your grandmother wanted me in black." To my own ears I was offering apologetic excuses to the child, and she promptly took advantage of such weakness.

"I won't stay in the same room with you!" she announced, and went flouncing out, brushing roughly past me, as though she would have liked to hurt me in some physical way if she could. I sat down in the chair she had left, feeling once more defeated and helpless to act.

"If you let her get the upper hand, the child can make you suffer in this house," Ian Pryott pointed out.

"What am I to do?" I said in despair. "No one here behaves in a reasonable, normal way."

"Then you must learn how to deal with those who are neither reasonable nor normal, mustn't you?"

Again I sensed that Ian Pryott weighed and judged me. Once more I wondered how to find my way past the guard he had set up against me. I could not, I felt sure, make any explanation concerning my own actions until Ian knew me

107

better. How could he have faith in what I might tell him as a stranger?

He had not returned to the writing I had interrupted, but sat watching me quietly. At least his manner was less chill this morning and he had not turned me out of the room so that he could get back to work. I seized upon a subject that must surely be of concern to him.

"With the captain gone, what will you do now?"

"I'll finish my work, I suppose. After that, who can tell? Perhaps Lien will give me a few odd jobs around the place in order to use my valuable talents."

He appeared to be mocking himself and somehow I did not want him to do that. "From what I've seen, your talent for carving is real. Why shouldn't you develop it, do something with it?"

He shrugged. "What I do can be done by a thousand others. Men at sea have amused themselves with whittling for centuries. There's no market for such carvings."

As I regarded him in troubled silence, he suddenly relaxed and smiled at me. "Don't set me down as lacking in ambition and backbone, Miranda. I've ambition enough in my own way, but the course I choose will have to be my own, and there's no great hurry. The captain promised me a small legacy and that will see me through for the time."

The atmosphere between us seemed to grow less tense, less antagonistic, and I found that it was possible to talk quite easily to Ian Pryott.

"I need your help," I said. "You are the historian—perhaps there's something you can tell me."

He sat back in his chair, waiting, asking no questions.

I began indirectly. "When did the *Sea Jade* make her first voyage?"

He had no need to consider. "In the spring of 1858. She was one of the last clippers to come down the ways."

"I suppose you've talked to the captain about that voyage? I suppose there are records of it that you've read?"

Now he sensed my direction and a look of sympathy came into his eyes. "The subject was a painful one to Captain Obadiah. He never liked to talk about it, and he had a secretive nature. But since what happened then could not be ignored, he had to tell me something about it."

"Is it true that Andrew McLean died on that voyage? Is it true that he was shot to death?"

"There's no question about that," Ian admitted.

"How did it happen that all three of the captains were aboard the ship at one time? Obadiah was master, wasn't he?"

"That's true. The ship was a dream of Andrew McLean's. He had her built even sharper than the earlier clippers and he wanted to sail her himself on that trip. But Captain Obadiah had his eye set on a new record and he was determined to make it himself. As owner, he had the final say-so as to who would sail her, though he did not keep Andrew from going along."

"Why was my father aboard?"

"As a partner he probably couldn't bear to be left behind on so historic a voyage. From what I've read in records and letters, there were some who were against the three partners sailing together, lest all be lost on a dangerous ship. But old Obadiah liked the idea, so sail they did."

I left my chair and went to stand before Ian's desk. "Do you know exactly how Captain McLean died?"

His eyes fell before mine, and I saw that he did not want to tell me.

"Don't you know?" he asked at last.

"Not really. My father never talked about it. Last night Brock told me what he believes to be the truth. I cannot accept his account. I knew my father too well. Yet if by some wild chance there is some truth in the story, then I think Andrew McLean must have done something to deserve what happened. He must have—"

"There was a trial," Ian said quietly. "When the *Sea Jade* reached home, there was a trial."

I leaned upon the desk to steady myself. "Tell me, please. Tell me the truth."

"If you wish it," he said. He rose, moving away from my evident intensity and went to lean against the mantel as he had done the night I had first talked to him. There he stared into the fire as if he saw the movement of pictures in the flames. Choosing his words with consideration, he began the story.

9.

"APPARENTLY CAPTAIN MCLEAN AND CAPtain Health quarreled during a violent storm on the homeward voyage of the ship," Ian began. "What the quarrel was about has never been revealed. No one seems to know and Heath would never say. The fact is that Heath was armed and McLean was not, and that Heath shot and killed his former friend that night. Obadiah had Heath put in irons and then he sailed the ship through the storm and back to home port. The trial might have gone badly for Captain Heath if Obadiah had not eventually told the court that McLean had committed an act of mutiny in a rage, so that Heath had performed his duty in shooting him down."

I must have made some exclamation of relief, for Ian turned from the fire, his look pitying.

"Heath was let off for lack of evidence, but there were those who claimed that Captain Obadiah perjured himself to save his old friend. Otherwise, why had he not spoken up sooner and prevented a needless trial? Afterwards Obadiah would not let your father captain another Bascomb ship and Heath sold out his holdings in the company and retired from the sea."

I returned to my chair and sat down. I knew my father. He had been a gentle, loving, considerate man. An intelligent man, and one far broader in his views that Captain Obadiah seemed to have been. He had opened the world to me, while Captain Obadiah had apparently believed that the world revolved only about Scots Harbor and Bascomb & Company. A notion which the McLeans appeared to share. Yet for all his broader outlook, there had been times when my father had withdrawn from those he held dear, turning to some narrow, inner place where he brooded in a depth of silence. The name *Sea Jade* was not to be spoken lightly in his presence, lest it lead to such brooding. Always there had been for me a sense of ominous mystery about the ship's first voyage. There had been as well my aunt's quick tears and refusal to tell me what was the matter. The story Ian had just related seemed to corroborate what Brock believed. As Brock had pointed out so callously, I knew nothing of my father beyond the doors of his own home. But in spite of such evidence, there was a fiery loyalty in me that would not accept as fact even the strongest of arguments against my father. There were times when the heart was wiser than all reason and my heart insisted that there was more to this story than was fully known; that if the truth were found my father would be exonerated.

So deep was the reverie into which I had fallen that Ian's voice, continuing, startled me.

"At least Captain McLean's death made little outward difference to Brock and his mother. The McLeans already occupied this house and afterwards the mother and son stayed on. McLean had gone deeply into debt to back some of his bolder experiments, some of which were unsuccessful. It took his holdings in the company, and more, to pay off what he owed. Thus there was little left for Brock and Mrs. McLean. Brock must have been about sixteen at the time, and already shipping aboard Bascomb clippers. Captain Obadiah saw to it that his mother was paid a handsome salary as housekeeper here, so that she could continue to live in the house, and he promised to settle large holdings in the company on the boy, when he'd proved himself as master of his own ship. Brock sailed only once as a captain and he made a good record, I gather. But that was the end of his sailing."

"Because of the war?"

"Yes. He was an officer aboard the sailing frigate *Congress* in '62 when the ironclad *Merrimac* cornered her at Hampton Roads. He was severely wounded in the shelling and his active life at sea was finished with the damage to his hip, though in time he learned to get about on his own two legs again. He went into the management and building end of Bascomb & Company eventually. If he could put old disappointments from his mind, he might live a satisfactory enough life, even now. He has served the captain well. It was expected that Obadiah would shape his will to make Brock his main heir. But for some reason the old man always put it off. There seems something strange about that postponement. As if he couldn't quite trust Andrew McLean's son."

The library was quiet. I sat with my hands folded tightly together as I listened, my thoughts flitting ahead of Ian's words, striving to find some way out of the puzzle that had opened before me.

"Listen to me, Miranda Heath," Ian said and I looked up, surprised by the tone in which he spoke my maiden name. "Be careful what you do and say. Don't stir up any more animosity in this place than you've already aroused. Sometimes I think Lien is right when she says the earthly spirits of the departed have been allowed to collect under this roof for too many years. Now there's a gathering of trouble in the air. Stay apart from it if you can."

"How can I stay apart when I'm married to Brock McLean?" I demanded. "Tell me what you mean. With whom must I be careful?"

He made a vague gesture of dismissal by way of answer. "Who is to say for certain? Perhaps I'm more sensitive to the climate of this place than some. I have the feeling that trouble is brewing. I'd like to see you well out of it. It's too bad I couldn't act in time and do what Mrs. McLean first wanted me to do."

"What are you talking about?"

He grimaced wryly. "She offered me rather a tidy sum if I would get you away from Bascomb's Point with all due speed. She suggested that I make love to you, marry you if necessary—do anything at all to get you away before the captain could force Brock into marrying Carrie Corcoran's daughter —Nathaniel Heath's daughter. I'm afraid she believes in the sins of the fathers being visited upon the daughters." There was a hint of laughter in his eyes, amusement at the expression I must have worn.

I could only gape at him in dismay. I had begun to trust Ian Pryott, and to respect the clear, straightforward way in which he appraised Captain Obadiah and his household. Now I felt suddenly betrayed.

"So that was it?" I said stiffly. "When I asked you to help me get away and you agreed, I thought you were being kind. I thought you were my friend. When all the time you were tricking me because of the money Mrs. McLean had promised you. No wonder you were annoyed when I married Brock."

He laughed aloud, unabashed. "When you're angry, Miranda, you stop being merely pretty. You begin to look quite terrifyingly beautiful. You throw out dangerous sparks. But since we are being honest with each other, let me say that

112

I wouldn't have done what Mrs. McLean asked merely for the money she offered me. Though—never having had any— I have considerable respect for money. However, once I'd seen you, you were inducement enough in yourself. But there was no time. You threw yourself headlong into marrying Brock."

"I didn't want to marry him!" I cried. "The captain was dying. And they were all against me. I couldn't stand alone and—"

"And of course this does solve your major problem rather neatly, doesn't it?"

He was not laughing now and I saw that he believed what Brock had believed. In consternation I began to wonder if the motives both Ian and Brock read into my actions were the true ones after all, and if I deceived myself most of all. Had I been willing to snatch at any straw to save myself from the unhappy existence that awaited me in New York?

Ian came quickly across the room, perhaps sensing my re-action. He put a hand on my shoulder, touching me lightly. "Don't mind my teasing. I suppose it's a defense. Sometimes I carry it too far. I'll confess that I was ready to condemn you at first. Too late I've learned to know you a little better."

For the first time I saw frank liking in his eyes—and something of regret. He took his hand from my shoulder and moved away.

"In any event, don't be too hard on yourself, Miranda. Who knows what drives any one of us? The captain gave me my chance. But it was because I was ready to take it that I got myself into a different sort of background. Sybil McLean has always looked down her long nose at me and I've no love for her, or for her son. But perhaps they are driven too. As you must be now—by the situation in which you find yourself."

Once more I felt baffled by Ian Pryott. He had a way of alternately dismaying, then winning me—a contradiction that left me with a certain uneasiness concerning his true nature. Had I met him elsewhere than in this disquieting household, I would have trusted him wholly and instinctively. But my treatment here had roused in me a wariness that set me on guard, even where I most wanted to trust.

I believe he sensed my confusion, yet he made no effort to reassure me, and the very absence of any pressure from his direction relaxed me a little and put me more at ease.

His warnings not to stir up any more animosity than I could help reminded me that the captain too had tried to warn me of trouble ahead. I repeated the old man's cryptic words to Ian, telling him how the captain had, in his dying moments, warned of reefs that I must weather.

"He said I had only half the story and that I must find the whole." In uttering the words a connection flashed into my mind for the first time. "Do you suppose he could have meant that there was more to the story of what happened aboard the *Sea Jade*? At the very end Captain Obadiah murmured that he had always meant to do something. But he died before he could tell me what it was."

"I'm afraid he has given you too little to go on," Ian said.

"There was something else. Something about a whale stamp —about *following* a whale stamp. What could he have meant by that? What is a whale stamp?"

Ian went to his desk, opened a drawer and took something from it. Then he crossed the room to put an object into my hands.

"There you are! That is a whale stamp. Though what the captain meant by his reference, I have no idea."

He had handed me a scrimshaw piece, carved from the sperm tooth of a whale. It was made in the form of a lady's hand set upon a wooden base. The ivory hand was intricately carved, with a fancy lace cuff at the wrist, and a delicate ring etched on one finger. The closed fist made by curved fingers formed the handle of what appeared to be a stamp. I turned it over and saw the outline of a whale cut into the wooden base.

"What is it for?" I asked.

"I don't know what connection there might have been in the captain's mind," Ian said. "Or even if this was the stamp he had reference too. There must be a number of such stamps about. When a whaling vessel had a successful day and a whale was caught, the outline you see there was stamped in the margin of the ship's log opposite the record of the day. When a whale got away, half the stamp was masked and only the tail was marked in the margin. This was common practice aboard whalers."

I turned the scrimshaw carving about in my hands, examining the delicate, skillful work, studying the outline of the whale. But it told me nothing. I gave it back to Ian.

"I don't know what the captain meant, but I'm not going to

give up searching for an answer. I can't believe the story that has been told about my father."

I could tell by Ian's look that he believed what Brock believed and I let the matter go.

"Growing up in Scots Harbor, how did you escape becoming a sailor?" I asked him. "Don't you like the sea?"

"Like it?" He sounded rueful. "I'm devoted to it! But only on paper. What voyages I have taken in famous clippers!—but all in my head."

I could understand what he meant, for I had done the same thing. "I've always wanted to make a real one," I said. "Haven't you?"

He seemed amused. "I prefer dry land under my feet and a pen or a chisel in my hand. I never cared for swimming as a boy. Water is not my element and I can barely get about in it. Grant me the right to other interests, Miranda. Not every Scots Harbor man must be a sailor."

We smiled at each other then, and there was growing understanding between us. When he turned back to his desk I would have risen to leave him to his work, but at that moment the library door burst open and Laurel rushed in, breathless and excited.

"You're to come at once, Miss Miranda! They're going to read the captain's will. Mr. Osgood says we must understand its terms at once, and he is here. He wants you present, and I may stay too, so it seems likely that the captain has left us something."

I looked at Ian. "Must I go? Mrs. McLean is sure to resent my presence."

"If Mr. Osgood requests it, you must go," Ian assured me. "Run along. And when it's over tell me what has happened."

"Won't you come with us? If the captain has left you a legacy—"

"I'll be notified in due time," he told me quietly. "It's hardly urgent and they'll not want me there."

Laurel plucked at my sleeve. "Oh, do stop talking and come! The captain always said he would leave me something special in his will. Something that would remind me of him. Not that I'd ever forget him anyway," she added, sobering.

I allowed her to pull me along, noting that someone had tried to brush her hair into a semblance of order, though the black strands were already slipping out of place.

"Who combs your hair?" I asked as we went out of the room.

She tossed her head resentfully. "I do. When I please. Mrs. Crawford is supposed to, but she hurts me, so I manage myself."

This was something I might be able to change, I thought, but this was not the moment to suggest it.

When we reached the front parlor we found the others there and waiting. Mrs. McLean sat beside Mr. Osgood on the rosewood sofa. The shell carving of its back lifted behind her head in a lovely curved line—in contrast to her own stiff lack of grace. Mr. Osgood was large and more than portly and his bulk was lodged solidly beside her on the horsehair upholstering. An oval-topped table inlaid with mother-of-pearl had been drawn up for his use and upon it he rested a portfolio of papers. Brock stood near a window on the far side of the room, and at sight of him my attention quickened distressingly. I would have preferred to be less intensely conscious of the man who was my husband.

Nearby sat the captain's wife, her unbound feet placed neatly side by side in their embroidered slippers, visible beneath the wide fall of satin trousers. Her head was slightly bent so that her face seemed foreshortened, her eyes hidden by powdered lids, her mouth a tightly folded red flower. What was she really like, this woman of China? I wondered. What did she think and feel? By what approach might she be reached?

Mr. Osgood had risen as Laurel and I came into the room. Mrs. McLean fixed me with her usual air of antipathy, while Lien did not look up at all. When Brock had seated me, he returned to the window and stood staring out across the veranda toward the road, as if he intended to show indifference for whatever the captain had done. Clearly he wished himself elsewhere and was here only because his presence was required. His mother, on the contrary, seemed fiercely involved and now and then she cast a look of repudiation at the silent, waiting Chinese woman.

Laurel curled herself upon a brocaded ottoman in the manner of one about to attend a play, and was very still, lest she be sent away. Once or twice she smiled rather shyly at Lien —almost as though she congratulated her on what was to come, perhaps allying herself deliberately against her father

116

and grandmother. Lien, however, gave no sign that she noticed.

It was quickly evident that Mr. Osgood was in anything but a good humor. He bowed to me curtly, his manner implying that I had kept him waiting. When I was seated he took his place beside Sybil McLean and fumbled among the papers before him. In spite of resenting delay, he seemed to be postponing an unpleasant duty. In fact, he sat so long considering his words, that Brock turned impatiently from the window.

"Let's get on with it, sir," he said. "I've work waiting for me."

The lawyer reproved him with a glance. "I must make it clear to you, Mr. McLean, and to Mrs. Bascomb—" he turned his look upon Lien, who stared at a ring of rose jade she wore on one finger, "—that I do not approve of such steps as Captain Bascomb took before his death. I understand the reason for them—to a degree—but I advised him against such risk. I would have preferred—and I so informed him—to have him make over the bulk of his estate to you at once, Mr. McLean, since that was his eventual intent. But he insisted that certain stipulations must be met first. Namely, of course, your marriage to the daughter of Carrie and Nathaniel Heath. While he accomplished this intention, it was his misfortune to die before the will could be changed to read as he intended."

"We know all this, sir." Again Brock spoke impatiently. "What is done cannot be undone. The sooner the matter is made clear, the sooner we can all rearrange our lives." His gaze rested briefly upon Lien's glossy black head and at once moved away.

What would she do, I wondered idly—this alien woman set down in stony New England soil—once she had power and wealth in her hands? Would she turn us all out and destroy Bascomb & Company? Somehow I could not care a great deal.

"Perhaps you do not as yet know everything," Mr. Osgood assured Brock curtly. "I will read you the captain's wishes and then you will understand."

As his voice droned into the legal terms, my attention wandered back to my own problems and how I was to solve them. The account Ian had given me of what had happened aboard the *Sea Jade* satisfied me no more than what Brock had told me. I thought again of the seaman, Tom Henderson, and his claim to knowledge that might interest me. I disliked and feared the man, but nevertheless I would now have to talk to him. And soon, before he decided to leave Scots Harbor. A resolve began to form in my mind. This very afternoon I would go down to the ship and find out what might be learned from him. Since he was the only source of information to which I could turn, then I must see him at once . . .

Mrs. McLean's gasp startled me from my thoughts and I realized that Mr. Osgood had spoken my name. He did not call me "Miranda McLean," but had used the name of Heath.

I looked at him inquiringly. "I'm sorry. I wasn't listening," I said.

His exasperation was probably justified. He glared at me, blew his nose loudly with a large linen handkerchief, and retraced his steps through the last paragraph he had read aloud. This time the astonishing import was clear. Captain Obadiah had not left the bulk of his fortune and the control of Bascomb & Company to Lien, his wife. To her had gone dower rights only. He had left the rest—the far greater part—to *me*—to "Miranda Heath" to hold and possess as I pleased.

With this reading only Laurel drew in her breath sharply and I knew she was staring at me with the same fixed gaze she had adopted that first day when I had ridden home with her in the carriage. This small thing I seemed to grasp—and nothing else.

Brock had given no sign of surprise, but now he left the window and moved to the table beside Mr. Osgood.

"How is this possible? The captain's will, as we all knew, left everything to Lien. What has happened here?"

"The change was made privately a few days before this lady arrived," said Mr. Osgood, nodding at me. "Captain Bascomb wished it done in this way. As I have pointed out, he meant to change the name of the main legatee as soon as this marriage was effected. In the meantime, he thought he would safeguard his wishes by making Miss Heath, the younger Mrs. McLean, that is, his legatee."

I felt shocked and somehow frightened. This was something I had been in nowise prepared for. Something I had never wanted. Sybil McLean was staring at me with unbelievable malevolence, while Brock's gaze turned upon me in an oddly speculative way I could not fathom. I stole a quick glance at Lien and found that she had ceased to study her rose-jade ring. She was looking at me openly, and with knowledge in her eyes. In that illuminating instant there was just one thing of which I was sure. Lien had known this was to be. She had known that the captain had changed his will before my coming. Even while she had been required to do the captain's bidding, she had not welcomed me to this house—and with very good reason.

"But I don't want the money!" I cried. "I can't possibly be in charge of—of a fortune, or of a business!"

"Fortunately," Mr. Osgood reminded me dryly, "you are married to a man who is well able to advise you in the management of every detail. Which, I surmise, is what Captain Bascomb regarded as a safeguard. Had he not married you before, presumably Mr. McLean would marry you now."

Brock made a sound like one of Lucifer's growls. I would have spoken again, but the lawyer silenced us both with a look and went on reading. I was forced to sit as quietly as I could, no longer daring to catch the eye of anyone in the room while his voice ran on through the various legacies. Ian was to have the sum he expected—payment for the work he was doing on the Bascomb history and which he was instructed to complete. There was even a gift for Sybil McLean, who had so long taken care of the larger house. To Laurel, bringing from her a cry of joy, the captain had willed a small tiger carving of black jade.

"He knew how much I loved it!" she cried. "Now it will be my very own. Lien, Lien—may I go and fetch it right away?"

"If permission is given," Lien said and looked at me.

Laurel did not wait to see the look. She took Lien's words to mean permission and flew out of the room to get her treasure from the captain's quarters. No one tried to stop her, though Mr. Osgood murmured that such haste was not seemly in a well-bred child.

For Brock there was nothing. No mention, no small stipend, nor words of gratitude for years of service. But then, as Mr. Osgood had mentioned, the will was considered temporary by the captain. When the expected change had been made, everything after Lien's share and the small legacies would have gone to Brock McLean. As it was, he would receive nothing, except through his wife.

When the reading had been completed, Mrs. McLean rose, gesturing to Brock. Mr. Osgood shuffled his papers and spoke hastily.

"I trust the management of the house will be left in your most competent hands, Mrs. McLean. In fact I will advise that this be done."

Mrs. McLean turned to stare at me deliberately, coldly. "It will not be done. I shall wash my hands of all responsibility at once. Whatever orders are to be given must be given directly to Mrs. Crawford by the person who has been placed in charge." She moved toward the door. "Will you come with me, please," she said to Brock.

She went out of the room and her son followed, leaving silence behind. When I glanced toward Lien's chair I found it empty. I felt bewildered, stunned by what had happened.

Mr. Osgood considered me with sober intent. "Are you able to spare me a few moments, Mrs. McLean?"

I turned to him at once. "There must be some way to undo this will. Since this is not what the captain intended, as we all know, a change must be made so that everything can be turned over to Mr. McLean in his own name. Perhaps you can arrange this?"

I think he had not believed my earlier words of repudiation, or expected me to repeat them, for he looked faintly surprised. His manner softened a little.

"If, after considered thought, this is what you wish, then perhaps something may be worked out, Mrs. McLean." He regarded the papers before him as though he wanted to say more, and found it difficult to form the words or meet my eyes. "If I am to handle your affairs—that is, if you should wish me to—"

"I hope you will, Mr. Osgood," I broke in. "You know more about these matters than anyone else, and the captain trusted you."

"That, I fear, is the point," he said. "Whether or not I approve of the step Captain Bascomb chose to take, I recognize that he was in complete possession of his faculties and that he had a right to do as he wished with his money. He informed me that there was a letter to be found among his possessions which would clarify the reasons for this action. There seemed some indication on his part that he intended the righting of an old wrong. Do you know anything of such a letter?"

"Captain Obadiah tried to tell me something before his death," I said, "though he mentioned no letter. It was some-

120

thing about a whaling stamp. But he did not finish and I don't know what he meant."

Mr. Osgood looked grave. "This morning, at my request, Mrs. Bascomb put her husband's papers at my disposal. I had hoped to turn up this information before the will was read, but I found nothing. A more careful search will be necessary."

"Then I hope you will go through his effects as soon as possible," I urged.

"I shall come tomorrow if I am able. But to return to your suggestion, Mrs. McLean—that is, your thought of turning everything over to your husband legally, may I—ah—inquire if all is amicable between the two of you?"

"I don't know what you mean," I said. "Or why it should concern you. This is a matter of law, is it not?"

"It is, indeed," he assured me. "Law and justice. Justice which must be considered from the captain's viewpoint, rather than from your own, or from mine. If he wished to make it up to you for some harm done long in the past, then he would not consider that this had been achieved if you were married to a husband who might repudiate you as his wife, once he had inherited, and leave you in an unhappy and dependent position."

I did not tell him that I could hardly find myself in a more unhappy position than now existed, with the trap closed and Brock furious about all that had happened. I sat staring at the wedding band that had replaced green jade on my finger, turning it absently, my head bowed.

Mr. Osgood cleared his throat and spoke in a more kindly manner than he had yet shown me. "There is another small legacy that the captain wished placed in your hands—though it is not mentioned in the will specifically. There is a box of old maps—charts of the voyages made by Bascomb & Company ships. The captain felt some sentimental attachment to these and thought they might interest you because of your father. I presume the box will be found among the other effects."

I had little interest at the moment in such charts and continued in my trouble silence.

"Ah, well—everything will eventually work out for the best, I am sure," said Mr. Osgood a trifle lamely, and began gather up his papers.

I would have gone with him to the front door, but as he

left the parlor, someone spoke behind me and I turned in surprise to see Lien standing in the shadowy corner near a window, where velvet draperies nearly hid her. My back had been toward her and I had not guessed that she was there. Mr. Osgood must have known, yet he had said nothing. Perhaps he thought it of no consequence that she should hear what was said. Clearly the woman had waited to listen, to learn, and now she meant to have her say with me.

The uneasiness I had sometimes felt in Lien's presence returned full force as she came toward me on softly slippered feet.

10.

"IF YOU PLEASE," LIEN SAID, HER MANner humble, her eyes downcast, "is it your wish that I move from this house?"

"Why should you move?" I asked, taken by surprise at the unexpected question. "This is your home, just as it was before."

She made a vague motion with her hands. "I am only a woman. My opinion is not worth anything. My wishes are of no account."

I felt impatient with her. "I'm a woman too, and I don't feel that your wishes are of no account. None of this has been my doing and I want to change nothing of the present arrangement in the two houses. As Captain Obadiah's wife, your rights will surely not be overlooked. This is your home for as long as you want to live here."

She slipped her crossed hands into opposite sleeves and bowed her head over them. "I am humbled to the earth before your goodness."

I suspected that she was less humble than she seemed, and that a disconcerting mockery underlay her words. While I hesitated, at a loss for anything else to say, she bowed to me politely and went out of the room.

When she had gone, I stood in the empty parlor trying to understand what had happened to me, trying to fathom the turnings of Captain Obadiah's mind. But the sense of unreality that I had so often felt in this house was upon me again. At every move some strange fate had forced my hand and brought undeserved distrust and hatred upon me.

There was only one person to whom I could turn in the face of these new events. Ian had said to come and tell him what happened. I would do so without delay. But when I looked into the library he was no longer there and I decided to see if he had returned to work on the figurehead.

I went to the lighthouse at once and found my supposition correct. In his workroom Ian stood before the figurehead, and I saw that a change in it was being wrought. Under mallet and chisel the rough planes of the head had begun to take shape.

"You've decided to finish her?" I asked. "You've decided about her face?"

He laid down his tools at the sight of me. "Perhaps. You look as though the sky had fallen, Miranda. What has happened?"

"For me it has. Except for Lien's dower rights and a few legacies, everything has been left to Miranda Heath. I don't know what to make of it. I find it most dreadful to contemplate."

Ian whistled softly in astonishment. He seemed no happier than I as he regarded me. When he spoke he put something of his distressed wonderment into words.

"An hour ago you were as poor as I—perhaps poorer," he mused. "You were a trapped, unhappy girl. I had even begun to believe that what has happened was none of your doing. Now you are heiress to the Bascomb fortune—an important and wealthy woman in your own right. We no longer occupy the same plane, do we?"

"That's foolish!" I cried. "Everyone else has turned away from me—you can't turn from me too!"

He regarded me in silence. Light from a window glinted on his fair hair, intensified the oddly unmatched planes of his face. For the moment all interest in his work had vanished.

"An hour ago you were my friend," I pleaded. "Don't change, Ian. Please don't change."

"How can I not?" he challenged me wryly. "Do you remember, how I wondered if Lien might grant me a few odd jobs to do after she came into control? Now it appears that it is you I must ask for such work. I'm not at all sure I like the change."

"I don't like it either," I said. "I don't like it at all."

He turned from me to pick up a chisel idly. "How did Lien take this shock?" he asked.

"I don't believe it was a shock. I think she already knew she would receive only her dower rights. I think the captain must have warned her of what he meant to do. That is why she took a dislike to me from the first. I'm sure of it."

"What makes you think she knew?"

"Everyone else was surprised, but Lien seemed quiet and humble and watchful. Not at all surprised. When Mr. Osgood left she came to me and asked quite calmly if I wanted her to leave the house."

Ian grimaced. "Humility is Lien's stock in trade. A useful tool when she needs it. Somehow I've never believed it was quite honest. In her country she was accustomed to a position of importance as the wife of a wealthy merchant. What did you tell her?"

"That she has the right to stay, of course."

"Of course," he agreed. "Nevertheless, for both her sake and your own, it might be better if she went home to China."

His attitude bewildered me. "Why do you say that? You've seemed her one friend in this place. You've been kind to her."

"Kind, but a little wary," he admitted. "Who could help but pity her friendlessness? But I'm not sure that I trust her. It may not be wise for her to stay."

I recalled his warnings, given not so very long ago. Was it Lien he distrusted as a source of possible danger?

He had begun to work with his chisel again, returning to his rough shaping of the head. I watched him for a time in silence. There was nowhere else I wanted to be. Wherever else I turned there were problems I did not know how to face.

"I hope you will finish the figurehead now," I said at last.

"So you can set her aboard the *Sea Jade?*"

His mocking words startled me and as I thought about them an unexpected tingling of excitement went through me. For the first time the significance of all that had happened began to reach me. It now lay fully in my power to bring the *Sea Jade* home if I chose, and if she was really in Salem I had only to give the order. In fact, it now lay in my power to do a good many things I had never so much as contemplated before. The sudden realization was heady.

"Finish your work!" I pleaded. "Do what you want with her!"

Ian must have heard the elation in my voice. "So it's gone to your head already? I suppose that's what money can do in the twinkling of an eye. Very well—I'll complete the figurehead on one condition. That you'll pose for me."

"Of course I'll pose!" I could not have been more pleased. I whirled about the room in giddy triumph. "We'll bring Sea Jade home and set her on the seas again! And she'll wear the figurehead you've carved and that I've posed for —just as my mother posed for the first one!"

"You're going a bit fast," Ian said quietly. "It's not so easy as all that. You'll need Brock's co-operation first. You can't just snap your fingers and bring her home."

"Then I'll get it!" I promised, running before the storm with my sails full and my confidence high.

Ian waved his chisel toward the door. "Then the opportunity awaits you. He's over there in his office now. Let's see what your giddy craft will do when it runs aground on New England granite."

My sails had a tendency to back and slacken at the immediate prospect of facing Brock and I ceased my gay whirling. Ian merely looked at me, waiting, and as suddenly as they had inflated the sails collapsed. I made one more effort in his direction.

"Everything is going to be difficult now. Every hand is against me, as I well know. But not yours, Ian. Please, not yours."

"My hand has never been against you, Miranda. It won't be now," he said more gently.

Yet I knew that he remained aloof from me, no longer so readily my friend. There was a certain independence about Ian. He seldom conformed to the expected—and he did not do so now. Unwillingly I went into the main room of the museum, moving more and more slowly as I neared Brock's door. Not even Ian Pryott was an anchor to windward now. I had no anchor anywhere, nor any safe port to which I could sail.

From beyond the door came the sound of a dropped book from Brock's office. He must have fled there to escape the importunities of his mother. And now he must deal with me. But there had been enough of my seeking support from others. As friendless as I had ever been since my father's death, I raised my hand and knocked on Brock's door.

When he called to me to enter, I paused for an instant to strengthen my own resolution. Then I stepped into the room. He sat at his desk without turning. I could see his unruly black hair and the hunch of his shoulders as he leaned on his elbows staring at something he had propped against a book. As I drew near I realized that he was studying the painting of the *Sea Jade* that I had previously seen hanging on a wall in the outer room. The stiff little waves which the Chinese artist had depicted, the neatly billowing sails, the background hills of Whampoa, seemed to absorb him completely. Surely this was a good omen.

"I'd like to speak with you," I said.

He rose from his place before the desk, picked up a wooden chair nearby and tipped it so that its burden of books and papers slid off onto the floor. With a careless gesture he waved me into the chair, still without looking at me, or speaking a word. Then he returned to his contemplation of the picture as if oblivious to my presence.

I seated myself on the edge of the chair, wondering how to begin. There seemed no simple way of launching into the several matters I must broach—matters more important than bringing back the ship. But I caught at the subject of the picture for an opening.

"Tom Henderson tells me the *Sea Jade* is in dock in Salem."

Brock ignored my statement about the ship. "The fellow is still about? I've not run into him. What does he want?"

"Money, I suppose." I watched Brock intently. "He promised me a story worth hearing if I'd come to the *Pride* and talk to him."

"You are not to go!" Brock said sharply.

"Why not? Is there something you don't want me to find out?"

His glowering look told of nothing except his distaste for me. "Don't be any more of a fool than you can help. The man may be dangerous and he's come here to make trouble. I'll deal with him myself if I can lay hands on him. What's he doing aboard the *Pride?*"

I wished I had not mentioned the whaler. It would be necessary to see Tom Henderson soon, before Brock could send him packing. In any event, this was not the subject I had come here to discuss. Since there was no way to lead into it gently, I changed the subject, leaping headlong.

"I want to talk to you about the captain's will."

"As far as I can see, there's nothing to talk about."

"If you will just listen to me and stop snapping my head off, there is a good deal to talk about."

For the first time his manner toward me softened a little and he looked at me as he had not before. In a sense it was a look of sudden discovery. I could feel my cheeks warm as I faced him without faltering. Now, at least, I could go on.

"I don't want this money, or control of the company," I told him with all the dignity I could muster. "It is ridiculous that either should be in my hands. I've assured Mr. Osgood that I want to renounce it all and sign everything over to you. I want nothing for myself. Or at least very little."

He stared in apparent disbelief. "You've decided on such a course? After due and considered thought, you've decided?"

"You sound like Mr. Osgood," I said. "I don't need to indulge in long and sober thinking about this. All I want is my freedom. If you will let me go quietly back to New York, I will sign all the captain has left me into your hands."

"You are willing to pay a high price for what you call your freedom," he said coldly.

"Don't let's argue about this," I beseeched him. "Just let me go. You don't want me for a wife any more than I want you for a husband. And you do want all that the captain has so absurdly left to me. We both know he never intended this as a permanent arrangement. We both know . . ." but in the face of his silent staring I could not go on.

While the echo of my words still rang in my ears, Brock reached out and clasped my wrist as he had done once before. This time I tried to snatch my hand away, but he only held me the more tightly.

"Be quiet," he said, and I was quiet, trembling inwardly before a force that frightened me, that both repelled and attracted at the same time.

"There is something you will have to understand," he went on. "Whether I have any use for you or not—and considering who your parents were, I could scarcely develop much liking for you—nevertheless, the captain placed you in my care. He felt a responsibility because he once loved your

127

mother, and perhaps for other reasons as well. From that responsibility I cannot be bought off. If you choose to follow the captain's wishes and place the company in my hands, I will accept what the captain intended me to have. But you will not buy the dissolving of this marriage. I am not, in that sense, for sale. I will do as the captain wished me to do."

He had made my fate clear. Under no circumstances would I escape from Scots Harbor and Bascomb's Point with his consent. I sat where I was for a few moments without moving. He had released my hand and turned back to his desk.

I could almost hear the echo of the captain's voice in my mind. I could hear him warning me that there would be reefs ahead, but that I was a good little craft and I could weather them if I tried. While I no longer had any hope of changing Brock McLean's mind about what he stubbornly considered his duty, nevertheless, I had not yet foundered. At least there was relief in knowing exactly where I stood. I need waste no more time hurling myself upon the reefs. I would not give up my intention to escape, but in the meantime there were other things I might do. I recalled the burgeoning sense of excitement, the dawning of realization I had felt in Ian's workroom. Why shouldn't I accept that feeling, let it come, let it command me? But before I could speak Brock looked around at me.

"Well? Is there anything else? I'm sure there must be work waiting for you at the house. My mother has placed everything in your hands and I fancy you'll need to give Mrs Crawford her orders. You are in full charge now."

He meant to mock and confound me, and this I would not permit. "My aunt brought me up well," I told him quietly. "The running of a household is not an unknown skill to me. I will speak to Mrs. Crawford shortly, though I should think it best for accustomed management to remain in your hands. First, however—" I leaned past him to touch the painting of *Sea Jade*, "—first let us speak of the ship. Why not bring her home to Scots Harbor, refit and repair her, set her upon the seas again?"

"That ship? Are you mad?" Brock reached out and turned the picture face down. "She's an evil craft. She brought nothing but tragedy to us all."

"Is that why you were sitting here alone studying her picture?"

"She was my father's finest creation," he said. "I can admire beauty and grace, and renounce evil at the same time."

"It is only men who are evil," I objected. "The ship is innocent enough. Perhaps if we bring her back, we can exorcise the legend of wickedness that haunts her."

Perhaps, though I did not speak the words, if we brought her back there would be those who would come forward and say what they knew of her, those who might tell what they knew.

"There's blood on her decks," said Brock. "My father's blood. Shed by Nathaniel Heath."

I leaned toward him eagerly, burying my resentment. "Decks can be sanded. Old wrongs can be righted. Old lies can be exposed."

For a long, silent moment we sat there, locked in a contest of wills so intense it left me shaken. When I could bear the strain no longer I went on. "Not everyone could sail her. You are your father's son and you've sailed the China run. Go to Salem and buy her back! Bring her home —and when she's ready put her on the seas as a Yankee merchantman, with yourself as captain!"

In a sudden violent gesture he brought his fist crashing down on the back of the picture. I heard the crack of breaking glass. Then he stood up and strode from the room without another word or glance in my direction.

I did not understand his violence or his anger, but I sensed that his outburst was directed more against himself than against me. Somehow I had managed to touch a sensitive nerve.

Carefully I turned the picture over and tapped broken glass from the frame. The *Sea Jade* still sailed her corrugated waves and jagged splinters had left no scar upon the painting. I studied it soberly. Somehow I would find a way to bring her back. The idea was taking on the force of an obsession in my mind. To bring her back might be to resurrect the past, to learn what had really happened. The conviction, I knew, had little that was rational behind it. It was a thing of the emotions, as impossible to touch with the finger of reason as it would be impossible to touch the wind that billowed those sails. Yet the wind existed and so did my feeling about what must be done.

Now there was all the more urgency for seeking out Tom Henderson, for finding out what he knew. I would wait no longer. I would do this now. I slipped from the room and past the door of Ian's workroom. If he knew what I was about he would stop me, and I did not mean to have that happen. I was glad to escape without his discovering me.

11.

AS I CLIMBED DOWN THE BLUFF PATH to the shipyard below, I saw that work was again in progress on the skeleton hull. The scene was brisk with activity. There were the incessant sounds of hammering, the heavy, hoarse wheeze of cross-cut saws and clank of calking irons. The air was pungent with the acrid smoke of wood fires beneath tar pots, and the not unpleasant odor of tar. There were gulls everywhere—in the air and on land and water.

As I picked my way through the yard, a man would glance in my direction now and then, and turn impassively away, curious perhaps, but hiding any interest behind a guarded look. As I walked past the rising timbers of the vessel, I saw that Brock had come down ahead of me. He stood a little apart watching the work with an alert eye. His interest was upon men on a scaffold and his back was toward me. I hurried by, knowing well that he would stop me if he guessed my errand. It was fortunate that he had not yet had time to seek out Tom Henderson himself.

Not until I reached the wooden steps to the dock where the whaler was moored did I glance behind. His attention was still upon the work before him. He had not seen me.

I hurried across the rough, splintery boards of the dock and ran up the gangplank that gave in a faint bounce beneath my feet as I trod upon it. The decks of the *Pride* lay empty to my eye. The hatch nearest the stern of the boat stood open, but for the moment I ignored it to make a quick round of the deck. Tom Henderson was nowhere in sight. It was possible that he was below and though I did not relish a search for him, necessity drove me. If I waited another day—another hour—he might be gone from Scots Harbor.

Once more, half shielded from sight in the prow, I looked over the ledge of beach and found no one staring my way. Brock was no longer in view. He must have moved around to the far side of the growing ship. The din of the work went on without cease.

I went aft to the open hatch and down steep, ladder-like steps. Storm lanterns hung from hooks set in a beam and I reached for one and took it down. Enough light fell through the opening to enable me to light the lantern. Its illumination seemed altogether feeble in the gloom below. As before, I had a sense of timbers leaning in upon me in these stale-smelling depths. Outside pressed the water—enemy to this derelict.

Once the echoes of my descent had died away, I realized that it was far from silent below decks. Somewhere I heard a skittering of sound, and held the lantern high, calling Tom's name aloud. Again echoes crashed disturbingly about me and afterward the silence seemed intense. No one answered me. Apparently my quest was fruitless.

The passageway in which I stood ended in what must be the captain's cabin in the stern and I regarded the closed door thoughtfully, recalling words Laurel had spoken the first time I had come aboard the ship. She had said the captain had kept "secrets" in his desk down here—"away from land-lubbers." He had told her he might some day show her the hidden drawers in the desk. It occurred to me that the mysterious letter the captain had mentioned to Mr. Osgood, and which had not so far been found in his effects, might have been hidden here. The captain had been, as Ian too had said, a secretive man. This sort of whimsical hiding place might have appealed to him.

For a moment longer I stared at the cabin's closed door with growing uneasiness. The very fact that every instinct urged me to flee to the sunny air above, was something to be conquered. Curiosity was greater than my fear of this place. I forced myself to walk in the direction of the captain's cabin.

The ship moved faintly with the lapping of the tide—enough to make me know she was alive and afloat, but there were creakings and whisperings and rustlings all about me as well. I closed my ears and mind to them and held my lantern firmly.

The narrow door of the cabin was closed and it uttered a

frightful squealing as I opened it. But the shadows did not mind and the old ship never ceased her normal whisperings. The stale, closed-in smell of the cabin was stifling and behind me the door swung shut of its own weight over the high sill. I did not turn to open it at once, for the sight of the cabin held my attention.

Everything in it had been built for the most compact use of space possible. Overhead the ceiling beams hung close. The captain's bunk was a narrow ledge, his table bolted to the floor. Only a single wooden chair stood free. A high ledge reached beneath the very beams of the stern, offering storage space, and above it were two portholes. I climbed to the ledge in an effort to loosen the fastenings and let in a little air, but they had not been moved for a long while, and I could not open them.

In any event, it was the captain's desk that held my attention. I found a hook on which to hang my lantern and left the door closed despite the stuffy air, feeling somehow more comfortable with a strong oaken panel between me and the dark reaches of the ship.

This desk was surely not one that had belonged to the captain of the whaler. It must have been brought here at a later day by Captain Obadiah. It was a delicate thing, made in the curious Chinese Chippendale style that had been so popular. I knew such furniture was often made in England and then shipped to China where the carving and decoration were done, so that often it took years for a piece to reach the buyer.

The curved front legs had been carved into dragon scales, with dragon heads forming the feet on which the desk rested. The front was a maze of oriental scenes and symbols. A drop-leaf panel came open at my touch and numerous drawers and compartments within were revealed. Some came open easily and were empty. Others resisted my touch. Eventually this desk must be made to give up its secrets. But I did not want to stay here too long today.

I closed the drop leaf and opened a deep lower drawer. Inside was a large flat tin box with a padlock slipped through the tongue. Lettered in fading purple ink on the lid was the name *Sea Jade*. Excitement stirred through me. The name alone would have been enough to catch my attention, but there was more. In the lower righthand corner of the lid was a less noticeable stamping—the outline of a whale.

The padlock had not been closed and I raised the tin lid of the box and looked inside. The contents consisted of a stack of old maps and sea charts on which appeared to be marked the routes which clipper ships must have followed on their way to China. Mr. Osgood had said that a certain box of sea charts was to be placed in my hands. By lucky chance I seemed to have come upon the very box.

As I fingered the yellowing contents, my attention was again arrested, for a series of tails had been stamped upon the face of one map after another. The tail alone—of a whale. But why such a symbol should be used in connection with the course *Sea Jade* might have followed, I had no idea. To hunt whales in a clipper would be like tracking elephants with a greyhound. Yet the captain had told me to follow the whale stamp—"on the China run!"

Hastily I shuffled through the charts and maps, finding on each one the same marking—only part of a whale. Then, in the bottom of the box I discovered a sea map that had been matted, as if for framing. And on this, full in the middle of the route around Cape of Good Hope, the complete outline of a whale had been stamped in the same, now faded, purple ink.

There was surely significance here—something the captain had tried to inform me of, warn me of, in his last moments. Around me the ship creaked and whispered and I knew this was not the time or place to puzzle the matter out. I drew the matted chart from the box, and chose several of the others at random. I would take them back to the house and study them at my leisure. Perhaps Ian could help me fanthom the mystery of the whole and half whale stampings.

When I had retrieved the lantern from its hook and tucked my findings under one arm, I reached for the knob of the cabin door. The door seemed to have jammed in closing and it did not respond to my tugging. Panic rose in me at the thought of being shut into this place, with no one to know where I was, and the air growing closer every moment. As I stood with my hand on the resistant knob, I experienced again one of those strange moments of ordainment, of prescience. It was as if I had been brought step by step to this moment in time—as if, now that I was here, some dreadful use was to be made of me. I did not then sense danger to myself. That was to come later.

Before I could shake free of this eerie feeling and exert

myself to open the door, the sound of a loud and ringing crash came to me from beyond the cabin. It was the sound of a heavy weight falling, sliding, clattering. I wrenched again at the door. This time it came open in my hand and I stumbled over the sill in my haste to be out of that tight, close little room. My lantern sent nearby shadows leaping, but the forward end of the ship lay in pitch darkness. Though not in quiet.

There were sounds near the forward ladder that descended to the lower hold. Sounds of labored breathing, of a groan, the clatter of stones rolling one against another. Then silence.

I wanted to drop my lantern and run to the safety of darkness myself. But I dared not abandon my light. The stern ladder to the upper deck was near and I started toward it, wanting only to flee this dreadful place and escape to the upper air. But before I could reach the steps, the groaning sound came to me again, and with it a weak call, as if for aid. The voice came from the lower hold beneath my feet and was so faint that I scarcely caught it. Yet it was a desperate cry, perhaps the cry of a life that was ebbing.

On my own level all was silent and I stilled my impulse to panic. This was no desperate deed, but an accident and I must go to the aid of whoever had uttered that feeble cry.

Even as these thoughts raced through my mind, I was finding my way down the nearest stairs. Once more the damp smell of ballast stones and ancient timbers rose to meet me. As I descended into that place of fearsome shadows, I held up my lantern and peered along the boards that made a walk fore and aft between ballast on either side. At the foot of the forward ladder something lay across the stones—a dark figure that did not move, but moaned faintly in pain.

I ran along the walk as swiftly as I dared, fearing to stumble and drop my lantern, fearing the flash of blazing oil about me if I were careless. The fear of fire was an atavistic thing in me, like my fear of flashing lights—the two seemed always connected. Only the need of the moment sent me to the aid of the man who was slumped across walk and rocks.

He lay upon his back where he had fallen and there was blood upon the stones where his head had struck. His eyes were open and staring and the shine of teeth was visible in the nest of thick black beard. The man was Tom Henderson.

I knelt beside him and spoke his name, calling to him urgently. His eyes rolled sightlessly and words came faintly from the open mouth. I bent to hear. He seemed to be wandering, not fully conscious.

"Paid . . . paid . . . to do it . . " The voice faded out.

I bent over him. "Who paid, Tom? For what? Tell me what you mean!"

His mouth went slack in the bush of beard and his eyes rolled back in his head. I had never seen a man die, but I knew he was gone.

Nevertheless, I tried frantically to call him back. "Hold on, Tom. Just hold on and I'll go for help!"

I knew it was too late even as I rose from my knees. I stepped back, looking helplessly down at the sprawled figure. At the same instant I heard a running on the planks above my head, the thudding of feet moving in haste—then ceasing to run, as though an escape had been made. Now there was only silence overhead.

I sprang for the ladder nearby. Up from the lower hold I went, and then a second ladder to the deck and open sunlight. I flung myself toward the rail of the ship and looked over—to see Brock McLean standing on the dock at the foot of the gangplank. Whether he had been going up or down, I could not tell.

I called to him nevertheless. "Come quickly! It's the seaman—Tom Henderson. He has fallen from a ladder. I—I think he is dead."

Brock came up the plank at a run, scarcely limping when he hurried. He caught up the lantern I still carried and hurried to the forward hatch. I could not go down there again. My knees had turned to water and I sank upon the planks of the deck and sat there trembling.

Brock came up again almost at once. "That was a bad fall —backward off the ladder. The man's dead. I'll get help to bring him up."

He stepped into the prow and cupped his hands about his mouth, roaring out, "Ahoy down there!" in a quarter-deck voice. I heard men in the shipyard answer him and in a few moments several came aboard and ran down to the hold. Brock came and raised me to my feet, and there was no gentleness in his touch.

"What were you doing down here? Must I forbid the ship to you, as I have to Laurel? Go back to the house, girl. It's not a pretty sight they'll be bringing up from the hold."

"I know," I said weakly. "I saw. The back of his head—he—"

"Stop it," he ordered. "Get ashore and out of this. The fellow must have died at once."

I pulled myself free of his touch. "No," I said, "he did not."

Brock was suddenly intent. "What do you mean—he did not die at once?"

"He tried to speak. He was mumbling something when I found him."

"Mumbling what? What did he say?"

I drew back in dismay from so ominous a questioning. "I—I don't know. I couldn't make out the words."

He shoved me toward the gangplank and forgot me. When I looked back, I saw that he had followed the others below. My legs recovered their ability to move me from one place to another. I went down to the dock and sat on a low piling, while the gulls wheeled about me. Work had been disrupted in the shipyard area. Men stood about staring at the *Pride*, waiting to hear what had happened. I looked upward past yardarms, watching mizzen and main and foremasts tilt gently against the blue of the sky. So peaceful it seemed—that sky. But there was no peace in my thoughts.

While I stood beside Tom Henderson, in the hold, someone had run along the planks over my head. Someone who knew very well what had happened. And when I came out on deck, Brock McLean had stood at the foot of the gangplank. Coming up, or going down—which had it been?

They were carrying Tom Henderson from the ship now, and Brock followed. If he saw me sitting there on the dock as they went by, he gave no sign. Only one of the workmen, a foreman, perhaps, noticed me and came to ask a question.

"Good morning, Mrs. McLean. You were below just now, I take it? Did you see what happened?"

I shook my head. "I heard him fall. I was in the other end of the ship and up one level. I went down to see what had happened."

"A bad fall," he said. "A nasty crack he got on his head, old Tom did. Funny thing—with him used to running up and down ships' ladders all his life. Hard to see how he'd lose his hold and go over backwards like that."

I concentrated on a gull lighting at the far end of the dock, and watched it settle its wings after flight.

"You didn't happen to see nobody down there, now did you, Mrs. McLean?" the man pressed me. "Could be somebody pushed old Tom off those stairs."

"No," I said, "I saw no one but Tom himself."

"Or heard nobody neither? Who could've run away, let's say?"

I managed to answer firmly, clearly. "No, I heard nothing at all. Only Tom moaning."

The man shrugged and stepped away from me. " 'Twas just a thought."

He went after the others and I left the dock and found my way slowly back to the bluff path and climbed it to the house. I saw no one as I went upstairs to my room. There I lighted the fire and sat before it in a rocker. I was terribly cold. Huddled in my mantle, with the several charts I had brought from the *Pride* stacked on my lap, I sat rocking, trying to gain some order in my thinking. The wedding ring upon my finger seemed loose, as though my very flesh had shriveled, and I slipped it up and down aimlessly.

Why had I not said at once that I had heard someone running away after Tom had fallen? Why had I not told whoever asked of those footsteps thudding on the planks over my head? If there had been someone there who ran guiltily away, then Tom had been pushed and what had happened was no careless accident. The word for it was—*murder*.

I tried to remember how the running had sounded. Had there been an irregularity in its beat? Or would that be likely in any case? An uneven gait could be wiped out when steps were hastened.

I wrapped my arms tightly about myself and rocked in my chair, back and forth, back and forth—trying to banish thought from my mind. The effort was futile. My thoughts ran on of their own volition and took me where I did not want to go.

It was my duty to report the sound of running I had heard. Yet because I had seen Brock at the foot of the gangplank when I came up on deck, I could not bring myself to do so. I had not told him what I had heard, or what I guessed. I had not dared to after he had questioned me so intently about the words Tom might have spoken before he died. Brock's interest in Tom's words had seemed too intense, too rough, too frightening, so that my only impulse had been to deny any knowledge of their meaning.

That I lacked understanding of such meaning was true. But I had indeed heard several words of what Tom had tried to say—that he had been paid by someone. Paid for what information? Paid to do what? To whom might his words apply? To whom might they be dangerous?

No one summoned me to lunch, and I was not hungry, in any event. The afternoon slipped away and I did not stir from my room. No one came near me until Laurel scratched softly at my dooor.

"What is it?" I called.

The child took this as an invitation to enter and opened the door, slipping sidewise through it, a small, thin shadow in her black frock, her limp black hair falling tangled about her shoulders.

"I've been in town," she said, watching me with a sly, knowing look. "I've heard about Tom Henderson—that he's dead. You were there when it happened, weren't you, Miss Miranda?"

There was no point in my trying to speak delicately with this all too knowing child. "I found him after he fell."

Laurel kicked the door shut behind her with an unladylike foot and came further into the room. There she stood staring at me with an avidity that reminded me of her grandmother.

"Did you really push him off the ladder, Miss Miranda? Did you kill him, the way your father killed my grandfather?"

I gasped. "How can you be so ridiculous? How can you think such a wicked, unkind thing?"

She seemed pleased that she had so upset me. "*I* didn't think it first," she said, tossing back her lank strands of hair the better to view me. "It's what they're whispering about you in town. There are people who say your coming to Bascomb's Point is very strange. Even Mrs. Crawford says that. Strange considering whose daughter you are. Why should the captain leave you all that money? Why should my father be pushed into a marriage with you? That's what everyone is asking, and they think maybe it's you who shoved Tom Henderson off that ladder because he knew about things you aren't telling."

Her words left me aghast. "Your father will stop such talk," I said. "He knows what happened and he will tell them that what I've said is true."

"Will he?" She allowed an ominous silence to follow the words while she curled herself upon the hearthrug at my feet as if she had come to stay. The flames gave an unaccustomed rosiness to her pale little face, but they hardly lighted the dark depths of eyes that were like her father's.

"I don't think my father will care one bit what happens to you," she went on. "Perhaps you're a witch, like the ones who lived around here in the old times. Perhaps the townspeople will stone you and drown you in the harbor."

"I think that unlikely," I said, and pretended great interest in one of the maps I held on my knees. "If you've come here merely to say unpleasant things, I think you'd better go. I don't enjoy your company."

She paid no attention to this. The leaping flames seemed to absorb her full attention for a few moments, as though she saw demons and witches dancing among the very coals.

"Lien would like that," she went on in the same sly voice. "I mean if they drowned you as a witch. If it weren't for you, she might have posed for the *Sea Jade* figurehead, the way she wanted to. Now Ian likes you best and he's going to use you as his model instead of Lien. He told me so. But Lien loves Ian. She'd like to marry him, now the captain is gone."

I stood up so quickly that the maps and charts scattered upon the floor. I went to the child and pulled her abruptly to her feet. She turned her head as she had once before, intending to sink her teeth into my hand, but this time I was too quick for her. I twined my fingers through a handful of hair at the back of her head and held on tightly so that any movement she made would hurt to the very roots of her scalp. She gave a yelping, animal-like sound and would have kicked at me if I hadn't kept free of her feet.

"If you stand still I won't hurt you," I said.

Abruptly she went limp, perhaps in surprise. I did not release my grasp, but using it as a lever I marched her to a straight chair and sat her down.

"Don't move from there," I said. "Stay right where you are."

Strangely enough, so commanded in a voice that I hardly recognized as my own, she sat quite still, staring at me. I went to a bureau drawer and drew out a clean hairbrush. At sight of it she made a horrible grimace at me.

"Nobody can spank me except my father!" she shrilled. "If you try that I'll—I'll—"

"I'm not going to spank you," I said. "I'm going to brush your hair. I've had all I can stand of looking at that dreadful bird's nest you wear around your head. Your mother would be ashamed of you. If she saw the way you look now she would probably burst into tears of despair."

Laurel ducked a quick, startled look at me from under the fall of hair. "What do you know about my mother? How do you know how she'd feel?"

I separated a long strand from the rest of the tangle and began to brush out the snarls as best I could. "You have lovely hair," I said. "It's fine and soft. But that makes it hard to care for. We must find a different way for you to wear it so it won't tangle so easily. I have some sassafras bark that I'll wash it with soon. And if I start giving it a hundred strokes a day it will begin to shine beautifully."

She winced under the tug of the brush, but she did not forget her question. "How can you know how my mother would feel? You don't have any mother of your own."

"We have that in common," I agreed. "But that doesn't mean I don't know what mothers are like. Often I've looked at my friends' mothers and wished they were mine."

"Have you done that?"

"Of course. Haven't you? I expect anyone would. I've seen a picture of your mother and I've heard about her. She must have been a kind, gentle, loving person. If she were here she would never let you go around with your clothes torn and your hair wild—as if you were a little animal. Who looks after your things?"

"Crawford is supposed to," Laurel said grudgingly. "But she thinks I'm a nuisance and she's afraid of me besides. Grandmother doesn't want to bother. She says I'm a change-ling."

"Of course you're not a changeling, any more than I'm a witch. Turn your head a little—and hold onto this piece I've combed out. What does your father say about the way you look?"

"He doesn't care anything about me," Laurel said. "The only time he talks to me is when he scolds me."

"I don't believe that either," I said. It had seemed to me that Brock often regarded his daughter with helpless concern. Being father to such a child, with so little help from the women in his household, would be far from an easy task.

Nevertheless, it was not the child's fault that she was allowed to continue like this.

"Tell me about your father," I said as I went on with my brushing, hearing electricity crackle in her locks as I worked. "What happened at the time when he was wounded? Have you heard the story?"

"Of course! Everybody knows how brave he was. Captain Obadiah asked Ian to write down an account of the battle. I've read it lots of times. Father was aboard the *Congress*, one of the ships in the blockade off Norfolk, Virginia, when the *Merrimac* made her first naval attack."

I had read of how the sunken United States ship *Merrimac* had been raised and rebuilt by the Confederates, who had armored her with railroad iron and sent her into battle to break the blockade. When Laurel saw she had my interest there was no need to urge her to continue. She went on eagerly.

"The *Merrimac* sank the *Cumberland*, and then she came after the *Congress*. My father was a Union officer on board. None of our ships could hurt the *Merrimac*. I guess those old cannon balls just rolled off her iron sides. She almost destroyed the wooden *Congress*. Most of the *Congress*' guns were damaged and men were dying all over her decks. Our men had to run their ship ashore and raise the white flag. But when the *Merrimac* sent tugs to remove the prisoners, the men opened fire on them with small arms and drove them off."

Laurel pulled away so she could turn her head and look up at me. Excitement and pride glowed in her eyes as she went on with her story.

"My father was badly wounded, but he wouldn't give up. He held himself erect at the rail and fired his pistol at those tugs that wanted to board the ship. When the Confederates called on the men to surrender—since the white flag was up —General Mansfield said, "I know the damned ship has surrendered, but *we* haven't." So the *Merrimac* couldn't take the men. She drew off and began to fire incendiary shots until the ship was on fire in lots of places. But the men never gave up. When it grew dark that old *Merrimac* had to haul off. So the crew of the *Congress* escaped ashore and took their wounded with them. My father was saved, and he didn't have to go to a Southern prison. But he was very sick for a long time after that and he could never walk properly again."

141

I think my own eyes were shining a little as I listened to Laurel's spirited account. There was nothing I liked better than a tale of heroism and I could well imagine Brock in the role he had played aboard the *Congress*.

By now Laurel's hair was brushed into a gleaming mass, with all the snarls gone. I found a length of red ribbon and tied it at the nape of her neck.

"That's a wonderful story," I said. "Thank you for telling me."

There was a lump in my throat as I watched the child cross the room to the dresser mirror and stand on tiptoe to look at herself almost shyly. She was a wild little thing, but perhaps she could be tamed. I would need her father's help, need his authorization if that was to happen, however.

The hovering memory of footsteps returned to my mind. What of Laurel's father? A man who had known violent action in the past might know it again. Had he been acting out some secret revenge in the depths of the old whaler? What of Laurel if this were true?

Already she had been badly hurt by her elders and there could be no telling what might result if she knew her father had been involved in murder. There was a growing urge in me to protect her, to comfort and strengthen her against the future. Perhaps to comfort myself a little, as well. There was nothing more soothing and quieting to the young than physical contact, than being gently held and loved with the warmth of another human being. Dare I offer this to Laurel?

As she continued to stare at herself in the glass, I spoke to her quietly. "Do you know the thing I missed most when I was little and had no mother?"

The child's dark, reflected eyes moved toward my own, looking at me out of the mirror, though she said nothing.

"Sometimes," I went on, "I would see mothers rocking their children. Because they were sick, or hurt, or tired, or just to show them love. My aunt never rocked me because she thought rocking wasn't good for children and she wasn't a demonstrative sort of person anyway. She loved me very much and I always knew that, but sometimes I wanted that one little thing that I'd always missed."

Laurel turned from the glass, her eyes surprisingly soft. "My hair looks nice," she said. "You didn't hurt me as much as Crawford does."

I wondered if I dared take the next step. I wondered if I

might coax her to sit on my lap, big girl that she was. Just to lean against me quietly while I rocked her back and forth. As I thought of how to bring her to me, she did a surprising thing. A little hesitantly she crossed the room and came up behind my rocker, so that I did not know what she was about until I felt the chair move. There she stood behind me, gently pushing my chair so that it moved smoothly on its rockers. The lump in my throat made it hard to swallow. I leaned back and closed my eyes, permitting the rocking to soothe me. Not until I felt she might tire did I stop the chair and look up at her, and I know my eyes were moist and alight with tenderness.

"Thank you," I said. "I feel much better now."

It was not in the child to be wholly friendly at once, and she recovered her normal manner by giving the chair a slight push and scowling at me, as though she disclaimed her own moment of weakness. The charts still lay upon the floor where they had scattered when I had jumped up earlier, and perhaps to hide her embarrassment, Laurel knelt to look at them.

She recognized them at once. "You brought these from the *Pride!*" she accused. "They belonged to the captain."

I nodded. "Yes. I thought they might be interesting to study. I wonder why those tail stampings are on them?"

Laurel picked up the map that had been matted for framing and sat cross-legged, her head bent, studying it. "This one has more than a tail. The whole whale mark is here."

"I know," I said. "What do you suppose it means?"

"I found these aboard the *Pride* a long time ago," Laurel said. "Captain Obadiah used to put things there sometimes. Things he wanted to hide from Grandmother Sybil. He told me he didn't want anybody to know about these charts for a while, but he wouldn't tell me what the whale marks meant. Afterwards he used to get mad when I wanted to talk about them."

"So the marks do mean something special," I mused. "I think Captain Obadiah tried to tell me about them before he died, but he never finished his words. There was something about the China run—"

Laurel pounced with her forefinger, as if to pin down the mark of the whale off Cape of Good Hope. "I know one thing! This is the place where my grandfather died in a storm. It was off Good Hope that awful thing happened

143

aboard *Sea Jade*—when your father shot Grandfather Andrew."

For a moment longer she stared at the marking and when she looked up at me her face had changed.

"I almost forgot about that!" she cried, jumping up. "I can never be friends with you—never, never!"

Before I could stop her or call her back, she ran out of the room, banging the door loudly behind her to emphasize her words. I made no effort to follow. A small beginning had been made, and for the moment I could hardly ask for more. I bent to pick up the matted chart she had dropped and sat for a while longer puzzling over it, wondering what it had to tell me. Half whales and whole whales—*why*? Why the complete marking of a whale across this particular part of this particular route?

What was it the captain had whispered with his last gasping breath? Something about only half a story, about my looking for the whole story. Had he meant that the whole whale stood for the whole story of what had happened aboard the *Sea Jade*—a story that had never been fully told?

But I could decipher nothing by staring at the map. When I had an opportunity I would show it to Ian, and tell him of my search for an answer. Perhaps he could help me to discover the key, if there was one.

I felt restless now. I could sit here no longer wondering what might be happening outside this room, wondering what might have been discovered by now about Tom's fall in the hold of the *Pride*. I could put no stock in the things Laurel had told me about mutterings in the village. As I'd learned in the short time I'd been at Bascomb's Point, very little that she said could be trusted. Often it was difficult to tell whether she dealt with fact or fantasy. I found it hard to believe that anyone would seriously think me guilty of such an act. On the other hand, I remembered the questioning of the foreman, as well as Brock's urgency. Was it really possible that I was being regarded with suspicion?

My restlessness grew. The room had darkened with early twilight, so that only the flare of the fire lighted it, falling with a rippling golden sheen upon the charts strewn across the hearthrug. I gathered them up and put them safely away in a drawer. It was time for me to face another problem.

144

12. I WENT DOWNSTAIRS AND OUT TO THE kitchen to speak to Mrs. Crawford. I found her sitting at the kitchen table, her hands resting idly before her. At an hour when pots on the big kitchen range should have been steaming and bubbling with supper preparations, its black top was bare and cold. Not even a kettle was aboil with water.

She looked up at me bleakly as I entered, neither rising, nor replying to my greeting. I drew up a chair and seated myself at the table opposite her.

"Could we talk a little?" I asked.

Her apathy and indifference were clear. She fell to staring at the red, swollen knuckles of her roughened hands. I stared as well, thinking of Sybil McLean's smooth, beringed fingers —the fingers of a woman who had withdrawn in all but name from the necessary work of running a house, leaving most of it to this thin, bony, hostile woman. A possible approach occurred to me.

"Do you think it would be a good idea to get in a hired girl to help you, Mrs. Crawford? From the little I've seen, you appear to have more work than you can comfortably handle."

At once she removed her hands to her lap, hiding them beneath the table's edge. Her words when she spoke were surly.

"So you're already complaining, miss?"

She had a way of putting me quickly at a disadvantage. "I only wanted to help," I began, but now she cut in on me quickly.

"As I told you once before, miss, I wouldn't work for that heathen Chinese woman. And I won't work for the likes of you either. Coming here and taking over from your betters, putting on airs!"

I held onto my fraying temper and managed to speak evenly. "You are leaving us then?"

I think she had not expected counterattack from me. Her

hesitation in answering told me the truth. Mrs. Crawford did not really want to leave. She wanted to lash out at me with her tongue, to put me, as she felt, in my place.

"I'm sorry that you wish to leave," I went on. "Sorry because I am in great need of your help."

"I can see that." She glanced with faint triumph at the cold stove, with its absence of cooking food.

"That's not what I mean," I told her. "If you don't want to get supper tonight, I don't blame you. You've had two long days with all that company yesterday and everything different today. There must be a good deal of food left over and I don't mind fixing supper. I can manage well enough in a kitchen. My need for help concerns Mrs. McLean. But since you are leaving—" I pushed back my chair to rise.

"What about Mrs. McLean?" she snapped, her attention caught in spite of herself.

This was what I wanted—her questioning interest—and I stayed in my chair. "Mrs. McLean is an unhappy woman. I can understand that her son's marriage and the possible results of the captain's will are difficult for her to face. She will be increasingly unhappy if management of the house is taken from her. You have been doing the actual work, I know, but she has felt herself completely in charge."

"She wants none of that with you here. She said so herself."

"That is why I need your help. You are the only one she might listen to. The only one who can help her to understand that her supervision and planning talents are still needed. I know you're her friend. Will you stay long enough to persuade her? Everything could go on as before if you can change her mind. There's just one duty I might take off your hands at present—the care of Laurel. I can see that you're too busy for that, and it's the one place where I could help immediately."

She was listening to me now and there seemed a certain relaxing of the stern New England set of her face, though she made no comment.

"You must have worked in this house for a very long time," I went on. "You must be a very old friend of Mrs. McLean."

The woman sighed heavily. "I was a girl when she brought me here. She was always a fine lady, but circumstances made things hard for her after her husband died—" Mrs. Crawford darted a quick, knowing look in my direction. "Mrs. McLean comes of a good family and she knows how to behave. You'd not find her coming here in the kitchen to sit at the table with me."

I could see how persistently she circled round to cut at me whenever she saw an opening. Boldly I gave her further opportunity.

"Did you know my mother?"

She sniffed, her resistance breaking simply because she would not miss a chance to hurt me if she could. "I knew her all right. A baggage she was—flirting with this man and then that, keeping them all guessing, instead of settling down like a decent woman should."

"But she did settle down. She married my father."

"She wasn't a young thing by that time. She'd had the village tongues wagging for years. She was past thirty when she married, and the three captains were close to ten years older, more or less. It put Captain Obadiah's nose out of joint when she married Nathaniel Heath. Andrew McLean's, too, though he had a wife of his own by that time and he'd no business casting eyes at Carrie."

I kept very still. Whether I liked her point of view or not, the woman was willing to talk about things no one else would tell me.

"So she married my father." I prodded her.

"She married him, and right away he went off to sea, the way a sailor must. He meant to build her a house when he came home, but for the time in between he put her in rooms over in town. And better than she was used to, I must say."

"Can you tell me where her rooms were?" I asked. "I'd like to see the place where I was born. Perhaps I can meet some of the people who knew my mother then."

A glimmer of surprise crossed Mrs. Crawford's face. "Born? In town? That's a queer thing to say, seeing as how you're here at Bascomb's Point. You weren't born over in town, goodness knows. Though you might have been, if Captain Obadiah hadn't got wind of how Carrie was having a bad time. He'd never got over the witch-spell she set on him. With Cap'n Nat away, he came storming over to town and brought her back with him, to have her baby born at Bascomb's Point. I remember very well. It was here you were born, young lady. And here in this house that your ma died a few days later."

I could only stare at her in astonishment. My father had

never told me that I had been born in the house at Bascomb's Point. I had been allowed to take it for granted that my birthplace had been the village of Scots Harbor. It seemed strange that no one here had mentioned the fact either.

Mrs. Crawford watched me with relish, eager to satisfy her greed with any sign of pain or distress on my part.

"You'd like to know all about that time, wouldn't you?" she asked, leaning toward me across the table, her bright, darting eyes studying every shade of expression I might betray.

"I don't know that any of it matters now," I said, stiffening against her prying eyes. "You haven't answered the question I've asked you. Will you help give back to Mrs. McLean a feeling that this house is in her charge? After all, it must be while I go away."

She pounced upon the words. "You're going away?"

"When I am able," I said. "Perhaps not for a little while. There are certain things I must accomplish first. But I won't stay here a moment longer than I have to."

"What will *he* say about that? Your husband, I mean."

"I believe that lies between him and me, Mrs. Crawford. Would you care to trouble yourself getting a cold supper for us? Or shall I manage alone?"

She pushed herself back from the table. "I want no outside woman in my kitchen," she said and I knew she had decided to stay. This small victory I had won and it gave me some satisfaction. Never before had I tried my mettle in just this way. It was good not to come off in defeat.

I left the kitchen and stepped into the hall at the same moment that the front door opened and Brock came in, bringing a man in uniform with him. He saw me at once.

"Come here, if you please," he said and his tone brooked no opposition.

With rising alarm I went into the front parlor as he held the door for me and gestured me into the room. Then he and the stranger followed. I busied myself with the lighting of a lamp and found my hands awkward and uncertain. The man was the town policeman and his coming here returned Laurel's words full force to my mind.

We sat in the cold, solemn elegance of the parlor, where Captain Obadiah's body had lain, and where Mr. Osgood had read the will that had so affected all our fortunes. Officer Dudley took his duties seriously, albeit suspicion of murder was not often his province. In Scots Harbor's busier days, when ships were often in port and seamen came ashore, there had been more trouble and a larger police force. Of late years the inhabitants of what had dwindled to a village were well enough behaved and caused little disturbance. Even the jail was not often used in these times.

Now it appeared that Laurel had been right. There was talk about town to the effect that Tom Henderson was not a likely one to fall down a ship's ladder. Especially not with such force that he went sailing backward through the air and cracked his head on ballast rock. It would take a push to do that, people were saying. And who had been aboard the *Pride* except that young woman from the outside, to whom the captain, undoubtedly in his dotage, had left most of his money? That daughter of Carrie Corcoran, who had so suddenly and queerly married Brock McLean.

Not all of this came out so exactly in the policeman's rambling and somewhat apologetic words. But I could read well enough between the lines. It was, he said, his duty to inform me of the trend of such talk. Maybe only gossip, or maybe there was something to it. This he was here to find out.

I sat on the edge of a chair with my hands folded in my lap and heard him in disbelief. What made the experience seem all the more dreadful was the fact that Brock should sit beside me in silence, watching, listening, yet never coming to my aid with so much as a word—though he was the one who must know the truth of my story.

"I don't understand what you mean," I said when the roundabout account was finished. "If you think that I somehow ran the length of the ship and pushed Mr. Henderson off that ladder, intending to kill him, you must be out of your mind."

Brock stirred restively in his chair. "Just give him an account of what happened, Miranda. Tell your story—as you told it to me."

As you told it to me. Were those the key words? Did they mean that I was to mention nothing else I might have heard—such as footsteps sounding overhead? Or the betraying words spoken by a dying man?

I did as I was told and the two men listened with so little expression on their faces that I could not tell whether I was believed or disbelieved. I explained that I had come aboard the *Pride* looking for Tom Henderson because he might have information about my father. Brock made a snorting sound that immediately stiffened my spine.

"Tom Henderson was first mate on the *Sea Jade*'s maiden voyage," I said with more spirit. "I might have learned something of value from the man if his tongue had not been silenced by his fall."

"Please go on with your account," the officer said.

I told him I had not gone forward in the ship until I heard the resounding crash of Tom's fall. By the time I reached him he was gasping his last few breaths. Again I said nothing of hearing steps overhead, nothing of Tom's mumbled words. But I did add somewhat heatedly that I knew nothing of the man that would make me want to injure him, that I was small and light, and would certainly lack the strength to push anyone so burly to his death.

Officer Dudley eyed me soberly for a moment. "It'd take no great strength with a man so placed. Pretty easy, it would be, to push him off balance."

"I wasn't anywhere near him when he fell!" I cried. "This whole thing is ridiculous. I had no reason to wish him ill. I've never wanted to injure anyone in my life."

The policeman sighed. "I told 'em you'd say as much." He stood up and looked at Brock. "Guess you don't need to worry none, since there ain't a mite of evidence. While there could be those about who had no liking for old Tom, there's no way of telling if one o' them was down in that hold today. You sure you didn't hear something while you were down there, Mrs. McLean?"

"There was a lot of noise," I hedged. "Some of the stones rolled after he fell. And I made some noise myself, running. Besides, the whole ship creaks and groans all the time."

"Not the sort of noise I mean," he said.

Brock showed the man to the door. I stayed where I was until he returned, my indignation surging hotly. The moment he appeared I hurled at him the angry words I had held back while the policeman was present.

"Why didn't you help me? Why didn't you say your wife was incapable of murder? Why did you sit there and let him insult me with such horrible suspicions?"

He stood in the doorway, waiting until I ran down. There was something of his mother's look about him today—that opaque stare that gave nothing away.

150

"You were doing all right on your own," he said. "You needed no help."

"What if that policeman had wanted to take me off to jail?" I demanded. "What if—"

"He didn't," Brock said curtly. "I knew he wouldn't. Have you anything else to say to me?"

In a moment he would be gone from my reach, and I hurried on, my words atumble.

"Yes—yes, I have! Will you tell me, please, why no one has ever let me know that I was born here at Bascomb's Point? Why no one has ever told me that it was in this very house my mother died?"

His air of impatience lessened a little and he came a step or two into the room. "Perhaps you never asked," he said reasonably. "Perhaps we never realized you didn't know."

"Of course I didn't know!" I told him. "Not a word has anyone ever spoken to me of these facts. And I don't understand why. It would seem natural for you to speak of it. Certainly it seems strange that your mother has never brought up the subject."

"She wouldn't," he said. "Though I remember the time well enough. I was a boy of fourteen when they brought your mother here."

He was silent for a moment, as if remembering, and I saw the tight lines about his mouth loosen surprisingly. When he spoke again a touch of the Scottish burr had come into his speech.

"I remember what a bonny wee babe you were. Not wrinkled and red, but a rosy babe who knew how to laugh from the beginning. Your disposition was better then—though I'll admit you could raise the roof with your yelling when something annoyed you."

I heard him, amazed—more astonished by this unexpected softness toward me than by his words.

"What of my mother?" I prompted.

"Matters did not go well with her—the birth and afterwards. But you were the darling of all our hearts for a time. Captain Obadiah doted on you and envied Nathaniel his fathering of you. He brought in not one doctor, but three to attend your mother, though nothing could be done to save her. She faded quickly and three days later she was dead. So we kept you with us until your father came home from his voyage and took you away. Perhaps knowing you as a babe helped to influence the captain's feeling of responsibility toward you later." Brock's face darkened as though some memory troubled him. "Especially since you suffered a mishap in this house."

"A mishap? What do you mean?"

"Do you perhaps have upon your person the scar of an old injury?" he asked.

Taken by surprise, I clapped a hand to my shoulder and he saw the gesture.

"It could hardly be otherwise," he said, and the new gentleness went out of him. Once more he was about to turn away.

"Wait, please! Will you tell me how it happened?" I pleaded.

"I will not," he said and the dark look was upon him again.

"Then I'll talk to your mother," I told him and started past him through the doorway. "I want to know more about the time when my mother lay ill in this house. I want to know——"

He caught me by the arm and whirled me about so that I stood close to him in the doorway. "You'll do nothing of the sort, my lass! You'll say nothing at all to my mother. The shock of what has happened aboard the *Pride* has upset her sufficiently as it is. She is in her room with a headache and I won't have all that's old and painful dredged up to hurt her again. She has enough to bear."

I tried to pull out of his grasp, but he held me with both hands and shook me a little, so that my head fell back and I looked into angry eyes that commanded my own until I went limp, ceasing to fight, ceasing to resist him. Incongruously, held like that, I felt an unexpected and disturbing desire to go into his arms and be comforted there. If only he would be gentle with me, if only he would be kind. But he set me away from him and went out of the house, his eyes still clouded with some inner fury, his jaw set and stern.

I leaned my head against the door jamb and tried to right my dizzied senses. I did not like what could happen to me with this man. How could I hate him so thoroughly, and with such good reason, yet be drawn to him so that in the midst of anger I was conscious of the touch of him and wanted to be held close in his arms? So that I looked at his mouth and wondered how it would feel to be kissed by him? Despising myself, feeling that such thoughts betrayed my father, I drew the parlor door shut and went into the quiet haven of the library where I could be alone and think about the revelations that had been made to me. I did not want to think more about my own intense reaction to Brock McLean.

I was sitting there in the gloom, without fire or candle, with only lamplight from the hall faintly penetrating the darkness, when Ian hurried into the house and came looking for me. He found me there at once and lighted a lamp. Then he came to me and took my hands in his.

"You are all right, Miranda? I've just heard what has happened. I went over to the village for something to eat and learned about Tom Henderson."

"Then you've also heard that I pushed him off the ladder on purpose and that the town policeman came here to question me?"

"Miranda—don't. This absurdity will die down quickly enough. People like something new to gossip about and they say things they are sorry for later. Why did you go seeking the fellow? You could only ask for trouble."

I told him I had felt I must see Tom and find out anything he had to tell me. My love for my father, my loyalty to him would not allow me to accept as truth the dreadful accusation that still stood against his name. But not even to Ian did I utter the words that continued to stop on the tip of my tongue—what Tom had said before he died. And of the frightening sound of running I had heard overhead. I could not tell anyone. And still I did not understand why.

Ian heard me with pity in his eyes and I knew he thought hopeless my quest for a truth that would exonerate my father. Nevertheless, he tried to comfort me and raise my hope for the future.

"You are in a position to take hold now, Miranda. You can do anything you wish. Accept the fact, then learn how to live with it. Use it. You can begin a new life for yourself any moment you choose."

"I don't want to live with it," I insisted. "I will stay for a little while until everything is settled. Then I will go away. Nothing will stop me."

He released my hands and took a turn or two about the room. "Perhaps this is the way it must be. Perhaps this is the wiser, safer way. But while you are here, will you pose for me? First we will finish the figurehead."

"You want that very much, don't you?"

I saw his face come to life. For an instant the shadows were wiped away.

"Yes, I want it. I've never had this feeling about a piece of work before. It is as if my hands already know every phase of the carving. I can sense that this will come right for me. Perhaps if I can create this one thing and do it well, I will find freedom too. Perhaps the only future that exists for either of us is to get away from Bascomb's Point."

"Then we'll begin tomorrow," I promised him.

With his hand beneath my chin, he tilted my face to the light as he had done once before. Then he bent to kiss me lightly on the cheek. "Thank you, Miranda."

It was as if I had bestowed a gift upon him, and he upon me. I think he did not understand how much I needed that anchor to windward. Often in my thoughts I found myself turning to Ian for advice and reassurance. Yet when I was with him I was never drawn by that dominant attraction which nearly mastered me when I was with Brock.

For the second time in that long day it was Laurel who broke in upon us with a summons. Since there was no fire in the library grate, the door stood ajar and she appeared in the opening abruptly. I noted that she had not removed the ribbon from her hair or allowed it to relapse into its wild state.

"Lien wants to see you, Miss Miranda." The echo of Lien's formal manner of speech sounded in Laurel's voice. "She humbly beseeches you to visit her as soon as it is conveniently possible."

I looked at Ian, but he merely shrugged.

"Did she say what she wants?" I asked Laurel.

The child's eyes were agleam with anticipation. "She's angry with you! But she didn't say about what. She took out the captain's pirate blade again this afternoon and looked at it. Maybe she would like to chop you up in pieces."

"No friend of mine talks to Miranda like that." Ian spoke so sternly that Laurel looked faintly abashed. "I'll come with you, if you like," he said and drew me from his chair. "If she has that sword out again, perhaps we'd better see her together. No telling what is going on in her mind."

Laurel trailed after us without invitation as we went through the door into the old house. Captain Obadiah's room seemed strangely changed without his lusty presence.

A fire had died to banked red coals in the grate and only

candles burned upon the mantel. The captain's chair stood empty in its place beside the hearth and without him the room had become an empty shell that the small woman from China could not fill. She came toward us out of the gloom, a ghostly figure in her white garments. Today no pin of gold filigree shone in her coil of black hair, though she wore rose jade upon her fingers.

Even as she gestured us humbly into the room, the look she turned upon me showed no meek humility. Behind us Laurel stole in unreproved and perched herself upon a hassock in the corner, as if she attended a play.

At Lien's insistence I took the captain's chair. Sitting in his place, my brief memories of the old man flooded back and I wished vainly that I could have come sooner to Bascomb's Point. If only he and I had talked this problem out. If only there had been time, perhaps none of these present difficulties would exist. But such musing was vain and it was Lien who now commanded my attention.

She invited Ian to sit down, but he refused, standing a little apart from the two of us, as though he knew that whatever battle was to be joined lay between Lien and me. But I think not even Ian expected what was to come.

Lien had learned enough of abrupt Yankee ways so that she could on occasion shed her oriental courtesy and elliptical phrasing. Now she came to the point without evasion.

"I have learned of the death of the seaman, Tom Henderson. I hear that you are the one to find him, Mrs. McLean. You will tell me about this, please."

Whatever I had expected of her, it was not this and I was tired of telling the story.

"What does it matter? He fell down a flight of stairs. I found him. That's all there is to it."

"Is it perhaps that you were searching for something aboard the *Pride*?" Lien asked.

"I didn't go there to search," I told her. "But I found some interesting old sea charts in the captain's cabin. Charts with the mark of a whale upon them."

I could sense the quickening of Ian's attention and recalled that I had not yet told him of the charts.

"This is all?" Lien inquired.

"Why do you ask?" I countered. "Is there something else he might have kept there?"

The silken shoulders moved in a faint disavowal of knowledge and I suspected that the gesture concealed more than she was telling. Lien, I realized, had not come enough into my reckoning.

"I went down to the ship to look for Tom Henderson," I continued. "He had hinted to me that he might have information to divulge."

Lien heard me without expression, her face a pale mask, her lips for once lacking their carmine. "This man comes also to me. He seeks money for his lies. I tell him no—he has frightened the captain and done much wickedness. I do not wish to hear him."

From the corner of my eye I caught Ian's faint movement and turned my head to see that he watched Lien intently.

"I'm not sure all he had to tell was lies," I said.

Her dark foreign eyes continued to hold my own, but she said nothing more. Laurel wriggled on her hassock and Ian went to a window and looked outside. He had not yet entered our talk, but left it between Lien and me.

"Perhaps you will return to China now," I said to her. "With the captain's inheritance you can live comfortably in your own country."

Beneath the white silk her bosom rose and fell in quickened breathing and I knew that I had said the wrong thing. She did not speak of her plans, but slipped away to another subject, clearly of importance in her mind.

"The figurehead that Mr. Pryott is carving—" she began, "—you are to model for this?"

I recalled that Lien had thought of posing for it herself, and I remembered as well the thing Laurel had told me and which I had shrugged aside—that Lien was in love with Ian, that she wanted to marry him.

"Perhaps the choice of a model is for the sculptor to make," I said gently.

For the first time she seemed agitated. Her fingers intertwined and the jade stones she wore shone softly pink in the candlelight. She seemed to strive for words, but before she could speak Ian went to a table and picked up a long-stemmed pipe with a tiny metal bowl. He brought it to her with a grave smile and she took it from him gratefully. When she had filled the bowl with a pinch of golden brown tobacco from a pouch, Ian lighted the pipe for her and she sat for a moment puffing. There could have been no more than three or four fragrant puffs in the bowl, but they seemed to soothe and calm her. When she laid the pipe aside, she was in better control of her emotions.

"Please forgive me," she said, addressing us both. "The moment of weakness has passed. It is not for me to say what face is to be used."

Ian spoke gently, persuasively. "We have to remember that the original carving was modeled with an occidental face. This was part of the charm and strangeness of the *Sea Jade*'s figurehead. I believe it signified a meeting of East and West on the seas."

I tried to help. "Since it's possible that the *Sea Jade* may be brought home to Scots Harbor and that the new figurehead may be used to replace the old when the ship is refitted, it seems only natural that the new figurehead should be as much like the old as possible."

We had forgotten Laurel in her shadowy corner, so still and rapt had she been in attending our small drama. Now she came whirling excitedly into our midst.

"Miss Miranda! Is it really true that you will bring the *Sea Jade* home? How wonderful that would be! Captain Obadiah would be pleased. He would be glad."

We looked at her in some astonishment and I sensed that her sudden outburst had broken the tension that had risen uncomfortably in the room.

Lien did not smile, but when she spoke whatever hostility she felt was hidden from view. "I am sorry if I have offended you, Mrs. McLean. For this I am sorry. It is you, the captain's heiress, who is alone in this house with every hand turned against you. You are a young person and inexperienced. This will change. But youth is difficult to endure while it is upon one. It seems unfortunate when a girl so young is given power she cannot handle and when she is without friends."

Lien was not without perception, but I could not take her words with grace. In my youth, I was indeed offended. I rose somewhat stiffly, bade her good evening and started toward the door.

Behind me she spoke to Ian. "Go with her, please. I have much to think about, much to plan."

Now that the play was over, Laurel went off ahead of us. As Ian returned with me to the upper hall of the other house, Mrs. Crawford was sounding the Chinese gong for supper.

He kept me there for a moment, ignoring the summons. He had sensed my depression and discouragement and I knew he searched for some way to cheer me.

"Don't mind Lien, Miranda. Give her time and she will get over this notion of posing for the figurehead."

I met his look directly. "Laurel says she's in love with you."

He made no attempt at evasion. "Perhaps this was inevitable, though I did not seek it. She was a woman alone, with a husband grown old and indifferent. I found her friendless in this place. We were drawn to each other in sympathy when she came to me for her English lessons. I could not be otherwise than kind."

"You are kind to everyone," I said warmly.

He studied my face for a moment. "Not always, Miranda. There are times when kindness is not what I intend."

I stepped quickly back from an implication I could not face. "Will you come to supper with me? There is something I want to show you, consult you about."

He sensed my withdrawal and accepted with a faintly mocking bow. "I'll be happy to join you," he said, and waited while I went into my room and took the sea charts from the drawer where I had put them. Then we started downstairs together.

I do not know what made me glance back on the way down. Some faint creaking of a door, perhaps, or the whisper of a sharply drawn breath. At any rate I looked and was in time to see Sybil McLean's door closing softly. How long had she stood there at the crack listening? Uneasiness lay upon me as I went downstairs to dine with Ian Pryott.

At least it was quieting to be with Ian. I doubted that Brock would be present tonight, and apparently Mrs. McLean was not coming down. Laurel of course had supped earlier. We sat beside each other at the round table and I tried to throw off the thought of that softly closing door upstairs.

13.

MRS. CRAWFORD SERVED US SULLENLY, setting out the cold meal with evident disapproval of this tête-à-tête. We could not help but be aware of her manner and we spoke guardedly while she was in the room. Not until the kitchen door had closed behind her did I show Ian the charts and point out the curious matter of the whale stampings. Though he pored over them, he could decipher no more of the matter than I.

"Will you keep them for a while and see what you can make of them?" I requested. "There must be meaning here that I haven't been able to translate."

Ian promised and set them beneath his chair. I started then to tell him of the information Mrs. Crawford had let drop—about my mother being brought to this house before I was born, and of her dying here. But I had broached the story with no more than a few words, when the door opened and Sybil McLean walked into the room, erect in her rustling black dress. She had decided to join us for the meal after all.

As she neared the table I saw that her skin seemed more sallow than before and her eyes were more darkly hollowed. Ian rose to seat her, but she barely thanked him for the courtesy. She rang the silver table bell for Mrs. Crawford to serve her, and during the rest of the meal she spoke to neither of us, her face drawn and strained, only her eyes moving watchfully.

I knew why she was here. She had heard us talking together in the hall and she had no wish for me to be alone with Ian, now that I was her son's wife. Once she had wanted him to take me away from this house. Now she must accept me and guard what she felt were her son's interests.

There must have been some demon in Ian that night. As he had warned, he was not always kind and considerate, and he had never liked Mrs. McLean or enjoyed her snubbing.

159

Now he turned to a deliberate baiting of her that frightened me a little because I so mistrusted the woman.

"Tomorrow," he announced with exaggerated cheer, "Miranda is going to pose for the figurehead I am carving. It is a replica of the *Sea Jade*'s famous figurehead, you know. I've been at a loss to find a model for the face, but Miranda has solved my problem. As her mother's daughter, she will fit the subject admirably."

The sallow hue in Mrs. McLean's cheeks gave way to a purplish tinge. "You will do nothing of the kind," she said arrogantly. "It is not suitable for the girl to pose for you."

The demon of mischief-making quickened in Ian, though I tried to catch his eye and signal him to stop. Perhaps he had suffered so long under Mrs. McLean's tyranny that he could not resist this opportunity to reverse the process and gain for once an ascendancy over her.

"I think you forget," he said with deceptive sweetness, "that the girl, as you call her, can now do exactly as she pleases. One thing she pleases is a plan to bring the *Sea Jade* back to Scots Harbor. She has had word, you know, that the ship is afloat in Salem now."

I gasped softly. I wanted this indeed, and had said so. But he was committing me to too much too soon. I had made no real plans since Brock had broken the glass of the picture.

Mrs. McLean put a hand to her mouth, as if to stop its twitching and answered a little wildly. "No—no! History must not repeat itself! I warned Andrew that he would bring bad luck upon the ship and upon all of us if he used Carrie's face for the figurehead. Yet she posed for him in spite of my disapproval. With his own gifted hands he created that monstrous image. I cannot endure to have this thing happen again."

Her look alarmed me and I reached out my hand to her. "Don't distress yourself, please. I couldn't bring the ship back without Brock's help and he has already refused me. So perhaps nothing will be done. You mustn't concern yourself. Ian likes to tease."

She threw me a look that thanked me not a whit for my effort to reassure her. "You!" she said. "From the time when you were a squalling babe in this house you've brought us nothing but trouble."

Brock had said I was not to speak to her of that time,

160

but now she had brought it up herself. I leaned forward eagerly.

"I'd like to know more about what happened here at that time. Will you tell me?"

The woman had barely touched the food on her plate. Now she pushed herself abruptly from the table. "Some matters are best forgotten. I am not feeling well. If you will excuse me——"

I could not let her escape so easily, now that the subject had been opened. "Carrie was my mother. I don't want her to be forgotten. I want to learn everything I can about her life, and about the time when she was in this house."

Mrs. McLean rose from the table and stood for a moment looking down at me. She did, indeed, look faint and ill, but she managed to rally her forces for a further effort.

"Very well. Come with me and you shall learn."

I flung a quick look at Ian. The mockery had gone from his eyes. I think he was a little ashamed of himself for baiting one who was momentarily helpless. He nodded to me to go with her and I left my place at the table.

As she climbed the stairs, Mrs. McLean clung heavily to the rail. In the upper hall she led the way to the rear and opened the door of the small room I had occupied upon my arrival. It stood as stark and empty and chill as it had on the day I had first set foot in it. She stepped into its emptiness and lighted a candle on the bureau. The door to Laurel's room was closed and I heard the child humming tunelessly to herself in the room beyond.

Sybil McLean had rallied a little. She moved to the center of the floor and stood looking about with a strangely gratified air—as if she took some pleasure in her memories of this room. As if she drew strength from the mere thinking of them.

"You were born here," she said. "Your mother died in that very bed."

The room's chill seemed to invade my bones. So innocently had I slept here my first night in this house, not knowing that my mother had lain in the same bed—in suffering and in death.

"The captain had the room shut up just the way it was when she died," the woman went on. "We did not open it again, until you came here to Bascomb's Point."

I could not speak. I wished she would withdraw her cold,

intent stare. It was as though she meant to relish any pain I might feel. As though she meant to search the very depth of my being and enjoy perversely the probing of wounds. I had asked for this, but I had not expected so hurtful a thrust of pain.

I tried to shield my vulnerability by speaking of practical matters. "Did you nurse her when she was here?"

"I?" Mrs. McLean shifted her gaze to the bed for a moment, as though she saw the sick woman there. "Naturally I did not! I would never have touched the creature. The captain knew that very well. He brought in a midwife from the village to nurse her."

"And afterwards?" I pressed. "After my mother died, who cared for me?"

She actually smiled at me, spreading tight, thin lips in a grimace. "I took care of you myself for several months. Until Captain Heath came home and took you away. You were, after all, a helpless baby, and I had no objection to tending you. It had been a long while since I'd had a child of my own."

I could not imagine her caring tenderly for Carrie's babe. If I had been in her care during my first months, I was perhaps fortunate to be alive. I thought of the scar upon my shoulder and what Brock had said of my injury. Yet I could not bring myself to question her about it. In this direction terror awaited me in the shadows of the past.

Perhaps she guessed the turn of my thoughts, for she looked almost amused. "Come," she said, motioning me from the room. "Since you've opened this door yourself, there are other things I can show you."

This time she led me to the big front bedroom that had once been Rose McLean's and was now mine. From the keys she wore dangling from her belt, Mrs. McLean selected a small one and unlocked the tall wardrobe closet. With a careless hand she brought out several dresses that hung there and flung them upon the bed.

"There you are! These are your mother's clothes—those she brought with her when she came here. The captain would not permit us to burn them as I wished, and after Rose's death we stored them here."

Under the woman's cold, elated look, I did not want to touch the garments that lay upon the bed. She saw my hesitation and reached past me to pick up a dress of soft

162

brown cashmere and thrust it into my hands.

"It must seem strange to know that your mother's fingers fastened these hooks, that this fabric clothed her body. Are you pleased now that you asked me? Are you happy to wallow in old tragedy? Does it give you satisfaction?"

I tried to return her look without wincing. "I'm happy to have something of my mother's. Thank you for showing me her things."

She flung the dress on the bed and went out of the room without another word. When the door closed after her I picked up the garments and sat in my rocker, holding them in my arms. A faint scent of old perfume emanated from the cloth, musty and stale. It was as if something of the girl who had been my mother came close to me for the first time. As though she stood beside my chair—a misty, formless figure, yet with the power to reach out and touch me over the long dead years. Almost I could hear the whisper of her voice—as if there was something she tried to tell me, some warning she urged upon me, and by which she sought to protect me.

The rocker creaked under my moving weight. A gust of wind rattled a windowpane and I sighed deeply. The garments in my hands were only a means of evoking dreams. They could tell me nothing. Dreaming was something I had put from me for good—unless I could dream to a purpose. I must not return to old habit again.

Reality lay in the fact of a man's body tumbled backward from a ladder, bleeding upon ballast stone. A man of the sea, who would never have slipped so easily from a ship's ladder, or fallen by accident with such force as to result in death. Someone overhead had run away and only I had knowledge of that running. All this was real. All this had happened.

More clearly now, I began to sense my own danger. I had held my tongue and no one knew what I had heard. No one knew of the words Tom Henderson had whispered. Yet what if there was one who feared that I might still speak out at any time? One, perhaps, who suspected me of greater knowledge than I possessed?

The very thought was frightening. I could not sit here longer with fear running through me, icy cold. I rose to hang my mother's dresses in the wardrobe and closed the door upon them. Then I went to tap lightly on the door of Laurel's room. The child at least would be company.

When Laurel answered, I went in and finding her in bed, sat beside her. For nearly an hour I stayed to talk and for once she did not fight me off, or try to hurt or alarm me. She had been reading herself to sleep and was already a little drowsy, which perhaps made her more tranquil and amenable.

Deliberately I spoke of plans for the days to come, broaching the question of whether or not the *Sea Jade* might be brought back to Scots Harbor. I spoke of the posing I would do for Ian. And so, at length and by roundabout ways, I came to Laurel herself.

"Tomorrow you must help me with your dresses," I said. "You can show me where mending is needed. Perhaps, together, we can make you some new things. My aunt always said I was very neat and clever with a needle."

A faint interest showed itself in the child's eyes. At least she was enjoying the attention I had given her. And a beginning had been made. Before I left her to fall asleep, I told her one of my father's tales of the sea—all about the courage of men pitted against an element so much more powerful than themselves—an element which they nevertheless bested, as brave sailors must.

Yet while I talked and Laurel listened drowsily, I could not give my attention wholly to the matter in hand. Another part of my mind was remembering Brock. Where was he now? In spite of my evasion, did he suspect me of knowledge withheld? And if he did, what measures might he take to assure my silence? Though I listened for his footsteps to mount the stairs and come down the hall to his room, I heard them neither then nor later. I must have been long asleep in my bed by the time that dark-browed, vengeful man returned to Bascomb's Point from whatever business he had been about.

During the following days, in spite of an anxiety that continued to haunt me, in spite of a new habit of glancing over my shoulder when I neared any lonely place, in spite of a growing sense of enemies about me, the time passed quietly enough and at first without event.

Mr. Osgood informed me that the legalities of the will might take many months to work out. He was as good as his promise and came at once to go through Captain Obadiah's papers, but he did not find the letter the captain had mentioned that would supposedly explain the motives behind his plan. I told the lawyer of secret drawers in the captain's desk aboard the *Pride*, but it seemed to go against Mr. Osgood's neatly legal mind to think that much of importance would be stored in such a place. He suggested casually that I might investigate this material when it was convenient and show him anything I thought important. For me, however, the *Pride*, so bright and shipshape above decks, was a place of oppressive evil below—a place where dark deeds had been committed. I did not want to visit it alone.

As far as Tom Henderson's death was concerned, rumors and gossip were still rife and on the two or three occasions when I went to the village I could see that I was not wanted there. Officially what had happened had been set down as accident, since there were no indications that could be regarded as evidence of anything else. Nevertheless, I had the feeling that the fact of murder—an awareness of that fact— lay close to the surface at Bascomb's Point. We who lived there did not speak of Tom Henderson among ourselves, but we watched one another with distrustful eyes. A shadow lay upon us—as if of some dreadful calamity that was still to fall. Only Ian seemed able to escape the shadow, coming seldom to meals at the house, slipping quietly in and out of the library to avoid Brock and his mother.

In those uneasy days there were three deviations from what I was coming to regard as the usual at Bascomb's Point. First, the black dog took to baying at the moon every night, wearing my nerves thin with the frightening sound. When I brought myself to speak to Brock about the matter, questioning whether the animal could be taught more silent ways at night, he merely laughed and told me that I might take on Lucifer's education any time I saw fit. The moon was full, he pointed out, and both men and dogs became restless and uneasy at that time. Eventually the baying would stop. The others in the house seemed to take no concern for the matter, perhaps being long inured to the sound. I tried to resign myself, tried to sleep in spite of the ugly clamor.

The second change had to do with my posing for Ian Pryott during the morning hours. On the day after I had promised to serve as model for the figurehead I had gone into the workroom and sat down. Ian was there waiting for me and the work was begun. When what was happening became evident there was a fuming among the others in the house. No one approved, but this condemnation did not at once break violently into the open. Mrs. McLean urged her son to forbid my posing on the grounds of impropriety. I heard him tell her carelessly that if she disapproved she could sit in at the posing sessions and play the role of chaperon. But this she could not bear to do.

Brock's own dislike for what we were doing did not cause him to interfere. I almost wished that he would. Anything would have seemed preferable to his remote disavowal of concern toward all that affected me.

Of Lien I saw little, though Ian reported that she had not forgiven him for using me as a model and that her mood was one of deep gloom. Since she would speak frankly to no one at this time, we could not be sure what course her thoughts were taking, or what plan she might be considering for the future.

At least these hours during which I posed and Ian worked on his carving, were the only tranquil ones during this time of waiting disquiet. As I quickly discovered, Ian had an uncanny talent for portraiture in wood. The face of the figurehead was growing remarkably into a likeness of my own. He was an exacting sculptor and at first he was dissatisfied with his work, regarding it critically every step of the way. Nevertheless it progressed day by day toward completion and as its excellence became evident Ian's discontent faded and a certain exultation took its place. He knew at last that what he was doing was good and the fact excited and heartened him.

In the afternoons, when the weather was pleasant I wandered about the Bascomb's Point area, exploring to some extent. I was still marking time, unwilling to fit myself into any pattern that might seem permanent. I had few duties around the house, since Mrs. Crawford did not welcome my help. She had followed my suggestion, however, and persuaded Mrs. McLean that nothing could be managed without her supervision. The two of them took up their duties once more, shutting me out as though I did not exist. Since I was still wholly concerned with my own unanswered questions, and blocked in the solving of my main problems, this did not disturb me.

The third change that came about during this time was in Laurel. She had shown more interest in the refurbishing of her wardrobe than I would have expected. Perhaps the novelty of a friendly, not-too-critical personal interest where none had existed before, was too flattering to be resisted. Slowly, a bit at a time, she appeared to be lowering the guard she held against me. She was still wary as some little woods' animal—as if she expected a trap—but she was less influenced now by her elders' disapproval of me than she had been at first.

Once or twice I caught Brock watching her with an air of baffled relief, and though he gave me no credit for this emerging change he did not oppose me, or interfere. Tacitly, without words, I had been given leave to do as I liked with the child. There were no more warnings to me not to interfere, Or perhaps, I thought, this was simply further evidence of his complete indifference to all I was, all I did.

In the end these things were indeed a mere marking of time. Beneath the surface our unrest and hidden discontents churned and tormented us all. Eventually, as must happen when suspicion and anger and hatred are too long contained, the pressure would rise, disaster would explode.

On the day when the threat that hung over us descended with the slash of a sword, I had wandered out upon the point of land beyond the lighthouse and climbed down to a broad ledge of rock where the sea cliffs plunged dizzily away at my feet. It was a gray afternoon of threatening storm, with a fierce wind blowing and the seas running high. I had dressed warmly and tied a thick wool muffler over my head, so I was well shielded from the blast.

I loved a day like this when the sea took on the grim look of the sky and rolled landward endlessly in mountainous corrugations. Ridge after swelling ridge would hurl itself upon the rocky shore and break with a crash, sending white spray so high in the air that specks of it flecked my cheeks and touched my lips with salt. Sea birds careened in the wind, sailing and diving in their wild play, alighting at times upon the rocks below. They had little fear of me since I sat as still as the very stones themselves.

It was here that Laurel found me and clambered down to sit beside me. A child born of the sea herself, she never tired of watching its moods and the changing of its face. I smiled at her without speaking and she sat beside me for some time in silence. We shared a kinship in our feeling for the sea and it was something we needed no words to express. Today her hair, beneath her green hood, was neatly combed, and no torn fringe of petticoat hung below her coat. I marked my work with satisfaction. She seemed less of the wild thing today—at least in appearance. I knew this was my doing and I took pleasure in this beginning I had made with the child. Whatever else was wrong with my life, in this one direction I was having some salutary effect.

After a time, when the silence between us grew long, Laurel began to talk to me in her impish, gossipy way. "I went in to look at the figurehead when you finished posing this morning, Miss Miranda. It is much more beautiful now that it has a face. It looks exactly like you, in spite of the Chinese headdress Ian has carved for it. My grandmother is angry. She is having headaches and lying awake at night because of it. She torments my father because he doesn't stop you from posing, or stop Ian from carving."

"I'm sorry your grandmother is upset," I said. "Perhaps your father knows there is no harm in my posing."

"Lien is upset, too," Laurel went on, a young Cassandra, always most cheerful when she could prophesy disaster. "She says the evil spirits of the flesh that belonged to the captain and that have been loosed at Bascomb's Point are getting stronger every minute. She says nothing will stop them until they wreak their wicked purpose." She shivered with eerie pleasure as she spoke.

"I don't feel this," I said—a bold statement that was not altogether true. "And I don't think Ian feels it. Yet if it were true, I'm sure he would be aware of the fact."

Laurel shrugged. "Ian likes making everyone squirm for once. I don't blame him. But sometimes I think he ought to be more frightened than he is."

"Ian frightened? Why should he be frightened?"

She reverted in a flash to her old manner and leaned forward to peer disconcertingly into my face. "Why shouldn't he be, with the spirits growing angry? You're afraid, aren't you? You weren't afraid before, but you're afraid now, because the dog is baying at night. And because someone wants you to be dead."

I reached out and clasped her by the arm before she could move away. "Stop that! You know you can't frighten me with such talk. If you mean to keep it up, you can go away and leave me alone. I liked it here in this quiet place before you came."

168

She was accustomed enough to adult rejection, to being sent off to a supper of bread and milk. But she was not accustomed to a rejection of her company on an equal basis, simply because someone did not enjoy having her near. This was not punishment but dismissal. Instead of snatching herself out of my grasp, she wriggled a little closer, her manner contrite.

"I'm sorry, Miss Miranda. I know you're not afraid. If you'll let me stay, I'll tell you things you want to know."

I said nothing, watching a great breaker hurl itself upon the rocks below and shatter like broken glass. The roar came up to us, followed by the echo of water gurgling away in caves and crevices near the water's edge.

"I know why Lucifer bays at night," Laurel persisted.

I held my tongue, and she went on, tantalized by my silence. "He's baying because Tom Henderson's ghost has left the *Pride* and come to Bascomb's Point. Lucifer's trying to tell us all that Tom means to take revenge because he was murdered."

Just as the child had disturbed me and taken away from the first eagerness of my arrival at Bascomb's Point, so she disturbed and shocked me now.

"You must not say such things!" I cried. "The police know the man fell—and that's all there is to it!"

She looked pleased at having upset me. No longer worried about being sent away, she nodded in a patronizing fashion. "Oh, I don't think *you* pushed him the way they say over in town. But someone did. Miss Miranda, don't you believe that wickedness can get into the air just like a sea fog? You can't touch it, and you can't blow it away unless a great wind comes up, but you know all the time that it's there and you can't see your way because of it. Don't you feel things like that, Miss Miranda? I do, and so does Lucifer. The bad thing is not to know where the wickedness is coming from."

Almost she persuaded me, this all too sentient child, for I had indeed sensed a miasma in the air. In her own way Laurel possessed a wisdom beyond her years. Or perhaps it was child-wisdom. A child lived closer to elemental things than those who had matured and substituted reason for feeling. Perhaps I was still young enough to feel this too, and I could not laugh at Laurel.

"Listen to me," I said. "If you hear anything, or learn anything that is real—not just talk about ghosts—come and tell me. Will you do that? Will you tell me first of all?"

I suppose it was unwise to let her know that I could take her so seriously. At once she preened herself, like a sea gull smoothing its wings in vain satisfaction. At once she began to perform for me. She drew up her knees and rested her chin upon them, wrapped her arms about her legs and closed her eyes as if she were lost in some embryonic trance.

"I can feel it now," she murmured. "It is coming close— very close. The wickedness is stealing toward us over the point in an evil mist. If we breathe it we will choke and die. It's coming so close that—"

Above our heads a foot struck a pebble and we both started violently and looked upward in alarm. The stone rolled over the ledge and went bouncing from crag to crag down the cliff, lost at last in the water's surging roar. Above us on the rocky edge of the precipice Brock McLean stood watching. There was that about his appearance and manner that seemed all the more disturbing after Laurel's eerie words. Once more an uneasy elation seemed to possess him—some strange mingling of triumph and satisfaction, laced with a more deadly potion that I could not place.

Laurel leaned toward me to whisper and I felt the quivering of her body. "I was only making it up, Miss Miranda. I didn't feel anything. It's not my father who is wicked! It's not—" she did not finish, but sprang to her feet and went leaping away over the rocks to climb to the top at another place, to disappear from view, fleeing in panic.

Her words left me aquiver as well, and for a single dreadful instant I looked down over jagged rocks and wondered what it would feel like to go pitching over, dropping like a stone until my body struck the water, or was dashed against the rocks themselves. Then I shook off my fright and this false sense of premonition, forcing myself to look calmly upward at the man above. Not for anything would I fly in obvious terror from his approach. I would not give him that satisfaction.

He climbed down to the boulder on which I sat and came to a halt beside me. I did not speak, but returned to my contemplation of surf breaking far below. I had no wish to look longer into that storm-ridden countenance, though the spell Laurel's words had set upon me was fading.

His voice when he spoke held so little animosity, verged

so closely on praise that I was pleasantly surprised and all too easily disarmed.

"There is a change in Laurel," he said. "I know this is your doing. She has needed a gentling hand. I am grateful."

I managed to answer tartly, hiding the rush of foolish delight that went through me at his words. "It is no thanks to your being a loving father that there is a change in her."

"I know that," he said with unexpected humility. "I have been too often wrapt in my own concerns, so that my only use with the child has been to admonish and discipline. She has lost all affection for me."

This I contradicted at once. "Your daughter loves you deeply. She admires you, though she would never admit it to you, and she longs to be admired. But when you give her nothing of praise, nothing of appreciation, what can she do but hide her feelings behind the pretense of hostility toward you that she wears?"

His gentler mood could last just so long and I sensed that my criticism ruffled its edges. Brock was not accustomed to women who spoke the truth to him so boldly. He stood in silence beside me and I went back to watching the sea, my blood pulsing to its rhythm.

After a time he spoke again. "The sea interests you?"

"Why not?" I said. "It is endlessly fascinating and I can watch it endlessly. If I'd been a man I would have been a sailor. I'd have gone to far away countries and brought back silks and jades and rare teas."

"That's the romantic side," he said and lowered himself to my rock, so that he sat with his elbow touching my arm. "The sea can be as treacherous as she is romantic. She's forever pitted against the ships that sail her. I've seen her when she has torn away the royals and cracked the mizzen in two and set the sheets snapping like to break. I've seen her sweep the decks with waves that threaten to bury a ship and send to his death any poor fellow whose numb hands will no longer hold to frozen rigging. You'd feel less sentimental if you'd seen her in that role."

"I'd still find her fascinating," I insisted. "You know her and you don't hate her." I looked at him then, into that broad, dark-browed face so close to my own that his breath touched my cheek and my own breathing quickened. I spoke more eagerly. "Anyone can read your love for the sea. It's in your eyes when you look at her, and in the sound of your voice when you speak of her. Perhaps you're unhappy because you deny her and turn your back on her."

He glowered at me more darkly than ever. "*I* deny her? When have I ever denied that I've loved her all my life? More constantly than I've loved any woman."

"Then your wife must have hated the sea," I said.

"Rose?" His tone softened as he spoke her name. "She hated nothing. But I think she was glad to have me home. She was a gentle soul—too gentle for this rough world."

He spoke as of someone gently loved and long lost, and I sensed that he no longer grieved over her death, as his mother had wanted me to believe he did.

Aware of this still tempered mood, I urged upon him once more the plan I had not mentioned since his first rejection of it.

"If you go to Salem and bring the *Sea Jade* home, you can refit her and have the chance to sail again yourself."

The sound he made in answer was harsh—a sound of repudiation and pain.

"But why not?" I persisted. "The ship deserves better than to be used ignobly. She was your father's dream come to perfection. There is nothing to keep you from setting her on the seas again if you so desire."

He gave me a sidelong, scowling look. "Why are you ridden by this obsession?"

I was not entirely sure myself why the vision seemed so clear in my mind—so fitting and right.

"She killed my father and destroyed yours," Brock went went on. "Why give her another chance? Who knows that she might not perform her old tricks all over again? Who knows what deadly force we might stir up by bringing her back to Scots Harbor?"

This—from Brock McLean!—was too much for me. I laughed in his face "So now I know where Laurel gets her talent for imagining strange visions. Is this a Scotsman's second sight?"

He looked straight into my eyes and there was no amusement in his own. "There is much in the world beyond your ken, my lass. Perhaps you'd be wise to stay out of deeps that do not concern you lest they close over your head."

"As they did over Tom Henderson's?" I said.

At once I sensed the rising of anger in him, but there was

172

a wariness as well, as though he suddenly stepped with caution.

"Are you afraid to sail again?" I taunted when he did not answer.

"I'm not fit to sail again!" he told me savagely. "There's no harder task on the seas than sailing a clipper ship to get the best from her. The crew must have a master they can respect. Not one who is only half a man."

For once his suffering was fully visible and I found myself shaken at the sight of it. Yet I did not relent. "Why do you discredit yourself? Why won't you take the gamble and prove to yourself what you are? Why must you be afraid of failure?"

I thought for a moment that he would lash out at me in fury and I braced myself against the expected flood. Instead, he startled me by laughing wryly to himself, as though something amused him.

"What a cocklebur you are, *Miss* Miranda! I can see how you work your spell with Laurel. Your insert yourself insidiously at a sensitive point and those who oppose you find the bur hurts less if they go in the direction you wish. Is that what you're trying with me? Because you want *Sea Jade* brought home?"

I did not really know what I wanted. It was as if some lodestar drew me without reference to reason.

"The new figurehead is nearly finished," I said. "We could set her upon the ship to replace the old, sea-battered one."

Brock's momentary amusement vanished. There was a change in him—unaccountable and somehow deadly.

"The figurehead will never go to sea," he told me flatly.

I could not let well enough alone. "But why are you against it? If you will only look at it, you may not feel so strongly. This new carving has nothing to do with my mother or with anything that happened in the past. It is my face Ian has depicted."

"I've no need to look at the thing," he said roughly and sprang to his feet in the seemingly light, quick way that never paid tribute to his lameness, though it must always cost him great effort.

I knew he would be gone in a moment and the promise I wanted from him to bring *Sea Jade* home was still far from given. I rose and put my hand on his arm, holding him there. He merely stared at my hand until I flushed and drew it away. Once more it was as though a strong current flowed

173

between us, quickening in my blood, carrying me along to some disastrous undertow of emotion. Whether he felt it or not I could not tell, but I fought the current, giving him back scowl for scowl.

"The least you can do is to come with me and look at the figurehead," I said.

He made a sudden gesture as if relinquishing all responsibility and turned toward the lighthouse. "Have it your way then. Come show me this masterpiece."

He did not wait to help me, and as I clambered upon the rocks after him I heard the dog in the distance, though not baying now, as he did at the moon. This howling came from the heart—a wild and grievous, lonely sound.

"Lucifer mourns his master," I said as I caught up with Brock. "Have you neglected him lately?"

"If you'll wait for me here," he said, "I'll get him now and take him with us."

This was scarcely what I had intended, but he gave me no chance to protest. Off he went, striding toward the kennel behind the Bascomb house.

What an exasperating man he was! I thought for the hundredth time. I regretted any recognition of that current that could leap the barriers of antipathy and charge me with a feeling that I decried every time it happened. I would not, could not, feel this way about a man I had every reason to fear and hate. Because I wanted to reject the slightest request he might make of me, I did not wait for him, but went up the steps and into the lighthouse. Perhaps he had known very well that this was what I would do.

The door to Ian's workroom was closed and I knocked upon it, not wanting to interrupt if he was working there alone. There was no answer and I opened the door. The room was empty. As always, the figurehead stood on its platform with its back to the door, leaning slightly out into the room because of the angle at which it was built to follow the curve beneath the bowsprit of a ship. Ian's tools had been put away and the work area was clear, as he always left it when he was through for the day. But on the floor below the platform were scattered small slivers and splinters of raw wood that had not been swept away.

I walked around the figurehead's platform and looked up at the Chinese lady in her painted robes. Looked with a

174

shock of horror into the utter devastation that had been wrought across the face that had once represented my own.

Someone had slashed the carved features violently across again and again, slicing, cutting, destroying. The likeness to my own face, or to any human resemblance had vanished. The nose had been splintered with the fury of the blows, the forehead gouged, lips and cheeks and chin were scarred with a crosshatch of cuts that spelled a ruin that could never be repaired. Nothing else had been touched—not the flowing robes or the crossed hands, but only the face. Horror rose in me in wave after sickening wave as that faceless thing that had once been Ian's work stared at me with ravaged eyes.

14.

FAR AWAY THE BLACK DOG HOWLED as if in anguish. Brock had not, after all, gone to quiet Lucifer, or to bring him back. Because he himself had not intended to return? Because he knew very well what I would find when I stepped into this room, and he had not wanted to be in my company when I discovered what had happened?

I remembered sensing his uneasy elation when I looked up at him on the rocks above me. I had felt some mingling in him of angry triumph, of violence suppressed—or was it already spent?

My flesh crept and the realization of my loneliness in this empty room where someone had taken a maddened revenge upon my image, came home to me. First the wooden face—next the reality? Laurel's words swept back to my mind "Someone wants you to be dead."

At that moment I gave no thought to the weapon that might have been used to do such harm. I thought only of escaping the horrid sight, of fleeing to some place of greater safety. But what safety was there with that unlocked door between Brock's room and mine? At least I must not remain here until he came, if that was what he intended.

Released from my shocked trance, I ran out of that

haunted place. Before I reached the outside door, however, someone opened it and came whistling into the main room of the museum. It was not Brock, but Ian Pryott, and I stopped in my tracks, staring at him in a mingling of dismay and relief. He had come when I needed him most, but until this moment I had been concerned only with myself, with my fear of the malevolence that must lie behind the attack upon the figurehead. I had been too wrought-up to consider the artist who must now face the destruction of his work.

He smiled at me in greeting, then saw my expression and sobered. "What is it, Miranda? What has happened?"

I could only wave my hand helplessly in the direction of his workroom. He did not stop to question me, but ran toward the open door. I followed, sick at heart for Ian now.

As I had done, he first saw the splintered bits of wood upon the floor and turned to look at the figure. His face was toward me as he stared up at the work he had created with so great a sense of excitement and hope. I saw the sickness in his eyes, saw despair wipe away all else. His hands went limp at his sides and he stood staring, the agony of an artist whose work has been destroyed showing in his face for anyone to read.

When he spoke it was so softly that I hardly caught the words. "I'd never done so fine a thing as this. Perhaps I never will again."

I forgot the enmity for me that lay behind the deed and tried to find some way to comfort this man of whom I grew increasingly fond.

"Surely you can use a new block of wood," I said. "I'll pose for you as long as you wish. You can discard this damaged part and start over. The rest of the figure is intact. Perhaps it will be even better next time."

There was defeat in his eyes, though he answered me gently. "It was carved from a whole piece of wood, Miranda. And such work doesn't come as easily as that. I don't often have the feeling of everything going exactly right. It isn't a thing to be casually repeated."

I went to him, longing to assuage his grievous wounding, aching within myself because of the hurt to him. "You mustn't say that! You mustn't believe it! Other artists have repeated their work over and over. Painters and sculptors, too."

"Only because the first efforts were never right. When the

thing becomes as fine as you can make it—then there's no use in trying to repeat. Besides, it was your face, Miranda—" he broke off and would have turned away.

My heart went out to him and I put my hands lightly, pleadingly on his shoulders. In a moment his arms were about me, and he was holding me to his heart, shielding me from the ugliness of what had happened in this room; shielding himself as well as me. For a moment I clung to him, feeling that we might support and protect each other, knowing the comfort of so human a clinging. But Ian did not leave it there. His arms tightened and he bent his head to kiss me.

But I could not hide from danger in Ian's arms, no matter how much he wished to hold me there. However brutally and shockingly it had happened—first with Tom Henderson, now with the figurehead—the cocoon of my childhood had been torn away forever. I no longer wanted to go back. Whatever must be faced and dealt with must be faced and dealt with because I was a woman grown and willing to depend upon myself.

As gently as I could, I withdrew myself from Ian's embrace. "For us this isn't possible," I said.

He let his arms drop from about me, not understanding. "For a moment I'd forgotten who you are. I'd forgotten the name you bear."

This was not what I had meant. I had myself forgotten the very detail that trapped me here as the wife of Brock McLean. I shook my head angrily, wondering how to make him understand without being cruel. He saw only that I was angry.

"Don't waste yourself in rage, Miranda," he counseled me. "If there is a way in which this problem can be solved, then we will find the way and solve it. If it cannot be worked out, then raging will only destroy us. I found that out long ago."

He had not at all understood that my withdrawal was not because I was the wife of another man, but for more subtle reasons that had to do with my own maturing, my own acceptance of a world of real responsibilities. But I could not now explain.

He turned his back upon the ravaged image and began to search the room with eyes that knew every corner of it.

"I wonder what instrument she used?" he said.

I caught only one word and echoed it: "She?"

"Of course. What else could this be but a woman's vindictive act? None of my tools seem to have been displaced. And I doubt that such slashes could have been managed with any such tool even if used in a fury."

"But—but I thought—" I began. "That is—I believe Brock knew this had happened, and—"

Ian turned abruptly from his tool shelf. "Brock? What are you talking about?"

"He knew something," I told Ian. "He was pleased about something in a queer, savage sort of way. And when I wanted him to come with me to look at the figurehead, he went off and let me find what had happened by myself. And he hasn't come back."

Ian shook his head. "It's hard to believe that Brock would be involved. Brutality I could expect from him—yes. But it would be open brutality. Not something sly and hidden and vindictive like this."

I was not sure about Brock. I knew nothing at all of what he might be capable.

"What *she* do you mean?" I asked.

"The captain's wife, of course. Lien."

Yes, I could imagine the woman attempting such a thing. She had wanted her own face represented on Captain Obadiah's ship, and she did not like me. It was I who had taken a fortune away from her, by her way of thinking. Yet it seemed unlikely that she would wish to hurt Ian by such an act.

"You've been kind to her," I pointed out. "Aside from the captain, you've been her one friend in the Bascomb house. Surely she wouldn't hurt you in this way."

He made no attempt at denial or evasion, but continued his search of the room. In a corner, dropped behind a roll of tarpaulin, he found what he was seeking and drew it out. I saw again the ugly blade of the Malay cutlass as he turned to me with it in his hands. He ran a careful finger along steel that had been blunted for most of its edge and showed me the tiny silvers, the powdering of wood dust.

"The sword came with her from China," he said. "It is the instrument she would use."

I stared at the pirate blade in revulsion. It was as if I could feel the cold slash of it upon my person—as if I were to be next after the carven image.

Ian started for the door, carrying the cutlass with him and

I cried out in alarm, for he did not look like the gentle man I knew. "What are you going to do with that?"

"I shall return the lady's property," he said and went out of the room, leaving me there with the ruined figurehead.

There was nothing I could do to interfere. Ian must deal with this matter in his own way. I did not believe he would hurt Lien, in spite of the destruction she had wrought, yet I could not feel easy in my mind as I followed him from the lighthouse.

I saw him moving quickly ahead of me as I walked more slowly through the gray and lowering afternoon. I had forgotten Brock's promise to return and join me until I saw the dog and his master coming toward me from behind the Bascomb house. Lucifer threatened to leap at me as they drew near and Brock held him back with a strong, rough grasp.

"Down, you brute! The lady doesn't care for your attentions." Lucifer obeyed and stood quivering beside his master, his eyes fixed burningly upon me. "Well?" Brock said. "I suppose you've found out by now?"

"So you did know," I accused. "And you knew I wouldn't wait for you, that I'd find it myself. I thought you were pleased about something. I suppose you have no idea of how much work and heart Ian has put into that figurehead. I suppose you are incapable of appreciating what a fine piece of work it was."

He laughed at me, and the dog snarled at the derisive sound. "I could see well enough. I've been following the thing through its entire blasted progress."

"You knew, yet you left me to find it alone! Didn't it occur to you that the experience might be terrifying?" Even as I spoke I knew that such words would have no effect upon him. I could expect no kindly treatment from Brock McLean.

"I wanted to speak to my mother," he told me. "And I expected you to come to no harm. But I found her shut into her room again with one of her headaches. There was nothing I could do for her, so I came back."

"Ian knows, too," I said, having no concern for his mother. "We've found the instrument that was used—that Malay cutlass of the captain's. Ian has gone to talk to Lien."

"Lien?" There was a curious inflection in the way he spoke her name, as though he found it difficult to connect the Chinese woman with this act.

"It must have been Lien who did this," I told him. "She wanted to pose for the figurehead herself, and she has many reasons to dislike me."

There was a long moment of silence between us. In spite of the evidence, Brock seemed unconvinced that Lien had committed the act of destruction. For the first time I saw the significance of his hurrying home to talk to his mother. Sybil McLean was surely of the temper to perform such a deed. And she liked me no better than did Lien. Perhaps she had even more reason to destroy a replica of the *Sea Jade* figurehead. In Sybil McLean old hatreds blended venomously with new.

We had turned and were walking slowly toward the house, the black dog pacing his steps to his master's gait. At least it seemed that my first wild suspicion of Brock himself had been foolish, though I did not know whether I felt relieved by this, or disappointed. It would please me to think as ill of him as possible. As if by thinking ill I might somehow protect myself—from myself. I glanced up at the man as I walked beside him, seeing once more the craggy carving of his profile, the strong muscles of neck and jaw.

"When did you discover what had been done to the figurehead?" I asked.

"Just before I came out upon the cliffs and saw you and Laurel on the rocks below. I was shocked at first, for all that you think me insensitive. I wanted to get away and clear my wits before I took any action."

"You were pleased too," I reminded him. "I could feel elation in you."

He offered no denial. "I've disliked this sculpture of Ian's from the first. It seemed an insult that it should be growing to completion on Bascomb property—forcing old injury down our throats. I can feel sympathy, as well as concern, for the unhappy creature who felt driven to destroy it."

"I thought you might have done it," I told him boldly.

He gave me a look of such contempt that I felt quickly ashamed, and turned away from me, hauling on the dog's chain. Without further word the two went off along the sea cliffs as they were wont to do when the master was perturbed and restlessly driven.

I let myself in through the white gate of the Bascomb house and started upstairs. I was wondering how Ian fared with Lien, and so lost was I in troubled thoughts, that I did not note that Sybil McLean's door had opened as I mounted the stairs. Not until I reached the second floor and turned down the corridor to my room, did I realize that she stood opposite in her own doorway, where she could watch my approach from the floor below. I must have started when I saw her there, for her tight lips quivered into a rather dreadful smile. Her hair was disheveled and she wore a wrapper of some drab, mustard-colored material, drawn loosely about her. She spoke to me not at all, but stood transfixed in her doorway, staring into my face for every step of my way along the corridor. Her deepset, colorless eyes did not so much as flicker and her silence was deadly with unspoken triumph.

I suppose the moment of my passing was short indeed, but it seemed to take me forever to reach the haven of my own door. I was nearly running by that time, which must have added to her perverse pleasure at so frightening me. Frightened I was. I had the hideous feeling that at any moment she might snatch at me with the same hands that had wielded the cutlass and that if she chose to put them to my throat, I would be no match for her in strength.

Then I was through the door and had closed it behind me. There was no key anywhere in this room. No bolt I could slide across—as there had been in the little room in which my mother had died. Why, I wondered, my cheek against the door panel as I held my breath listening, had there been a bolt in that other room? Had the captain put it there to protect my mother from the hatred of this woman?

Across the hall there was silence. No sound of a door closing reached me, nor was there the fall of a foot in the hall to indicate that she might have crossed to my own door. Simply that blank silence. I felt almost impelled to open the door a crack to see what she was doing. But I did not need to. I knew very well. Mrs. McLean was standing where I had seen her, with that fixed smile on her lips, that blank expression in her eyes—simply standing, without the movement of an eyelid, looking straight through the panel of my own door to the quivering spectacle of fear I was making of myself.

I found a chair with a strong back and propped it beneath the doorknob, thus bolting it after a fashion. Across the room Brock's door stood closed as always, but I had no chair to prop against that. If she chose to enter his room from the hall . . . ? I fled to the window and stood beside it, where I could at least fling it open and scream if there should be need.

From that vantage point I could look out and see that Brock had turned away from the cliffs and was coming home after all. I drew back from the window and went to fling myself across the bed. There I lay with my heart pounding and my thoughts making no sense at all because I was, at that moment, so thoroughly ruled by fear that I could not think.

From across the hall came the whisper-soft closing of a door, followed by the sound of footsteps across the bedroom floor beyond. Mrs. McLean's vigil, at least, had ended. I lay cheek down upon my pillow, with my heart pounding, waiting for some disaster to fall.

And nothing happened. Nothing at all.

The time was not yet ripe. The slashing of the figurehead's face was only a rumble of distant thunder. The storm was brewing, but though the winds of tension had begun to rise, the breaking point had not yet come.

The time was not yet ripe.

15.

NOTHING OF FURTHER NOTE OCCURRED until after supper. Since I wished for neither the company of Brock nor his mother at the evening meal, I invited myself to dine early with Laurel and we had a moderately amusing time in the kitchen, for all that Mrs. Crawford's disapproving presence set some blight upon us.

Laurel did not yet know about the figurehead, and I made no effort to enlighten her. Perhaps it would have been easier for her if I had. But the child had seemed so much improved in the last few days that I did not want to bring up a matter so disturbing. I would deal with it in the morning.

Not until later that evening did I see Ian again. After

supper, when Laurel had gone to bed, I sought the library as the one cheerful room in the house and lighted a fire there. I sat toasting my toes at the hearth, trying to concentrate on a romantic novel by Sir Walter Scott. Usually Scott's tales of noble highland lords and ladies enthralled me, but of late such romancing appealed to me less and less. The events of my immediate life loomed to a menacing degree, claiming all my waking attention. So, though the fire burned cheerily on the hearth, and print on white pages lay ready to invite my eye, I felt neither involved nor interested. The printed story would not take hold.

When the door opened suddenly and Ian came in, I nearly dropped my book. So had everything in this house begun to startle me.

"I hoped I'd find you here," he said.

He swung a straight chair about and straddled it, facing me with his arms resting across its back. The look of strain was still there in the set of his mouth. He appeared weary, with a discouragement, perhaps a hopelessness upon him, that I had never seen before. The destruction of his work was taking its toll.

He sat for so long in silence that I questioned him gently. "You saw Lien? What did she say?"

"Only that the cutlass has been missing from the captain's rooms for two days. She went to the village, she says, and when she came home it was gone. She meant to tell me when she saw me—but I had not visited her recently."

I could sense that there had been reproach in Lien's words. "Then she denied destroying the figure?"

"She did indeed. Most vehemently. Whether she was telling the truth or not, I don't know. I have heard her lie to the captain glibly enough when it served her purpose. Her mood is not a good one. She is hurt and angry."

"Angry with you?"

He gazed at me then and I saw in his eyes the look I could not meet. I lowered my own to the meaningless pages of the book. From Ian I wanted friendship but not love and I knew this must somehow be made clear to him. There was in him a quality I had always sensed—an inner vitality that he had been forced to suppress in this house. Given release, it might sweep everything before it. Ian might be a quiet man, but he was no weakling. Yet I still shrank from hurting him further when so severe an injury had been done him.

I repeated my question, avoiding his eyes. "Is Lien angry with you?"

"She is angry with me, and she is angry with you as well. I think she senses what has happened to me—because of you. And she's angry as well because of the trick she feels the captain has played on her about the estate. Until shortly before his death she had expected the whole, and she is not without greed. Yet I can blame her for none of this."

I did not want him to explain his meaning. "Brock believes it was his mother who destroyed the figurehead's face," I told him.

His look sharpened, as if he considered for the first time this new idea with all its ramifications. Apparently he had been so convinced that Lien was behind the act that he had thought of no one else.

"It seems a possibility," he said at length. "Our glowering Sybil would have every reason for the act because of her feeling about Carrie and the ship, and about you. Still—it is more likely to be Lien. I think your husband has not hit upon the true answer, Mrs. McLean."

"Don't call me that!" I cried. There was a tendency in Ian to twist the knife at times, and to mock himself as he did so.

He left his chair to move about the room—up and down, pacing until I turned unhappily to watch him. He caught my look and came back to the fire.

"What a fool I was!" he cried. "If I'd had an ounce of sense the day you came, I'd never have waited to get you to that train. I'd have kidnapped you at once, galloped us both away from this place and from all Captain Obadiah has done to you. But I waited. And now it's too late. A step is taken, a direction is pointed. A path is beaten—and there is no turning back."

I could wish it had happened that way too. Then I would never have felt Brock McLean's strange spell. I would never have been both drawn and repelled as I was by the man who had become my husband. But none of this could I say to Ian.

While I sat in silence, staring into the fire, he went to the desk where he had worked for the captain. "I'll return the sea charts to you," he said. "I've been able to make nothing of the markings." He spoke indifferently as he laid the maps in my lap and I suspected that he had been too concerned with

184

other matters to give attention to a quest he did not wholly believe in.

I set the chart that had been matted for framing on top and studied it for the dozenth time. How romantic sounding were the lettered names: the Horse Latitudes, the Doldrums, the Variables of Capricorn, the Northeast Monsoon. And of course the Roaring Forties, where ships rounding Cape Horn for Australia took advantage of the "brave west winds" on both outward and homeward passages. Around Cape of Good Hope ran the way to China, and there, set boldly below the tip of Africa was the stamped outline of a whale that so puzzled me: "on the China run," as the captain had said.

I shook my head despairingly at Ian. "I'll take them to my room and study them further. Perhaps some inspiration will come to me."

Ian was not concerned with the charts. He came behind my chair and dropped his hands lightly on my shoulders.

"Good night, Miranda," he said. I held myself very still until the hands upon my shoulders lifted. From across the room I felt the draft as the library door opened and Ian went away.

Had my mother felt like this long ago when she was young? Perhaps loving one man—my father, yet not wanting to hurt others who loved her, and thus hurting them more than she intended? I must make Ian understand that no matter how kind to me he had been, or how grateful I was, I could not love him. Love would not turn as one might wish. Had I loved Ian, I could have better accepted my own feeling. As it was, I was drawn in unhappy fascination toward another man, only to resent that very fact.

I gathered up the charts and went to my room. In the hall I cast a fearful look at Sybil McLean's door before I closed my own. At least no open crack indicated that I was spied upon. If Brock had come upstairs while I was in the library, I had not heard him. Beyond his door there seemed the quiet of emptiness.

When I dropped the sea charts on my bed, the one with the cardboard mat fell face down and I saw that the whale mark—the outline of an entire whale had been repeated on the backing. I knelt on the bed, my fingers moving idly over the cardboard, over the face of the chart. Then I began seeking with intent. The mat was well glued but I pried up one edge and ran a hatpin beneath until it was fully loosened all around. Working carefully, I drew the chart itself from the backing sheet. Beneath it lay a thin sheet of rice paper, face down.

Knowing the fragility of such paper, I picked it up with delicate fingers. Across the sheet ran faded brown script that I recognized at once. It was the same bold hand that had invited me to come to Bascomb's Point. The writing was Captain Obadiah's.

A heading in slightly larger script than the rest brought my own name leaping to my eyes from the page:

For Miranda Heath when she is grown, in the hope that this will be found after my death. I write these words to clear my conscience of an old wrong, and so that the truth may be known.

I carried the single sheet of paper to my chair and sat down to read the brief, terse words that stated again the well-known fact that the three captains were aboard the ship; that the storm which broke in fury over the *Sea Jade* was one of Good Hope's worst; that there had been a quarrel among the captains. So far I knew all this. There was nothing new—no explanation of the quarrel. Then, in conclusion, a statement, bald and unadorned:

Nathaniel Heath did not kill Andrew McLean. It was I, Captain Obadiah Bascomb, who shot Captain McLean.

That was all. I read the words over again with my blood pounding in my ears. Apparently these lines had been written while I was still very young and because the captain had wanted me to some day know the truth. It seemed that it would have been a more valuable gesture had he spoken out during my father's lifetime. But at least Captain Obadiah had now cleared his old friend's name.

This was a confession, though without detail. It might be enough to exonerate my father in this house, yet it did not tell me all I wanted to know. Then I saw that something had been added as a sort of postscript in smaller writing at the bottom of the page. Again a name leapt to meet my eyes.

Tom Henderson of Scots Harbor was first mate on this voyage. He was witness to all that happened. He will corroborate this confession.

But Tom Henderson would corroborate nothing. Tom Henderson was dead—as the three captains were dead. It was possible that Tom had been murdered. But who could have such a stake in what had happened aboard the *Sea Jade* all those years ago that it had been necessary to silence Tom Henderson? As far as I could see, there was no one.

Unless . . . ? A new thought occurred to me. What if something about Andrew McLean was being hidden—something that his son would not want revealed, even at this late date? Certainly Brock's feeling for his father was one of such fierce and loving pride that he was willing to carry his hatred for his father's murderer down through the generations—even to me.

Realization on another score broke through my bewilderment. Truth lay in these starkly simple words—a truth the captain had hidden all his life, but which fully justified my belief. Nathaniel Heath had never committed murder. Thus there could be no further reason for Brock, who was Andrew's son, to continue his resentment of me on this account. I would now be able to vindicate my father's name with this statement, and I would remove the largest, most sinister block that stood between my husband and me.

For the first time since that night in the captain's room I had accepted Brock McLean as my husband in my own thoughts. The realization unnerved me. It was as though one weight that had long thrust me down had been suddenly lifted and left me free. But free only to take on a new weight.

Free to put myself in mortal danger perhaps? I saw again in my mind's eye the ravaged face of the figurehead. That deed, with all its wicked implications, returned disturbingly to haunt me. And the far worse memory as well of Tom Henderson muttering his life away in the hold of the *Pride*. He had tried to tell me something and I had not understood. Who had paid Tom Henderson—and for what? Why, if he knew the truth of what had happened aboard *Sea Jade*, had he kept silent for all these years? If he had meant to blackmail the captain, why had he waited? It would seem that his return was the catalyst that had brought all these stormy elements into motion, from the moment when his sudden appearance had so startled the captain, to the fall that had caused his own death.

I was dreadfully cold. I had not troubled to replenish the fire and I shivered as uncontrollably as I had the first night I had gone to bed in this room that had once been Rose McLean's. With fingers that seemed stiff and fumbling I

187

worked myself free of hooks and drawstrings and put on my nightgown. Then, still shivering, I slipped beneath the sheets.

What was it that I feared so terribly? Was it the ominous threat that had seemed directed at me in the slashing of the figurehead? Or was it more than that? Was it always, always, that my mind returned to the sound of guilty footsteps hurrying overhead—and the sight of Brock McLean at the foot of the gangplank when I had come out upon the deck of the *Pride*? Tears burned at the back of my eyes and I blinked them away desperately.

It was a long while later that I heard Brock come up to his room, heard the crackling of his fire next door, heard him whistling softly to himself as though no worry of any sort had marred this day for him. As well might be, since his wife had perjured herself to protect him.

Now I began to weep in earnest. I did not want him to hear me, so I gulped and sobbed into my pillow, choking back the sounds. The force of my weeping frightened me, yet I could not stop myself. There was so much that was dreadful to think about, so many frightening pictures to turn round and round in my mind, and I seemed to have lost all ability to stop them.

In the midst of my weeping a knock sounded on the door between Brock's room and mine. I knew I couldn't bear it if he came in and found me with all defenses down.

"Go away!" I wailed and buried my face in my pillow again.

I might as well have said, "Come in," for he opened the door. Light and warmth from his room spread in a broad shaft into mine. He came to my bed and I turned my head away so that he could not see my face. His words when he spoke astonished me.

"I've brought you a key," he said. "It will lock both the door to the outer hall and the door to my room. While I'm gone, see that you use it."

"Gone? Where are you going?" I choked.

"Word has just come that Henderson's claim about the *Sea Jade*'s presence in Salem is true. I've decided to go there and look the ship over."

My attention was caught in spite of my other concerns. "Then you've changed your mind? You'll bring her back to Bascomb's Point?"

He answered me curtly. "She was my father's ship. If she's seaworthy, I'll bring her home myself."

I was still shivering, but my weeping had been arrested. He crossed the room and I heard the metallic click of a key dropped upon the marble mantel. Then he turned to consider the quaking of my bed.

"What's the matter with you? That sounds like chattering teeth."

"What isn't the matter! Everything is wrong that could be—everything!"

He came to put a hand on my shoulder and felt my shivering, my chill. In his usual ungentle way he turned my head so that I faced the light from his room and he could see my swollen, reddened eyes, and my cheeks puffed with crying. He asked no "by your leave," but simply gathered me up in his arms, quilts and all. I could not even struggle as he carried me to his room and kicked the door shut behind him. Again with his foot, he jerked a big armchair before the fire and plumped me without ceremony into it. With a careless hand he picked up one of my trailing quilts and tucked it around me. I found myself in a warm nest with the firelight hot on my face and the tears drying upon my cheeks. Brock leaned toward me and pushed wet locks of hair back from my face.

"Now then," he said, drawing up a second chair next to mine, "suppose you tell me what this is all about."

I peered at him and saw that he looked more amused than sympathetic. In his obtuse way he probably understood nothing of the emotional turmoil I had experienced since coming to this house. The fact made me angry. I wanted to rub that smug amusement from his face. If he thought of me as a weeping child, I would show him otherwise. So— for all the wrong reasons— I finally told him the truth.

"I heard your footsteps on the deck the day Tom Henderson died! I heard you running away overhead after you'd pushed him off that ladder!"

I had the satisfaction of seeing all amusement wiped instantly from his face—though the expression that replaced it was far from reassuring.

"What are you talking about? What footsteps?"

"Yours!" I wailed. "When I went to see what had happened and found Tom, I heard you overhead. When I came up on deck and looked over the rail, there you were going down the gangplank."

"I could hardly go down it when I hadn't been up it," he said in exasperation. "Why didn't you bring up this matter of someone running away before now?"

"Because I thought it was you," I said bleakly, and all my anger ebbed futilely away.

He stared at me. "Despising me as you do, you still kept silent about what you thought? Why?"

"I—I wanted to tell you first. But there was never an opportunity. I thought you ought to—to have a chance to answer before I simply went around making accusations."

"Thank you," he said gravely. "I would have expected less mercy at your hands. If it's of any reassurance for you to know this—and if you can believe me—I was not in the hold of the ship until you called me and told me about Tom. I happened to be approaching the gangplank because one of the men in the shipyard had seen you on the way to the dock and mentioned the fact to me. I came over to find out what you were up to. I'd reached the foot of the gangplank when you looked over the rail."

A relief that was like weakness spread through me. For the first time the quaking inside me stopped.

"You should have told me at once that you'd heard someone running," Brock went on. "Then I could have investigated. Since no one came off the ship while I was there, whoever it was could have hidden in any dark place below decks and been safe enough. There was no talk about Tom having been pushed at that time. Later there would have been ways to leave the ship and slip away in the direction of town, with no one any the wiser."

"Then—who do you think it could have been?" I asked faintly.

He did not answer directly. Instead, he leaned toward me and took one of my hands in his. "That's better. You've stopped shivering at least. Your face is a sight, and your nose is red, but your teeth aren't chattering. I find it hard to believe that you were weeping all those tears because you thought I was a murderer and you were afraid to face me with the fact."

His words made my suspicions seem all the more absurd. He had some justification for thinking me an utter idiot. Then he spoiled my new sense of relief.

"Since you've said nothing so far, I'll ask you to keep silent a little longer," he said. "Will you promise me to say nothing of this matter, at least until after I return from Salem?"

"But why?" I asked. "If there has been a crime, then we shouldn't let the trail grow colder. I should think—"

He reverted at once to sharp command. "You'd better do no more thinking. You've done enough damage by not coming to me with this at once. Now you'll leave it to me to deal with. Don't you think you'd look pretty foolish if you reversed your story with Officer Dudley? He might suspect that you really have something to conceal."

All this was true, but it was what lay behind his words that troubled me. For if Brock chose now to keep silent, it would only be because he was protecting someone. If not himself —then his mother? But I lacked the courage to fling this new suspicion in his face. Instead, I did something that had not been in my mind at all five minutes before. I told him of the captain's dying words that had directed me to follow the whale stamp. I told him of finding the charts in the hold of the *Pride* and of my search for meaning that had culminated only a little while before in the finding of Captain Obadiah's confession. In what detail there was, I told him what the letter said.

"So you can see," I finished, "that it was not, after all, my father who shot yours aboard the *Sea Jade*. By his own words it was Captain Obadiah who fired the shot."

Brock was looking at me strangely, almost benignly. Had this story meant so much to him? Could he now forget whose daughter I was and abandon old bitterness against anyone who bore the name of Heath?

"Miranda!" he said, and the name, astonishingly, could be a caress on lips I had never dreamed could speak with so tender a cadence.

Moving in his quick, light way, he took me up in his arms again and then sat in my chair, holding me cradled against him. My head fell all too willingly into the hollow of his shoulder and my arm went about his neck. In a moment he would have kissed me and I would not have turned my mouth from the touch of his lips. But at that instant the hall door to his room was flung open with a crash and a woman stood there in her flowing night robes, a tall pewter candle-

191

stick in her hand, its taper lighted. Sybil McLean was staring at us with wild, accusing eyes.

As deftly as he had picked me up, Brock put me aside and rose to face his mother—all in a quick, smooth gesture without shame or awkwardness in it.

The fixed cold mask was gone from the woman's face. It looked alive enough now, with every line distorted in anger. "I heard you in here together!" she cried. "I knew you'd brought her to your room! Do you think I will allow this, Brock? Do you think I will permit you to be false to your father's memory?"

Under the effect of an anger that verged on madness, I curled into my quilts, pulling them around me, as if for protection. But her words had no effect on Brock. He went straight to her, took the candlestick from her hand and set it on a bureau.

"Miranda is my wife," he said. "What goes on behind our doors is no concern of yours."

She took a step toward me, as if in threat, but he held her by the forearms and after a moment of struggle she went limp in his grasp.

"It's time for you to look at what you are doing," he told her sternly. "I've understood and sympathized with your suffering, but this cannot go on. It isn't my father's memory that troubles you. It's your jealousy of Miranda's mother. It is because of Carrie Corcoran that you're eaten with hatred. The time has come to return to your senses."

Drawing her with him by one arm, he came to where I cowered in my chair. Before I knew what he intended, he reached out his free hand and pulled the quilt from about me, ripped the top of my gown from my shoulder to reveal the scar he knew was there.

"Do you see?" he said to his mother. "Are you reminded of a murder you nearly committed? Do you see the brink you're verging on, if something doesn't stop you?"

Once before, since I'd come to this house, Sybil McLean's eyes had rested upon my scarred shoulder with a gloating satisfaction I had not understood. But now she stared as if in fear and shrank from the sight—or would have if Brock had not forced her to face me.

She began to whimper a little wildly. "I never meant to hurt the babe! I only meant to look in and see why she was crying. I never meant my candle to touch the muslin of the crib. It went up in flames before I knew. But I screamed then. I screamed for help. And you came, Brock, and snatched up the babe and beat out the flames that were burning her garments. So she lived, did she not? I called for help and she lived. The girl has no more than a scar to show for what happened. I never meant her death."

Brock looked at me. "Go back to your room, Miranda. I'll quiet her. I know what to do."

I caught up my quilts and fled from the warm chair and fire, back to the chill of my room. I closed the door behind me and stumbled in a darkness to which my eyes were now unaccustomed till I found the mantelpiece. There my fingers searched for the key on icy marble. My hand shook as I locked the door to the outer hall. Then I crept between cold sheets and thrust the key beneath my pillow.

The door to Brock's room I did not lock.

His voice went on beyond the door, softly, so I could not hear the words, but with a note of sternness in the sound. After a time I heard him take his mother back to her room. When he returned to his own, he stood beyond our closed door and spoke to me in a low voice.

"Are you all right, Miranda?"

I told him I was all right. I did not tell him that I was cold again, chilled now with fear, yet all the while longing for him to open his door and come for me again. From his room came the sounds of a man packing for a trip, and sometimes the clink of the fire dying. He did not speak to me again. Nor did I to him. I lay thinking, not of the events of the day, not even of the frightening fact that as a baby I had nearly died at the hands of Sybil McLean, but only that Brock had regarded me with unexpected tenderness, that he had held me to his heart, with my head upon his shoulder. I ached to be held so again, longing anew with all my being for the inevitable caresses that would have followed. But longing went unassuaged. The door between our rooms remained closed, and I had no confidence that the moment of promised fulfillment would ever come again.

As time passed, longing subsided and fear returned. I wished that I dared plead with Brock to take me on his journey to Salem tomorrow—not only because I wanted to be with him, not only because I could wish to return in his company aboard the *Sea Jade*, but also because I was afraid to remain in this house when he was no longer present to

193

stand between me and the forces of evil. Strangely enough, in this man of dark moods and uncertain temper I had found a trusted protector. Tomorrow he would be gone and I would be left to deal with that half-mad woman across the hall. A woman who had once nearly caused my death, and who had perhaps thrust Tom Henderson from a ladder in the hold of the *Pride*.

Yet I could not bring myself to plead with Brock. His mood had already changed and I dared make no such appeal. I must deal alone with whatever might beset me, and with only the key beneath my pillow to offer me protection.

Because there is no better aid to wakefulness than one's own teeming thoughts, I slept little that night. When Ian's light flashed on in his lighthouse room, I lay for a long while watching the oblong it made on my ceiling. And I thought once more of Ian and the affection he offered me. What if I were mistaken about Brock? What if I had been right in the beginning and was utterly wrong now?

The light on the ceiling was blocked by shadow. Then it dimmed and vanished. Some lines I had read of Bulwer Lytton's returned to my mind:

> "Two lives that once part are as ships that divide
> When, moment on moment there rushed between
> The one and the other a sea . . ."

Already, in the very pulsing of my own blood, I could hear the sound of that rushing, dividing sea. Suddenly I wanted to plunge into its tumult and swim for my very life to the haven that was Ian Pryott. It was Ian who spelled safety, not Brock. Yet I knew I would not make the plunge. I had already chosen dangerous waters.

In the early morning hours I fell at last into slumber. When the sound of Lucifer's howling brought me wide awake, Brock was already gone.

16.

THE NEXT DAY WAS FRIGHTENING AND ominous from first to last. I will always recall it under the name I gave it at the time: *The Day of the Dog*. The animal must have known that Brock had gone away, for he kept up the hideous sound of his howling for hour after hour.

Once, in the early morning, the sound quieted for a time and I walked among the bare bushes of the rear garden toward the kennel. There I found to my surprise that Lien was feeding the beast. She seemed unafraid of him and he took meat from her hand and allowed her to fill his water dish without threatening her with so much as a growl. Somehow I was not reassured by this friendship.

She did not see me, but when she had finished and returned to her kitchen in the old house, I moved closer to the fence, watching Lucifer tear at his food with those strong teeth and jaws. He looked up and saw me there, and at once he began his wild cries again. The sound seemed a portent of disaster to come. I left the garden hurriedly and went back to the house, followed by the dreadful howling.

Somewhat tardily I thought of Laurel, wondering if she had discovered the destruction of the figurehead as yet. Probably not, or she would have come running to Ian and me. I had seen her at breakfast and she had said nothing. When I asked Mrs. Crawford where the child was, the woman said she had gone to the village on some errand. I resolved to catch her when she returned and tell her what had happened.

Ian was working in the library, but I did not seek him out. For one thing I feared that he might read in my face some evidence of the night's happenings, and attempt to question me. The thing I dared not betray was the fact that Brock had asked me to say nothing of those footsteps I had heard in the ship. This restriction lay uneasily upon my conscience. What Brock intended I did not know, or whether he would

195

give the murderer over to the law if he was convinced of—her?—identity. However strong an attraction he might hold for me, I did not truly know the man who was my husband.

How empty the house seemed with Brock gone! How uncanny the howling of the dog! I could not sit quietly in my room with my door locked, but found myself wandering upstairs and down aimlessly, my senses alert for any untoward detail, for any hint of threat to my person.

Nothing disturbed me until I was climbing the stairs for the dozenth time and looked up to see Sybil McLean in the hall above. I stifled an impulse to turn and run in order to avoid her at all costs. But I would not allow myself to retreat in terror.

For once she gave me no blank stare. There was a certain avidity in her gaze, and I liked this expression even less than the other. Her smile was paper thin, as artificial as a cutout.

"Come visit with me for a while," she invited, and made a slight gesture toward her room.

After last night, there was nothing I wanted less than a tête-à-tête with Sybil McLean. I said nothing as I finished my climb and came even with her in the upper hall. She must have sensed resistance coming, for she put out a hand that was almost coy in its uneasy gesture of friendliness.

"You mustn't hold that old accident against me, child. I never meant you to know. Brock should not have blurted it out as he did."

I regarded her in astonishment. Could she wipe from her mind so easily her actions of the night before? Could she forget the way she had burst in upon her son and me in wild anger, indifferent to decent privacy, intending harm to me?

"What happened when I was a baby doesn't matter any more," I said. "But what happens now does."

"Of course!" she agreed with greater animation than I had ever seen in her. "This is what I mean. We must begin to be friends, Miranda, you and I. My son wishes it. He is all I have now. I must not make him angry with me."

Had Brock told her of my hearing steps that ran away on planks overhead the day Tom Henderson had died? Did this unconvincing gesture of friendship mean that she knew she must coax for my silence with a pretended change of attitude?

As I hesitated, the dog bayed wildly, mournfully, and Mrs. McLean reached out and laid a hand upon my arm. Through the cloth of my sleeve I felt the deadly cold of her fingers, as though warm blood no longer flowed in her veins.

"Come," she said again.

I could not escape her grip without snatching my arm away and revealing my own fear. To show courage was to be safer than I might otherwise be. However unwillingly, I was drawn through the door of her room and seated before a smoky fire.

The woman picked up a poker and stirred the embers until flames licked up to her satisfaction, cutting through the smoke. When she had added more wood, she seated herself opposite me and looked at the portrait of Andrew McLean where it hung above the mantel.

"My son has told me something very strange," she began. "He gave me some tale I think he scarcely believed himself about your finding a letter—a confession, he said—written by Captain Obadiah."

"It's true." I felt relieved if this was all she wanted to speak about with me. Perhaps if she knew the truth, she would cease to hold her husband's death against my father, perhaps her attitude toward me would really change. I hurried to tell her more of the letter and of how I had found it.

She listened with that bright, avid gaze that was so different from her blank staring, and which reassured me not at all.

"So it is by this means that you hope to win my son over," she said when I had finished. "But you are wasting your time, you know. There's something else that changes everything. Something I have known since the time your mother was brought here. Perhaps I guessed it even before."

I listened uneasily, though never suspecting the direction her words would take.

"I've decided to tell you the truth," she announced abruptly. "The secret should be kept no longer. If it was Captain Obadiah who shot and killed my husband, then you are still the daughter of a murderer—for you are the daughter, not of Nathaniel Heath, but of Captain Obadiah Bascomb."

I stared at her, neither comprehending nor accepting her words.

She went on almost cheerfully. "I always suspected as much. I could see what was going on between your mother and the captain. He was the only one who could lead her down that road willy-nilly. She played with the others and she teased them. But she lost her head over Obadiah. He had

197

a fascination for women in those days. And she resisted him no better than the rest. He was the father of her babe—yet he would not marry her. Always he said he was never the marrying kind, that he liked his loves in every port. So she waited for him through the years and would not marry any other. He was the father of her babe, though I think he did not know the child was coming. She had that much pride, at least, so she wouldn't beg him to marry her in her need. No —it was to Nathaniel Heath—that soft, gentle man who could be easily used—that she went with her trouble. And of course *he* married her." The woman's voice rang with scorn.

I could not speak—I could not believe her. She must have taken satisfaction in my stunned expression, for she gave me her paper smile and went on in the same falsely animated way.

"Captain Obadiah was fit to be tied when Carrie up and married Nathaniel Heath. He never believed she could give him up, or that the time might come when he couldn't do with her as he pleased. He knew well enough the baby was ahead of its time and that he was the father. When it was about to be born Nathaniel was at sea and Carrie was in a bad way. So Obadiah brought her here to give her care that came too late. As you know, she died in this house, a few days after you were born."

Listening to her, it was as though all my childhood, all my early life, all the love between my father and me, between my aunt and me, had been torn into scraps like old newspaper and flung to the winds. I could almost feel my life blowing about me in scraps—a paper thing with no solid existence of its own. My doubting of her words had begun to fade. There was the ring of truth in all she said.

"I guessed the truth," she repeated, "but I didn't see it set down in black and white until Carrie wrote a letter a day or two before she died. It was a letter to Obadiah, but I found it in her room and read it before he did. In her own words she told him that he was the father and that Nathaniel had married her knowing this. So the captain had it down in her writing, as well as in his knowing. I've kept silent all these years. Even when I knew he was bringing you here because he wanted to see his daughter grown, I kept quiet— even with Brock. But I didn't think Obadiah would ever go so far as to leave the bulk of his fortune in your hands."

Now I could see why Captain Obadiah had wanted me

married to Brock. He could have changed his will over to Brock then and left me well cared for—or so he thought. But in the meantime, to safeguard me, he had made his secret will with me as his heiress. But I could not think of him as my father—never, never!

"When Nathaniel's ship came home, he hurried here at once and took you away," Sybil said. "Not even Obadiah could stop his doing that. Nathaniel knew Carrie had not wanted Obadiah to raise you. By law Nathaniel was your father, so Obadiah could not block him without admitting everything and sullying Carrie's name and yours. In his mule-headed way the captain had principles that wouldn't let him do that. As if she had any name to worry about—that one! But Nathaniel Heath took you to his sister in New York and raised you there."

Still I could not believe, could not accept. I could only sit looking at this woman who had torn up all my safe and happy past life and flung it in my face.

Suddenly her expression lighted with a new thought. "If this matter you've been telling me about a confession is true, then Obadiah must have had his revenge on Nathaniel. He let him take the blame for something Obadiah did. Maybe he even hoped to get you back by making Nathaniel yell for help."

This I could see. Perhaps Captain Obadiah had said to Nathaniel, "Give me my daughter and I'll save you." But Nathaniel Heath had quietly stood his ground and given up the sea rather than put me in Obadiah's hands. In the end, of course, Obadiah had saved him from a prison sentence—he had not been able to carry through what must have been a bluff. Nathaniel had come to live with his sister and me in New York and had never sailed on a ship again.

"Mr. Osgood mentioned a letter the captain told him would explain everything," I said. "I wonder if he meant not only this confession that he wanted me to find, but also the letter from my mother. Do you know what has become of it?"

Mrs. McLean stiffened perceptibly. "The letter no longer matters. It has long since served its purpose. I should think the captain would have destroyed it."

Her sudden vehemence made me wonder. She seemed too anxious to dismiss the very letter that spoke of my parentage.

"I will ask the captain's wife," I said. "Perhaps she has the letter now."

I closed my eyes against the swirling fog of my own thoughts. It was as though I could grasp only one strand of meaning at a time. I reached for another such strand now.

"When I first came to this house, when I was first in this room, you told me that my father—that Nathaniel Heath—had shot your husband. You wanted me to believe, as Brock did, that I was the daughter of a murderer. You emphasized that again last night. Yet even if Nathaniel had been guilty, it wouldn't have mattered because you knew I was Obadiah's daughter. So why—"

She fixed me with the bright malice of her look. "You are Carrie Corcoran's daughter. I could ask nothing better than to hurt you at every turn when I had the chance."

It had been foolish of me to think for a moment that Sybil McLean might change in her feeling toward me, or want to change. I left my chair and moved blindly toward the door. With deadly intent her voice followed me.

"And now we know that you really are the daughter of a murderer—if, as you say, the captain's statement tells us this. You are daughter to the man who killed Brock's father. When he comes home we will tell him this—you and I."

I managed to get through her door and across the hall into my own room. I stood beside my window and looked out upon the jutting of land that formed Bascomb's Point. I said to myself, "Nathaniel Heath is not my father. I am the daughter of a man who committed murder and let a better man take the blame. I am the daughter of a man who seduced my mother and did not marry her. All these things are in my blood, all this guilt flows through me."

Yet I could not believe or accept a word of it.

What a fortunate thing nature does for us in a time of shock. When there is too much that is dreadful to be comprehended all at once, we simply cannot absorb what has occurred. By the time the enormity of what has happened reaches through our daze and is fully realized, there has been some slight healing. Some meager ability is given us to accept and endure. Perhaps greater suffering sets in later, yet we are stronger by that time, better able to meet it and live.

So it seemed to be with me at that moment. I was more dazed than anything else. My mind could not yet encompass what had been presented to me. I could still reach for only one strand at a time to pull myself along.

Certain things there were that I must do. I must find out if

Laurel had returned from the village. I must seek out Lien. I must recover my mother's letter. That was the one thing that mattered, that became paramount. Perhaps in her own words Carrie would give me meaning to cling to: some slight thread of truth upon which I could begin to string the beads of my life again.

As I stood at the window looking out at the lighthouse and toward the rock cliffs, with the sea beyond, I began suddenly to listen. There was a strangeness in the air that I could not place until I realized that the dog had ceased to howl. I wondered if he had given up, resigning himself at last, even though he had no way of knowing whether his master would ever return.

Breaking this uneasy silence came an explosion of barking from the direction of the lighthouse. My unseeing eyes focused and I saw to my horror that Laurel was there on the walk and that she had that great brute of a dog by its chain. The child was not leading the dog. Rather, Lucifer was dragging her along, barking furiously the while.

I ran downstairs without bonnet or mantle and flung myself through the front gate, running desperately in Laurel's direction. I did not know what I could do, but only that I must somehow come to the child's aid before she was harmed by that great, savage beast.

Lucifer heard me coming and jerked around with blazing eyes. His chain slid through Laurel's helpless hands as he came at me. The little girl cried out a warning and hurled both arms about the creature's neck, letting him drag her weight along with his own. As she struggled with the dog, a long black garment she carried slipped from her grasp and fell upon the ground.

"Stay where you are!" Laurel shouted. "Don't come toward him in a hurry."

The dragging of her limp body halted the dog. He stood still, quivering, staring at me with those wild eyes. I obeyed Laurel and stopped on the path, realizing that the child was far less likely to be harmed by the dog than was I. When Laurel was sure I would come no closer, she unwound her arms from Lucifer's neck, picked up his chain and stood beside him, speaking to him soothingly, softly. When his shivering quieted, she smiled at me.

"There—he's feeling better now. It's time he got to be friends with you, Miss Miranda. He's so frightened of

201

everybody and he tries to hide it by growling and barking and springing at people. Just hold out your hand for him to smell and I'll bring him to you."

Somehow I managed to stand my ground as the two approached, the little girl whispering in the dog's ear, while Lucifer hesitated and dragged his feet, not in the least anxious to become better acquainted with me. When at last, at Laurel's insistence, my hand met that black, ugly muzzle, it was all I could do not to snatch it fearfully away. Oddly enough, Lucifer did not sink his teeth into my hand as I expected. He sniffed me a bit and studied me, while it was my turn to stand shivering.

"Speak to him," Laurel said. "Then he'll stop being so nervous about you."

How did one speak to so terrifying a beast? "Lucifer," I ventured inanely, "—good boy, Lucifer."

He snuffled at me doubtfully—a gesture Laurel seemed to regard as loving acceptance.

"There!" she cried triumphantly. "You're friends now. My father will be pleased if you and Lucifer like each other."

I doubted this, but I did not argue the point. I was very cold, both from anxiety and from the chill bite of the wind. The black garment on the ground that Laurel had dropped was a cloak and I picked it up and flung it about my shoulders. As I drew the hood over my head, I caught the perfume of sandalwood and knew it was the cape I had seen Lien wearing.

"You shouldn't have put that on!" Laurel's distress was so extreme that for the first time I forgot the dog and regarded the child who looked more like the witch girl I had seen on my arrival than she had done for some days. She pounced on me, holding Lucifer by one hand, and would have pulled the cloak from my person if I had not stepped aside. At her movement Lucifer growled as if he might come to her aid.

"Stop it!" I commanded her. "You're upsetting Lucifer again!"

Laurel let the cape go. "I suppose you've spoiled the scent anyway. Now I'll have to find something else."

"Something else for what? Laurel, what is it? What are you doing?"

She flung a despairing hand toward the lighthouse. "The figure-head! Someone has destroyed it. Miss Miranda, someone tried to murder you the way Tom Henderson was murdered."

I blamed myself for not having warned her, for postponing too long the task of telling her what had happened.

"I know about the figurehead," I said gently. "But as you can see, I'm very much alive. It was only the face of a wooden figure that was destroyed."

Laurel regarded me uncertainly. Lucifer had quieted and sat upon his haunches, alert and listening, seeming a more intelligent animal than I had thought him.

"I went to tell Ian the minute I found it, but he already knew," Laurel said. "He thinks it must have been Lien who did this awful thing. I went to ask her, but she was different —not one bit friendly to me. When she sent me away, I picked up her cape in the hall and brought Lucifer from his kennel. I was going to make him smell the cape and then walk around inside Ian's workroom and see if he could pick up Lien's scent. That's the way they do in stories. Then we'd know for sure if it was really Lien whom the evil spirits have possessed."

I shook my head ruefully. "I don't think it works exactly like that, Laurel. Besides, Lien must have gone into the lighthouse many times, so you couldn't tell a thing, even if Lucifer was willing to play bloodhound for you."

Laurel sighed deeply and her shoulders seemed to droop as purpose went out of her. "Something is dreadfully wrong. I'm frightened, Miss Miranda."

Something was indeed dreadfully wrong. For me it was far more wrong than it had been before. I knew too much —and too little. I smoothed back a strand of hair that blew over Laurel's forehead and touched her cheek lightly. "Go put the dog away, dear. Just think what would happen if he ever got loose."

"Nothing would happen," Laurel said. "He'd just go down to the docks and wait there for my father to come home. That's why he howls. He wants to go there and we won't let him."

I nodded. "Nevertheless, you must put him back in his kennel. Then in a little while come to my room and we'll talk. I've something to show you."

I would wait no longer to explain matters to Laurel. She had a right to know and I would try to make clear to her whatever I could make clear.

She smiled at me more agreeably and tugged at Lucifer's chain. He went bounding along with her as she hurried in the direction of the kennel.

I held Lien's cape around me as protection against the wind as I started toward the house. The garment gave me an excuse to visit the woman to whom it belonged. Despite any uneasiness I might feel, I would postpone seeing her no longer. It was Lien who could find my mother's letter for me. It was Lien in whom the captain might have confided.

I went through the front gate of the Bascomb house, but this time I did not go in by the front door. I went instead to the door of the older house and raised the brass knocker. Inside the echoes raced hollowly up the stair well.

17.

AT MY SECOND KNOCK THE CAPTAIN'S wife came to the door. I held out the cape, explaining that Laurel had borrowed it, and she took it from me, offering courteous thanks.

"May I speak with you for a moment?" I was equally polite.

Lien bowed her assent, inviting me in. It was as if we fenced with each other using the delicate weapon of polite conduct. I took no encouragement from these extremes of courtesy, for I knew there was a state of war between us.

Lien's foreign visage was strange as ever to me and in it I could read neither welcome nor rejection. My mind's eye held remembrance of the ravaged figurehead, and I was not eased of my fears.

Today she wore her white jacket above dark Nankeen trousers, but there were smudges on the white, as though she had worn it for cooking and cleaning. Her hair was not as smoothly combed as when the captain had been alive and there were evidences that despair and discouragement had brought her to a careless state. This change in her gave me no reassurance. Despair could lead easily to acts of

204

desperation. But I must not give way to my own fears before I had said what I had come here to say.

Surprise would be the best weapon to use with her. When I had seated myself in the captain's big chair at her invitation, I spoke in a manner that I hoped would seem quiet and matter-of-fact.

"This morning Mrs. McLean told me that Captain Obadiah was my father. Do you know if this is true?"

"It is true," she said without evasion, and seated herself on a hassock not far from me.

If I had hoped that Lien might contradict Sybil McLean's words, her answer ended my last doubt. Whatever Lien knew she would know from the captain himself.

"But why did Captain Obadiah keep this from me? Why did he bring me here, yet not tell me the truth?"

Lien showed no hesitation about answering. "He was a devious man. A man with no gods and a troubled soul. He wanted to win you to him first. He feared that you would despise him when you knew, if he did not first win your love."

"Yes," I said, "I might have. But he didn't tell Brock the truth either?"

"No. All this would have been revealed gradually to both of you after the marriage, once he knew all would go as he planned. He wanted your forgiveness for many things. He had on his conscience the killing of Brock's father and the way he let Nathaniel Heath take the blame."

"I know about this too," I said. "But I've come here to ask about a letter the captain must have had in his possession. A letter written by my mother before she died. Do you have it?"

"I have seen such a letter long ago, but I do not know where it can be," Lien said. "It is possible that the captain placed it in the desk he kept in the cabin of the *Pride*. He felt his secrets were safer there."

I had feared as much. Now I knew I must brave the depths of the ship again. I wanted to hold the letter in my hand. I wanted to read whatever Carrie Heath had written with my own eyes. And I wanted to know if there was something further that Sybil McLean held from me.

"This seaman, Tom Henderson," I said, "what do you know of him?"

There seemed a quickening of attention in her, though she met my question with waiting silence. I went on.

"Who could have wanted the man dead?"

Again her answer was evasive. "The captain was afraid because of what this man knew. After the voyage on which Andrew McLean was killed, the captain paid his first mate well and sent him away to Burma, to Ceylon. Every year he sent him money to stay far away. But the captain was growing old and this man feared the money might stop coming at any time. So he returned to see if he could get more by threatening to tell everything he knew. When the captain saw him, he was afraid, lest all his plans be defeated. Especially he feared what Brock would do if he learned the truth about who had killed his father. The shock, as could be expected, was too much for the captain's heart."

Much that I had puzzled over was coming clear—but not the matter of what had happened in the hold.

"If Tom Henderson was pushed from the stairs, as they say, it was not the captain who pushed him," I pointed out.

"Who is to know?" Lien's gaze was strange and distant. "When a powerful and evil force is set into motion, where is it to stop? Evil breeds evil without end."

I had no answer for this and tried another approach. "Do you know what happened the other time? I mean when Andrew McLean died aboard the *Sea Jade*?"

"Mr. Henderson has told me. He wished to speak with me away from this house, so we met and talked where no one would hear."

I stiffened, remembering Tom's words—that he had been paid by someone. Had he meant the captain long ago? Or was it some more recent payment he had meant? By Lien, perhaps?

She went on, speaking as if to some shadow across the room. "The three captains sailed together on the first voyage because they wished to observe the behavior of the new ship. Though only Captain Obadiah was master. On the way home in a storm off Good Hope Captain McLean became angry, claiming that Captain Bascomb did not know how to sail such a ship. He said Obadiah would wreck the vessel and drown them all. Captain Heath agreed with Captain McLean, who had designed the ship, and he asked that McLean be permitted to take charge and save the *Sea Jade*. Mr. Henderson was at the wheel at the time and the others were nearby. He saw what happened. He heard everything.

"Captain Obadiah drew a gun and commanded the other two to stand back or he would shoot them down as mutineers. He said he had the right to do this. McLean would not give way and Captain Heath tried to stop Obadiah. He struggled with him to save McLean's life. But the gun was discharged. Whether by chance in the struggle, or because Obadiah meant to kill, Mr. Henderson could not be sure. Afterwards Captain Obadiah proved his skill by sailing the *Sea Jade* safely through the storm. He placed Captain Heath in irons, accusing him of McLean's death."

"Why?" I said. "Why would he do such a thing? Captain Obadiah would not have been held guilty, as master of the ship."

Lien lifted her white clad shoulders eloquently. "Captain Heath was the only man who ever defeated him. Captain Heath married a woman Obadiah had loved. He had taken Obadiah's daughter for his own and he would not give her up. Of course Mr. Henderson did not tell me such things. But I knew the captain well. He would have said, 'I will save you if you will give me the child.' But Captain Heath was a good man and this he did not do. In the end the captain was forced to save him from prison with another lie."

These things too I had guessed, and with Lien's corroboration I knew they must be so. Yet I felt oddly baffled, listening to her. I did not understand the nuances of her oriental nature. The Chinese, I knew, did not respond well to questions that were blunt and rude. Yet I had to ask a blunt question and I watched for her reaction.

"Was it you, Lien, who destroyed the figurehead?"

She laughed softly, as though I had said something funny, something that pleased her. "I am a humble person from a distant land. This you know. You are a young lady of great wealth, but you are of more uncertain birth than I. So which of us is to command the other to speak?"

"I'm not commanding," I said. "Ian thinks you did it. He is very angry. His best work had been destroyed."

Lien was not impressed. "He is well served. Always he was kind to me, attentive. Always I thought that when the captain died Ian would take me as his wife. We would have the wealth and the power together, and all who had scorned us would be as nothing. Then you came—and all

207

was different. From the time you first appeared, I could see that his kindness to me was only kindness. You won him to you with your face that is of his own people. You won him with your unhappiness, your danger, your need."

I made some small sound of remonstrance, but Lien raised her hand in an imperious gesture, perhaps learned long ago in a more elevated station of her life.

"Ai-ya—let me finish! These things in you Ian could not resist, but he has it in him to be cruel as well as kind. I remember one day when he sang your praises to me—as if I had not feelings of my own. As if he did not know how greatly I loved him. When I heard these things, I could have wished you dead in my first anger. How could I endure it that he chose you to model for his carving?"

"So you destroyed his work?" I said.

"Yes—it was I. And now that you know, what will you do? Do you think it will stop there? How will you escape from what is sure to come?"

I looked into her bright dark eyes and saw that the delicate mask of a Chinese lady was gone. Lien was looking at me as a woman enraged. A woman who clearly meant me harm.

I waited on no dignity but sprang up and fled the room. Behind me I heard her laughter ring out—high, silvery, scornful. And I heard her cry following me: "Run, little rabbit, run!"

When I reached my room my heart was indeed beating like any hunted rabbit's, and it did not quiet until I grew reasonably sure that she had not followed me.

I sat for a long while, trying to think, to understand. I could see Lien with that pirate blade in her hands slashing savagely at the figurehead. I could see her as well in the hold of the ship pushing Tom Henderson from the ladder, her fury aroused. Because he had threatened her in some way? Because there was more to the matter of her meeting and talking with him than I understood? Where had she met him? In the hold of the ship, perhaps, on the day he had died?

I got up and locked both doors of my room with the key Brock had given me. He had intended that I lock them at night, but the enemy he saw was a different one. Then I returned to my chair and sat rocking, rocking. I was increasingly afraid.

208

It was necessary for Laurel to call to me twice through the door before I went to answer her. I had forgotten that I had told her to come to me here. I was glad to hear her voice, for now I must comfort her and assuage her fears and thus put my own aside.

"You said you had something to show me," she reminded me as she came in.

I gave the captain's confession to her and watched her read it with widening eyes and a dawning of new realization. When she had finished she came exuberantly to fling her arms about me in a show of affection I had never expected.

"Now I can love you, Miss Miranda!" she cried. "Your father didn't kill my grandfather after all! So there's no need to hate you as my grandmother wishes."

I held her close to me. "Wait—you must neither judge nor forgive so quickly. Are you sure you must hate Captain Obadiah for what he did so long ago?"

She drew away to look into my eyes. "No, of course not! I could never hate the captain."

"I cannot either," I said. I could not tell her all the truth as yet. I could not yet tell her that I was Obadiah's daughter.

She turned abruptly to another subject. "When will my father come home?"

I could give her no answer to that and merely shook my head.

"I shall watch for him," Laurel said. "Tomorrow I'll go up in the lighthouse tower to watch. I want to be the first to glimpse the *Sea Jade*'s sails when they come over the horizon."

"You must call me as soon as you see them. I want to watch for her too."

She peered at me closely, though not with her former antagonism, and her words took me aback. "You love my father, don't you, Miss Miranda?"

I was altogether disconcerted. This, in so many words, was the thing I had wanted to conceal even from myself. There had been moments of longing, moments when I relied upon Brock for physical protection, as well as the realization that I must turn away from Ian. But I had stopped my futile dreaming and I dared not think of love between Brock McLean and me.

"I love him too," said Laurel softly, and slipped her hand into mine.

In that close and gentle moment we sat before the fire together and there was growing affection between us. Laurel had flung wide a door I had been afraid to open. I knew it would not close again.

Once more I was lost in dreams and this time I made no effort to stop the flood. The child beside me was dreaming too. Only once did she break the enchanted silence that lay between us.

"We will watch for the *Sea Jade* together," she said.

I clasped my fingers tightly about hers in promise.

18.

FOR ME THE DAYS THAT FOLLOWED were filled with unrestrained longing and dreaming. But where former dreams had run through my head like a fog, without substance or reality, the new ones focused upon a core that was real—the person and mystery of Brock McLean, and my love for him. He was my husband and I wanted him. But how was I to win him? How was I to know what he wanted of me when our relationship had been one of contradiction and often of stormy conflict?

Yet he had held me in his arms. This had been real, if only for a moment. My new dreams relied upon my heart, but now my mind was awake too and I turned from dreaming to planning. To plan was to dream with purpose.

I began to take more of a hand with the house, helping Mrs. Crawford in quiet, unobtrusive ways that did not threaten her authority. She had relaxed her guard against me just a little, and she was not above commenting on the change I had brought about in Laurel.

Nevertheless, these days were laced with uneasiness as well. There was a sense of our marking time, of awaiting the next move of that force that lurked beneath the surface and whose source I had begun to pinpoint with certainty. My last encounter with Lien had given me the deadly an-

210

swer. At least Lien and I avoided each other for the time being and I was on guard against her.

Sybil McLean had returned to having her meals in the dining room and she set her own mark of inner gloom and brooding upon Laurel and me whenever we were with her. She too was apparently awaiting the *Sea Jade*'s coming with a dread that was visible, even though she did not put it into words. I had the uncomfortable feeling that old hatreds were building within her toward some explosion, stirring about that irritant, that symbol of all she hated—the ship, *Sea Jade*.

Of Ian I saw little. From afar I knew he watched me and there was a heaviness upon his spirit. Matters between us had been brought to no final resolution. Yet there was no way in which I could reach out to him. Brock stood between us and I knew I would not have it otherwise.

A night I slept behind locked doors. During the day I sometimes remained in my room, pondering my identity. I could not think of Captain Obadiah as my true father. Yet now my own dear father, Nathaniel Heath, had slipped away into mists of obscurity and seemed lost to me. I felt lonelier than ever before, and I dreaded the moment when Brock must be told the unhappy facts of my identity. All this must come as a blow to him as well, for he had been devoted to Captain Obadiah. Now he must accept the captain in a new light with respect to Andrew McLean.

At least when Brock returned he and I could go together to the *Pride* to seek my mother's letter in the captain's desk. Each day I grew more fearful of visiting the whaler alone. Tom Henderson was gone, but his murderer remained and I feared to offer myself as a target in that place of ill-omen. The thought even occurred to me that the letter, if it was really there, might be a bait to coax me away from the house, away from human company.

Once at dinner, when Laurel had been excused from the table, Sybil prodded me concerning my mother's letter. "Did you ever ask Lien if it was among the captain's things?" she demanded abruptly.

"Lien thinks the captain may have kept it in one of the drawers of his desk aboard the *Pride*."

"Have you gone there to look?" she asked.

I wondered at her persistence. "Not yet. The ship seems an unpleasant place to me. I'll wait until Brock comes home. Then perhaps he will go there with me and help me search."

This plan did not please her. "The letter is of no consequence," she told me. "It will inform you of nothing you do not already know. Don't involve Brock in this sordid story." She seemed both interested in the letter's whereabouts and at the same time anxious to warn me away from it.

Her words made me all the more determined to read whatever my mother had written to Captain Obadiah in the time just before her death. But for the moment the letter could wait. I would not go to the *Pride* alone.

Sometimes when the day was bright, I sat upon the rocks above the sea and watched the horizon, as Laurel watched from the lighthouse tower with the captain's spyglass. Sometimes we watched from that high place together. But such sails as showed themselves on the horizon in nowise resembled the sails of a clipper ship.

Then one afternoon, when I sat reading in the library, Ian came in and I saw the excitement that quickened him.

"Come!" he said. "The *Sea Jade* is due this afternoon. I was in the village and the word has arrived by telegraph to Bascomb & Company."

I sprang up with an excitement greater than his own. "Then we must go to the tower at once!"

"Yes, we must go to the tower." There was a strangeness in his tone. He took my two hands in his. "The time is nearly here, Miranda. Are you ready? Ready to choose?" He waited for no answer, but dropped my hands and held open the door. "We must hurry so as not to miss her. This is a historic moment for the company, for us all, you know. It's not every day in our time that a famous clipper ship sails home."

As a captain's daughter, I could respond to this—though now the old, half-boastful label carried less pride with it. It was one thing to be the beloved daughter of Nathaniel Heath, who was a man of honor, and quite another to be Obadiah Bascomb's daughter.

As I went with Ian toward the lighthouse, the thought of seeing Brock became an increasingly exciting and troubling thing. When he returned I would be less afraid in the house than I was in his absence. Yet I could see no way for the two of us to come together as husband and wife, and I dreaded the tension, the rising of further anger between us.

Longing and anxiety were intertwined and I did not know which was the stronger.

Ian spoke only of the *Sea Jade,* so that I quieted a little, and tried to take heart.

Laurel had brought Lucifer to the tower, as if he too might welcome a sight of the ship that bore his master home. From the gallery beneath the lantern they heard us coming and the dog set up a great barking until he saw who we were. He accepted me now with a certain resignation, more as one who had been thrust upon the family, than as a friend, but at least he no longer snarled at my approach, or shivered, as Laurel claimed, in terror of me.

There was no need to tell Laurel of the message. She started a great screeching the moment she heard us on the stairs. "Come up! Come up quickly! The ship has just come into view. I know it's the *Sea Jade* this time and not another ship to fool us."

I reached the top, breathless, with Ian close behind, and we went out upon the gallery where the sea wind tore at us. I tied my bonnet more firmly beneath my chin and took the captain's glass as Laurel handed it to me.

At first I saw nothing but small circles of sea as I turned the lens this way and that. Beside me, Laurel plucked at my elbow and tried to correct my direction. Then something focused in the glass, and I saw her—the beautiful white bird sailing gloriously, gracefully over the horizon and across the ocean toward Scots Harbor!

I forgot all else in that moment, for I knew I was witnessing one of the miracles of the sea. As my father had often told me, most talk of a ship being under full sail was careless. Rarely did the right combination of fine weather and a light, steady breeze nearly dead aft occur so that all sails were set. Even when it happened, the men who sailed a ship never saw her dressed in all her glory, for the sight could never be seen from her decks. Once as a boy my father—Nathaniel Heath—had crawled out upon a bowsprit to a place where he could witness such a sight. Now here was I on this lighthouse tower seeing it for myself.

Mainmast, foremast, mizzen—all flew their full complement of sail, from flying jibs, mainsails, and topsails, through topgallants and royals to the tiny sky sails at the top. A great pyramid of white canvas rose against a blue sky as the *Sea Jade* flew toward us over the water.

Laurel grew impatient for the glass and we took turns after that. Once she even tried to press the spyglass to Lucifer's reluctant eye, explaining to him over and over that Brock was coming home. He understood the name, and perhaps he caught something of our excitement, for he prowled the tower restlessly and would have gone downstairs if Ian hadn't looped his chain around a bar of the railing.

Before long I needed no glass to see the ship clearly. How marvelously she skimmed blue water, with blue skies and white clouds above her full white sails. My throat tightened and my eyes misted. After all her years of slavery, *Sea Jade* was coming home in full pride and beauty. And Brock McLean was sailing her! Brock, whose father had designed and built her in the first place. If ever there was poetic justice done, it was now. I surmised that there would not be a man aboard who did not serve the temporary master of this ship with all the respect and obedience due him—because he was wholly a man. The measure of a man did not lie in a halting walk alone, and now Brock would know that this was true.

Ian touched my arm. He was watching me and not the ship. "Miranda!" he said and I caught the sudden tension in his voice. "Come back to shore, Miranda!"

I did not want to hurt him, but I had long made my choice and at the sight of those sails everything had fallen into place. I could not hide my joy because Brock was sailing home, nor could I concern myself with Ian just then—even when he drew his hand abruptly from my arm.

Laurel had tired of peering at the oncoming ship and she began waving her glass around, focusing here and there on nearer objects. Suddenly she turned it intently in the direction of the *Pride*, nudging me with her elbow.

"Miss Miranda, look! Why do you suppose Grandmother is going aboard the whaler?"

I took the glass from her and focused it on the smaller ship. Sure enough, Sybil McLean, still dressed in the black garments she had put on at the captain's death, was mounting the gangplank.

Ian watched her, too, puzzled by her actions. "Whatever is she up to? I told her that Brock was coming home today and she started getting ready for him at once, and giving orders in the kitchen. What can she want down there?"

Suddenly I knew. There could be only one reason that

would take Sybil McLean aboard a ship, when she so hated ships and the sea. From the moment when she had first mentioned my mother's letter, she had not wanted it to come to light. When I had said that Brock and I would seek it aboard the *Pride*, she had been markedly anxious to discourage such a plan. Now she must have taken matters into her own hands, determined to retrieve Carrie Heath's letter before anyone else could find it. I did not know her motive, but I knew that I must stop her before she could destroy the words my mother had written.

"Help me, please," I begged Ian. "Come with me to the *Pride*. Mrs. McLean told me of a letter my mother wrote to Captain Obadiah before she died. I've reason to think he hid it in his desk down there. It mustn't fall into Mrs. McLean's hands."

Ian hesitated and I sensed his reluctance. I had rejected him quite finally and I could not blame him for turning away from any demand I might make of him. But I could not face Sybil McLean alone.

"Oh, please, Ian—please!" I said urgently.

He gave me his old, mocking smile as he relented. "Of course, Miranda. We'll go down to the *Pride* at once and see what the woman is up to."

Fortunately, Laurel did not complicate matters by begging to come with us. Once more her attention was fixed upon the wonder of that lovely ship. The *Sea Jade*'s sails were slackening now as she prepared for harbor sailing. I saw her hesitating between the sheltering arms of land, almost as if she curtsied like a lady about to make her entrance at a ball.

Ian and I hurried down the tower steps. When we emerged below, Sybil McLean was no longer in sight.

Anxiety spurred my feet and we ran together, Ian and I, around the Bascomb house, with a short-cut through the garden. We dashed through the little patch of woods that edged the lip of the bluff, and when we came into the open I paused in headlong flight, for Lien stood on the bluff's edge. Her black cloak covered her and the hood was over her head. She turned at the sound of our footfalls and I glimpsed the pale ivory of her face, the bright, venomous darkness of her eyes when she saw the two of us together.

"The captain's ship comes home," she said. One arm was hidden beneath the cloak, as I was to remember later. She raised the other and made a wide dramatic gesture so that

215

the black garment lifted like a wing in the wind. I knew that she meant no captain but Obadiah.

As we left her and started down the bluff path, we could see the *Sea Jade* sailing into the harbor. The men were gone from the shipyard below us—gone to join the throng that crowded the waterfront. Already small boats were putting out from shore to welcome the sea queen home. Joyful hands had begun pealing the bell of a white steepled church, and soon other Scots Harbor churches were joining in the clamorous welcome. For this moment in time history had rolled back its pages and the great days were come again.

Neither Ian nor I had spoken to Lien. Nor did we pause to watch the *Sea Jade*'s triumphant conquest of the harbor in our plunge down the hill. Ian took my hand when we reached the timberstrewn area of the yard and we ran together hand in hand, dodging barrels and piles of gear, zigzagging toward the dock. Only once, when I stopped for breath, did I look back up the bluff. Lien no longer stood like a black-winged figurehead above. She had started down and was halfway to the bottom. Somehow the fact made me hurry all the more.

We ran up the steps of the dock, across creaking boards, and up the gangplank to the *Pride*. Ian sprang to the deck ahead and caught me about the waist to lift me down. I stood within his arms and suddenly all hurry fell away from him.

"There's still time to escape from Brock, Miranda. There's still time to save yourself. Once I thought it was too late, but I was wrong. Come away with me now—before he sets foot on shore."

I felt the tightening of his arms and resisted with all my being. He understood at last that my choice had been truly made and his arms dropped from about me.

"Come then," he said. "We'll look for Sybil McLean."

He went first down the open hatch nearest us in the stern. In a moment he had lighted a lantern and I followed him down. Beyond the stairs, in the after part of the ship, the door of the captain's cabin stood open. Sybil McLean was there, as I had known she would be, going through the drawers of the captain's desk.

I ran toward her at once. "The letter is mine! If you've found it, give it to me!"

"Do you think I would?" she cast the words at me angrily.

216

"Do you think I'll have my son read the lies that creature wrote?"

"Lies? Lies about what?" I demanded.

"About me! Vicious lies that my son shall not read. If the letter is here I will have it before he comes home!"

She continued to tug furiously at drawers and compartments, opening those that could be opened, trying to force the others.

Ian stood back and did not interfere.

"You might as well stop," I said. "I've told you the letter belongs to me."

She whirled to face me, and saw Ian standing behind me. At once her face came alight with a look more malevolent than I had ever seen in it before. It was as if all the hostility and hatred that so consumed this woman, had flared up to find a living outlet.

"So!" she cried. "It's you! I suppose you've come back to the scene of your crime!"

I knew the woman had stepped over the borderline of sanity at last. She was completely mad and I plucked at Ian's arm to draw him away, but she came toward him furiously.

"Wait," Ian said to me, "let's hear this out. Suppose you explain what you mean, Mrs. McLean."

"I talked to the Chinese woman this morning," she told him scornfully. "I said I wanted Carrie's letter. When she claimed she didn't have it, I threw something else in her face. I asked her why she had left the door unlocked so Tom Henderson could come upstairs that night he frightened the captain and caused his death. She had the gall to laugh at me and deny that she'd had anything to do with the door. She said it was you who planned this, Ian Pryott. You who unlocked the door and told Henderson to watch his chance to get upstairs to the captain."

I flung myself back from the hateful stream of her words and pulled again at Ian's arm. "Don't listen to her! You can see that she is mad. No one will believe anything she says."

Ian smiled at me wryly. "They will believe easily enough. People leap at this sort of thing. Just as they were ready to suspect that you might have pushed Tom Henderson off the ladder."

"It wasn't Miranda who did that. And I'm not in the least mad!" Sybil cried. "It was you—*you!* Because Tom was going to tell his story—that you'd let him into the house deliberately, knowing the captain's heart was weak, hoping for his death before there could be any changing of his will to Brock. You would have paid the fellow when Lien inherited, I suppose. But you didn't know, as Lien did, that the captain had already changed his will over to Miranda. You thought Lien would get all the money and then you would marry her and have everything you've always thought was due so clever a scoundrel as yourself."

Her words touched me with horror. "Tell her it's not true, Ian!"

He answered me dully, without denial. "Everything would have been simple enough if you hadn't come into the picture, Miranda. I never meant to love you. My plans seemed sound enough at first. But one desperate step led to another, and each forced me into the next. There was never any turning back. And now I'm done for."

He caught up the lantern and ran up the stairs. Mrs. McLean returned frantically to her search in the captain's cabin and I started up the steps in bewilderment to follow Ian.

At once he shouted down at me. "Stand back, Miranda!"

There was a ringing in his voice that made me obey. I sprang off the steps toward the center of the ship and a moment later Ian's lighted lantern came hurtling down, smashing as it landed, bursting into oily flame that spattered the old dry wood of the stairs and began at once to burn furiously. I stood horrified, listening to the wild, immediate crackling of dry tinder. Beyond, Sybil slammed the door of the captain's cabin in terror, shutting herself in.

"Come out!" I called to her. "Come out at once. You'll burn to death if you stay in there."

Beyond the door she began to scream, but she did not open it, and I remembered that it could stick. Ian's voice reached me above the sound of spreading flames.

"Go to the forward stairs, Miranda. Come up them at once and you'll be safe. I'll get you off the ship."

I paid no attention, my entire focus upon the frightened woman shut in the cabin, with the flames reaching surely toward the door. There was still an open space behind the burning stairs. I stared at it for a terrified moment, all my old fear of flaming light upon me. But I could leave no one to so hideous a death and this was Brock's mother.

I fled toward the open space, slipped through beneath the

slanting steps and reached the cabin door. The heat was already intense as I put my shoulder to the door and burst it open. The woman cowered in helpless terror on the captain's bunk, and did not move or answer when I called to her. I slapped her across one cheek sharply, and when she roused I caught her arm and pulled her bodily toward the door. At the wall of flame that faced us, she tried to shrink back, but I clung to her as Laurel had clung to Lucifer. The space was still clear beneath the stairs and I found a strength I had not known I possessed and pushed her toward it.

Her mantle was on fire and my bonnet was burning by the time we stumbled through. I tore them off, scarcely feeling the pain, and flung them toward the flames, beating out the sparks that would have kindled the rest of our clothes.

Air—we had to have air to breathe! Smoke was choking me and Sybil was coughing. I tugged at the woman desperately and now she found strength enough to come with me as I pulled her toward the forward ladder.

Scattered oil had done its work and already the entire stern was ablaze. Flames were making a chimney of the after stairway. I managed to drag her forward. Our one escapeway lay through the open forward hatch.

As we reached the steps, the breath of air was momentarily welcome. I looked up and saw the light of a blue and sunny sky, saw Ian kneeling on the deck looking down at us. As had happened to me twice before, since I had come to Bascomb's Point, I had the sudden intense feeling that all this had been ordained from the first, that somehow I knew what was to come. Yet I held up my hand to him in desperate pleading.

"Help me! I can't get her up the stairs alone. You must help me!"

But though he bent toward me, he did not extend his hand. "I'm sorry, Miranda. Remember that I loved you. That I could have loved you. But never as much as I love my own life."

The hatch slammed down above. I shouted Ian's name in disbelief, but my only answer was the sound of something heavy like a barrel being rolled upon the door over my head.

I ran up to where I could put my shoulder against the hatch cover, but whatever blocked it was heavy and would

219

not budge. Above on the deck I heard footsteps running—running away, just as I had heard them that other time. It had been Ian then—easily able to hide himself aboard the ship because I so foolishly kept from Brock the fact that I had heard someone running.

Mrs. McLean had crumpled to the floor at the foot of the steps and I went down to crouch beside her. Here near the floor, the air was better than it was on the ladder close to the ceiling. In the stern of the ship the fire burned furiously, fed on every hand by ancient timbers, spreading even as we watched. Worse than the flames was the thickening smoke, more immediately dangerous than the fire itself. Already it was filling the ship below decks with a choking blanket. The very taste of it was acrid and bitter in my mouth, burning to my lungs.

Yet it seemed that death could take a long and painful time in coming. We clung to each other, coughing and fighting for breath, when a sound—a sound from the world of air and sunlight overhead!—came down to us. It was the barking of a dog. No dog but Lucifer would bark like that, and I roused myself to call to him as if he could understand my words.

"Good dog!" I shouted. "Go get help, Lucifer! Go get help!"

But even as I cried out to him I knew my voice was too faint, knew that his barking could not bring us aid in time. Then, abruptly, a strong foot kicked the barrel away from the hatch. The door was yanked open and I looked up to see Brock above us. Fire and smoke roared toward this new vent, but Brock came down, caught up the unconscious figure of his mother and carried her up the stairs, shouting to me to come after him. I scrambled and fought my way up the steps.

In the cold sharp air of the deck I gasped painfully till I could breathe again. But we could not linger there. The whole after part of the ship was ablaze, with a great column of smoke rising to the sky, and cinders raining about us. Lucifer leaped and bounded frantically, his chain clattering. I caught up the end of it as we hastened from the burning ship.

Now there were ready hands to aid us. Mrs. McLean was taken from Brock's arms and carried ashore. But Brock stayed with me. Until this moment, he had not spoken, except to command, but now he drew me roughly to him, held me hard and hurtfully, murmuring over me the while. He touched my hair, my shoulders, my dress, seeking for any harm that had come to me.

"I'm all right," I told him. "Oh, Brock, Brock!" And I clung to him knowing not only that my husband had come home, but that I had come home, too.

I tried to tell him a little then, through my shock and my horror of what had happened. "It was Ian—it was Ian all the time! He rolled that barrel over the hatch to keep us down there. He would have sacrificed us both because your mother knew what he had done!"

"Hush," Brock said. "Don't fash yourself, lassie. He had a way with him, Ian. But this time he hasn't got off with it. Look, my darling."

I raised my head as we started along the dock together. At the far end stood a figure in a long black cape. The hood was flung back from her head and the pale ivory of her face was turned toward the water. Both hands were revealed now and in one of them she held the pirate blade. I stared at her for a moment of further shock and then followed the direction of her gaze.

From a small boat men were lifting something from the harbor water and my hand tightened on Brock's arm. I could not speak my question, but he answered it.

"Lien was at the end of the dock when he tried to escape, and barred his way. She had the sword in her hands and I think she would have killed him with it. So he chose the water. I saw it happen as I came along."

Ian, who so feared the sea, and could scarcely swim! Again there was fitting irony, but I could take no pleasure in it. I did not want him dead. I wanted him alive and good and trustworthy. All that he had never been, save when it served him well or cost him nothing.

"How did you know?" I asked Brock. "How did you get to us in time?"

He took Lucifer's chain from my hand. "The dog came down to the docks and I knew someone must have loosed him, knew something must be wrong. I hurried for the short-cut path toward home and that's when I saw the fire aboard the *Pride*. Lien was on the dock and she told me where you were."

We had reached the ledge of slanting ground that was the

shipyard, and I halted in sudden understanding to stare up at the lighthouse, high on the cliff. Laurel must have seen the fire and she had done the only thing possible. She had loosed the dog, knowing he would go to the place where he always waited for Brock.

But Laurel was no longer there in the tower. A small figure came hurtling down the bluff path to hurl herself into my arms, to cling to me breathlessly, and look with shy eagerness at her father.

On the beach women had come from the village to assist Mrs. McLean back to the house. Brock and Laurel and I climbed the bluff together, and my husband's arm was about me all the way. No longer did the things I had to tell him seem to matter very much. No longer did it concern me that I was Obadiah's daughter. For if I had changed, Brock had changed too. Clearly he had come alive, and surely he had left old hopelessness behind. There would be much to work out, but we could manage it together now.

We had nearly reached the house before I remembered my mother's letter. It was gone in the burning ship. I would never read what Carrie Heath had written, and sadness touched me. Her words might have been something of my mother to possess. But at least I knew now where my true love lay and never again would I give my life to futile dreaming.

Nearly a year has passed since the burning of the *Pride*. These final words are being written aboard that gallant ship, the *Sea Jade*. The taste of smoke no longer seems constantly on my tongue, or the smell of it in my nostrils.

I am the captain's wife aboard this ship, sailing with my husband as so many wives of clipper captains have sailed before me. Though there have been storms and vicissitudes, we have weathered them well. *Sea Jade* is no longer a strong young ship, for ships that are worked too hard must age, as men must age. But she is still a beautiful lady, and if she carries any memory of blood upon her cleanly sanded decks, she gives no sign. I think there is no man aboard that believes her a vessel of ill-omen today.

With what love were her wounds and scars repaired in the Bascomb shipyard! And with what pride she flies the yellow flag! Only her scarred and battered figurehead has not been retouched. Weathered and brown, with cracks showing in the wood, it nevertheless breasts the seas proudly—the strange figure of an eastern maiden, wearing the face of a western girl. A face no longer beautiful, perhaps, but one, I think, that is wholly brave.

It has been a long voyage, this trip to China. During its course my husband has given me a priceless gift. He has given my father back to me. He has made me know that it is not always blood and birth that count for everything. Nathaniel Heath was the father who chose to keep and love me as his daughter, and it is he who will always be my true father. Captain Obadiah seems more like a grandfather —someone exotic and distant in my life, related, it is true, but not bound to me by love as Nathaniel Heath will always be.

Only at such times as stubborn determination to have my own way rises to take precedence in me, do I recognize Captain Obadiah's blood in my veins. But at least I live in reality now. For one thing, I know that a husband does not live his life in the role of romantic lover—except on occasion. And since love is so much more than I had thought for both of us, I am content.

Lien is aboard our ship. With her portion of the captain's fortune she will return to her homeland a rich woman. Perhaps she will even find a suitable husband there. I have Lien to thank for a great deal. If Brock has given my father back to me, Lien has given me something of my mother. With Ian's villainy exposed and Ian gone, she no longer holds his love against me. One day during this voyage she came to me and spoke of my mother's letter. She remembered it well. Not word for word, perhaps, but much of its meaning. In it Carrie had told Obadiah that Sybil had admitted encouraging Obadiah's interest in Carrie. She had actually urged him to seduce Carrie with the sole purpose of stopping Andrew McLean's infatuation for her. It was these words Sybil could not bear to have Brock read. And though it can hardly matter now, I will never tell him.

But there was more in the letter, for Carrie spoke of her love for Nathaniel Heath, once the madness in her blood had quieted. And she spoke with loving tenderness of her babe who must have every chance to grow to womanhood free of ugly shadows. Through Lien's repeating of these words, the warmth of my mother's love has touched me over the years.

Brock's mother has been very ill and is still weak. Yet I think there has been a change in her since those terrible moments in the hold of the *Pride*. Perhaps when we return home she will be better able to accept me as Brock's wife.

For the present Laurel is away at a young ladies' seminary in Boston, associating with girls of her own age for the first time. She has gentled and no longer hides her love for her father as once she did, and he is learning the ways of a more understanding parent. Laurel and I are loving friends and when *Sea Jade* sails home we will have her with us for good. My husband has found himself in his own eyes on this voyage and he will not need to sail again. We both know that his work for the company lies at home. He is more a builder than a sailor, and he is not afraid of the change to steam and iron, as Captain Obadiah always was.

During the hot nights when the Southern Cross swings low behind the *Sea Jade*'s rigging, I have sometimes entertained thoughts that are long and sad. Thoughts of Ian Pryott, who destroyed himself and his fine talent. I know more about Ian now, and about his unhappy younger days in Scots Harbor. I can better understand the path upon which his feet were early set by those around him, and even in turn by Captain Obadiah. Yet a man must, in the long run, take responsibility for his deeds, and we cannot set our own blame upon others. That there was good in Ian as well as evil, I know full well, and I grieve for good so hideously wasted.

Tomorrow we should make landfall in Hong Kong and I will see the places of my youthful dreams. Perhaps it is there my baby will be born. Brock says that if it is a girl, it must be called Carrie, because he knows I would like that. There is no point in arguing. I know the babe will be a son and there is only one person I want to name him after —Captain Brock McLean, of course. I wonder if our son will grow up with a love for the sea? And will he listen raptly to tales of the days when the *Sea Jade* sailed on the China run? Days when the world was young and very different from that world in which he will grow up—a world in which the thrum of steam engines is heard on every hand, and the great white wings are gone from the seas.